PRAISE FOR

CARDSLINGER

Reader, I'm warning you now: this book is bursting at the seams with so much action-packed fun, you better saddle up, grab the reins, and hold on tight. A pair of savvy heroes, a whole heaping of unscrupulous villains, and a story chock-full of action, adventure, and lore make *Cardslinger* a must-read for anyone!

—Brooks Benjamin, author of *My Seventh-Grade Life in Tights*

Rowdy, rollicking, and riveting, *Cardslinger* is a fresh and original hold-on-to-your-hat adventure!

—Dan Gemeinhart, author of *Scar Island and Some Kind of Courage*

The world's great myths and legendary tales of the American West collide as Shuffle Jones embarks on an epic quest full of action and mystery. A big adventure with a big heart, *Cardslinger* is aces!

—Michael Northrop, *New York Times* bestselling author of the TombQuest series

CARDSLINGER

M. G. VELASCO

CAROLRHODA BOOKS
MINNEAPOLIS

Carolrhoda Books®
An imprint of Lerner Publishing Group, Inc.
241 First Avenue North
Minneapolis, MN 55401 USA

For reading levels and more information, look up this title at
www.lernerbooks.com.

Image credits: Morphart Creation/Shutterstock.com (snake); Evgeny Turaev/Shutterstock.com (eagle); Varlamova Lydmila/Shutterstock.com (bottles); Flat_Enot/Shutterstock.com (circus). Design elements: AlexGate/Shutterstock.com; hugolacasse/Shutterstock.com; Andrey_Kuzmin/Shutterstock.com; Compack Background/Shutterstock.com; Here/Shutterstock.com.

Jacket illustration by Monica Armino.

Main body text set in Bembo Std regular 12.5/17.
Typeface provided by Monotype Typography.

Library of Congress Cataloging-in-Publication Data

Names: Velasco, M. G., author.
Title: Cardslinger / by M.G. Velasco.
Description: Minneapolis, MN : Carolrhoda Books, [2019] | Summary: Thirteen-year-old Jason "Shuffle" Jones embarks on a quest across the American West to find his missing father, the creator of a popular fantasy card game that may hold clues to his whereabouts.
Identifiers: LCCN 2018033705 | ISBN 9781541554641 (lb : alk. paper)
Subjects: | CYAC: Card games—Fiction. | Mythology—Fiction. | Adventure and adventurers—Fiction. | West (U.S.)—History—1860-1890—Fiction.
Classification: LCC PZ7.1.V4424 Car 2019 | DDC [Fic]—dc23

LC record available at https://lccn.loc.gov/2018033705

Manufactured in the United States of America
1-45782-42664-1/3/2019

For Jodie, Conner, and Charlotte.
You inspire me every day, and this would
not have existed without you. Thank you for
joining me on this journey.

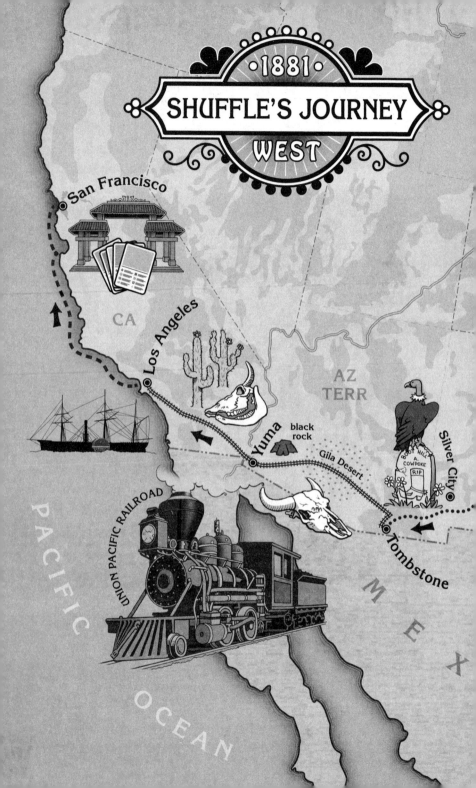

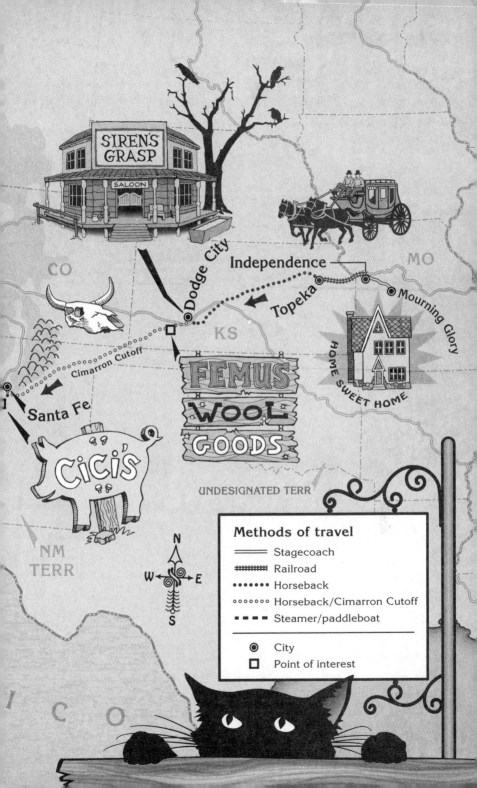

CHAPTER 1
MYTHIC

Shuffle Jones dodged a bullet.

Or rather, a covered wagon, barreling through town.

The driver didn't even acknowledge the near-fatal trampling. He just cracked the reins like they were made outta licorice. However, the little girl riding with him stuck out her tongue, as if to say, "Lucky you."

From the town square, the tower bell rang. Eleven o'clock. The sun hid behind gray clouds, and a wind blew in from the north. Despite it being late March, winter didn't want to leave. It was the same every day. Too cold. Too rainy. And too many mudholes.

Didn't matter, Shuffle had bread to deliver. Easiest money there was for a twelve-year-old, working for the only baker in Mourning Glory, Missouri. The mucky cold and the rampaging wagon weren't gonna stop him from making his last run of the morning. He closed Dad's wool coat, clutching the collar against his throat. At least a part of him stayed warm. Katana, his black cat, sat on his shoulders.

For his final stop, he hit up the haberdashery. White shirts, gray suit jackets, and felt hats hung on the walls. A box of ties and leather belts filled the center table. The old fella at the counter waved him over.

After an exchange of rye for coin, Shuffle realized he'd been paid too much. "Excuse me, sir. You gave me five cents extra."

The haberdasher waved his knobby hand. "Keep it."

Shuffle jingled the coins as he headed out the store. Adding it to his day's wages, he'd have enough scratch to buy the latest Dash Darkwood dime novel. Or flowers for Mama. It'd been a long time since she'd gotten fresh lilies.

As he made his way back to the bakery, Shuffle noticed that the prairie schooner that had nearly run him over was hitched to the dead tree in front of the general store. A sign that read *MYTHIC GAME* in blood-red letters now hung on the side of its canvas cover.

Mythic. Game. Two words he thought he'd never see together again.

Did he read it wrong? Maybe he needed some spectacles. No. Without a doubt, the sign said *Mythic*. It showed as plain and stark as a cavalry battle flag.

The game shouldn't exist. Not out in the world, being sold from a wagon, anyway. It was a game he and Dad had created about mythological heroes and monsters. It was never played beyond their table or the circle of lantern light, when they dueled late at night while Mama was asleep.

When he was seven years old, he'd perfected shuffling the cards. The schoolhouse kids were amazed because they spilled cards everywhere when they tried, but for him, it was as easy as riding a penny-farthing. Soon, the kids gave him the nickname Shuffle, which Dad loved.

That was five years ago—not long before Dad died, and Mythic with him.

Shuffle held on to Katana, sinking his fingers into her fur. Maybe he was hallucinating, which happened sometimes when he skipped breakfast—except, Mama had made him eggs and bacon. So it could be a mirage. Or a phantom.

Or it was a coincidence. For all he knew, this Mythic could be like Old Maid. Dad's Mythic was no simple child's game.

Soon, townsfolk gathered around the wagon, bedeviled by the salesman standing on the tailgate and yelling into a cone.

"Behold, folks. Mythic is here. The exciting card game played by living legends like the outlaw Billy the Kid." The salesman slid his hand down his greasy mustache. "He's the best Mythic player in the West. Ninety-nine wins, one loss. That's more than the number of men he's gunned down."

Katana's tail whipped about, and a ridge of hair rose along her neck.

Shuffle stroked her whiskers to calm her down. "No need to get riled up. Not yet, anyway."

The salesman snapped out a game card from his pocket and flashed it to the crowd. "On the other hand, the James gang play but don't care for strategy. They can't even read; they like the pictures. When a loss seems inevitable, they shoot their opponent for trying." He put the card up to his face, peering through a bullet hole.

Laughing, the cram of suckers drew closer. That wasn't surprising. Anything to do with gunslingers, outlaws, and lawmen got folks' attention. Heck, Shuffle liked shootouts, saloon brawls, and train robberies in stories, but in real life, that stuff wasn't funny. The thought of taking a lead plum for winning a game sounded less appealing than jumping off a cliff.

The salesman directed the cone at a group of ranch hands clutching their wages. "Care to partake in this new form of entertainment?"

Dying to know if the salesman was peddling rummy or something too close to home, Shuffle weaved his way to the front. "Billy the Kid don't play a child's game. Are you selling us hogwash?"

"This is the gen-u-ine article." The salesman tipped his bowler hat adorned with a rattlesnake head, fangs and all, frozen in a grin. "Mythic is wildfire, not a children's game. It's about mythological gods like Zeus and Odin. The ones who threw down lightning or unleashed beasts on unbelievers."

It was definitely not Old Maid. But how was this possible? Dad died, yet Mythic lived. No stinking way.

The crowd buzzed.

The salesman widened his eyes. "There are monsters like *manitou, yao guai,* and the flying serpent."

In a dark flash, those creatures appeared in Shuffle's mind. They ripped into each other, but instead of blood, game cards poured out of their wounds. Then a lightning bolt crashed, and Shuffle rocked back on his heels, aware of the salesman raising a small burlap sack.

"Packs of a dozen random cards for a nickel. Complete decks are ten cents—ready to play, outta the bag. Courtesy of Stan Slythe, printer of fine dime novels, quality tarot cards, and superior boudoir photographs." He stomped on the platform, rattling the chains holding up the tailgate. "Now who wants to become a legend?"

A leathery rancher shoved Shuffle aside. "Guess you want none."

Katana hissed and swiped at the man, unfortunately missing by inches. That should've given folks the idea not to be rude, but despite her warning, the horde surged in a frenzy of elbows and hands, sending Shuffle to the end of the line.

Being tossed around like a steaming tater was the least of his gripes. It seemed that his and Dad's game was indeed being sold, but could he even trust the salesman? The only way to be certain was to look at the cards and read the rules. Only then would he know if the game was the real deal or a rip-off.

Rocking a pair of coins between his knuckles, Shuffle made his way to the tailgate.

The salesman tilted his head, and on his hat, the viper's eyes seemed to follow. "You want some cards or are you going to give me trouble? And I don't sell catnip."

Katana leapt to the ground, slinking away.

"Pack." Shuffle slapped down five pennies. "Don't know if the game's fun enough to buy more."

"You're a hoot." The salesman produced a pack from the dark recesses of a box.

With the cards in hand, Shuffle retreated to a spot under a crooked tree. The word *Mythic*, in white rune-like lettering, spread across the solid black wrapper. Tricky folds kept it together. A simple message on the back folds read: *Stake your claim to adventure and to dreams made real. Stan Slythe Publishing, San Francisco, California.* He tore away the wrapper and revealed the first card, a *Hoplite*. A black spade. Black for Greek, spade for the Power faction. The Greek soldier held a spear over his helmeted head and a shield to his side.

He flipped to *Kitsune*, the Japanese fox spirit.

Then to *Ocelotl*, the Aztec jaguar warrior.

Shuffle studied each card closely. Dad used to worry about cheaters ruining the game with forgeries. He'd wanted to use something like a unique watermark to distinguish real from fake, but he'd never gotten around to that.

The icons, the colors, the factions, the abilities—all of them matched the rules of his and Dad's game. The paperboard finish of the cards was nicer than their home-made ones, but those differences didn't matter, because the rules defined Mythic. And the art style looked a lot like Dad's. The lines and shading appeared rough, and some of the strokes weren't as confidently drawn, but overall, the art seemed close.

Finally, Shuffle came across *Hermes*. Messenger of the gods. God of commerce, thieves, and games. The artist painted *Hermes* holding a staff entwined with serpents and wearing winged sandals.

No denying it now. The game's name, theme, and rules weren't coincidences. They were evidence of a no-good theft, and maybe of Dad's murder.

Five years ago, Dad—an antiquities professor by trade and a treasure hunter at heart—had left home for an expedition to Arizona, hoping to find a long-lost Spanish cache of artifacts. Six months later, out in the desert, his camp was attacked. The authorities didn't find anything but bullet casings and blood, not even bodies to bury. With no suspects to find guilty and hang, the law declared Dad and his companions dead.

That's four years of not really knowing, of hoping he would come home.

Four years of no Mythic.

The *Hermes* card lay crushed in Shuffle's grip. He tossed it, with the rest of the pack. More than a game,

Mythic was a connection to Dad. All the hundreds and thousands of moments spent talking and playing and laughing over the cards lived within the game. There was no way he was gonna let an idea-stealing, money-grubbing, bad-drawing thief kill that, too.

Someone had ruined the last four years. Someone needed to pay for their crimes. The salesman was probably innocent, but he might know the low-down, dirty imp who was guilty.

With his bootstraps tightened, Shuffle stormed the wagon.

CHAPTER 2
PROVE IT

Shuffle bellied up to the tailgate. Someone had stolen Dad's ideas and notes for Mythic, maybe even killed him.

"Excited for more?" The salesman shined a dime on his sleeve.

"I wouldn't say that."

"Then what's got your axle bent outta shape?"

Four years of frustration was what. No justice, no real closure. Only a piece of paper from the law that declared Dad dead. Case closed.

Except someone had attacked Dad and his colleagues and was now using stolen notes to make Mythic. That thief needed to be exposed and face their crimes.

Shuffle stabbed out a few breaths, ready for a fight. "Who made these cards?"

The salesman snapped his fingers. The dime vanished, and in his other hand, a pack of cards appeared. "Says on the back."

Stan Slythe. He could be connected somehow. At

the very least, he was profiteering from a thieving, a killing, and a plagiarism. What a swindler.

"No, not who published the cards. Who designed and developed them? You know, who created the game?"

"I don't know, kid. I just sell them. Why's it matter?"

Shuffle slapped the tailgate. "My dad and I made the game, that's why. He was killed, and his ideas were stolen by the murderer."

The salesman slid off his long coat, showing off his pistol. It stuck out like a snake's rattle. "I don't know what to tell you. That's a serious accusation about a serious man. If what you say is true, then you might just have a beef with Mr. Slythe."

"Who's got beef?" asked a girl coming around the wagon. It was the same little girl who had stuck her tongue out. She handed the salesman a small leather pouch. "The general store bought a case of each, Pa. I also sold a handful to the deputies at the jail."

"Nice work, Angel." The salesman kissed the tip of her tiny nose.

The girl, ten years old or so, crossed her arms over the pleats of her flowery blouse. "Who's the boy?"

"Angel, this here is one of the original creators of Mythic." The salesman weighed the sack in his hand before locking it in an iron box. "And he's questioning the validity of these cards."

"You calling us crooks?" The girl cracked her knuckles.

"No. That's not what I'm saying. I just can't believe this game even exists when my dad or I didn't have anything to do with it."

"Pa, this boy is loony. He thinks he made the game. A kid from a nowhere town." She looked Shuffle up and down. "If you made this game, you're good, right?"

Compared to Dad, he was decent, and that made him second best. *Good* would work, but not wanting to sound arrogant, he shrugged. "I'm okay."

She wrinkled her nose. "Just okay? What a joke. The creator oughtta be better than low to middlin'."

Mama always said it was a sign of weakness to boast. "Compensating for something," she'd say. But being called out by a stranger, a little kid, was too much to take. "Well, I happen to be better than Billy the Kid or any cardsharp who thinks he's big noise."

She drew out a deck. "Prove it."

"What?"

"Play me. Or are you a yellow-bellied lizard?"

Shuffle coughed out a laugh. He'd been called a coward plenty of times, but never when it came to a duel. Then again, he played Mythic with one person, and Dad never blustered. "Those are gaming words. But I need a full deck."

A small burlap sack landed at his feet.

"Courtesy of Stan Slythe," the salesman said.

Slythe, my boot. Shuffle swiped the deck. "Fine. Let's game."

CHAPTER 3

SPEAR OF VENGEANCE

A blanket-covered, termite-eaten crate served as the battlefield.

A bird circled in the overcast sky. A hawk, maybe a vulture.

Shuffle claimed a spot across from his opponent, Angel, the little girl with the tiny nose. There was no backing out now. Once a player had taken a seat, then it was game on until the end, win or lose—well, maybe except for supper.

"This is gonna be fun, Pa," she said, readying her deck.

The salesman knelt beside her. "Angel, the boy claims he created the game. Claims he's the best player in town. He's accusing our employer of criminal acts and saying we're selling lies. He's threatening our very livelihood."

Shuffle raised his hand, like he did at school so the classmarm wouldn't smack him with her pointing stick. "I didn't say those things, I—"

The salesman winked and turned to his daughter. "You ready to slay the beast?"

Angel slapped his shoulder. "Ready, Pa, for I am the sword."

Okay, this girl had to be suffering from rabies.

The salesman armed himself with the cone. "Listen up, folks. We have a battle of the gods. Which player will prevail? My sweet little angel or this bully?"

Shuffle nearly fell back. "Bully? I'm not—"

A rumble of chatter spread among the spectators as they formed a gladiatorial circle. Some folks placed bets. Others heckled him. And those were the people he knew. So much for being a hometown favorite.

Ignoring this cold-blooded treason, Shuffle halved his deck and bridged the cards, fluttering them together into a single stack. He'd have to win to save some face and not be forever known as a liar. Mostly, he needed to protect Dad's legacy. Losing would be like letting Dad be defeated by the scoundrel. Not going to happen. A victory would prove Shuffle right and, in a way, get revenge.

Besides, how hard could it be to outplay a little girl?

The salesman yelled into the cone. "There are three ways to win. First way's to crush your opponent's Belief. Each player starts with thirteen Belief points. Imagine them like flags. Lose your flags, lose the game."

Shuffle set thirteen clay chips that came with the deck across the crate, using them for Belief markers. At home, he'd use river rocks. The feel of a smooth, cold stone in his hand would set his mind on the right tactical play.

"The second way to triumph is to raise your Belief to twenty-one." The salesman nudged a skinny boy standing in the crowd. "It's hard to win that way when your opponent is attacking on every turn. Never seen it done."

Shuffle closed his eyes, remembering the third way to win. *Complete three Quests and win the game.*

He hadn't played a real match in five years, since the night before Dad left on his expedition. That evening, a breeze had rustled the drapes and brought in the smell of the rose bush, but the wind didn't mess with the cards.

"Can you stop me before my next turn?" Dad had leaned back in his chair.

"I've got a bit of flash and dash left." Shuffle played his best card, the hero *Odysseus* along with *Silver Thread*.

Dad's eyes widened. "You completed your third Quest. Amazing." He got up from his seat and offered his hand for a shake.

Like any good sportsman, Shuffle took it.

Dad pulled him into a hug. "I'll miss you."

"Do you have to go?"

The light of the room faded. Dad's shadow whispered, "I'll come back. No matter what."

He never did.

"Get on with it already," shouted a man.

Shuffle opened his eyes, back to the showdown.

"Love the furor," the salesman said, tipping his hat. He patted Shuffle on the shoulder like it was happy trails.

"What you get?" Angel asked, gesturing at Shuffle's deck.

Realizing he hadn't even looked at his cards, Shuffle tasted something sour, like curdled breakfast, at the back of his throat. For all he knew, his cards were the worst set out of the whole lot. Quite possibly, the salesman knowingly gave him horsepile.

Hoping for something decent, he flipped the deck over; the bottom card, now face up, was a black spade *Hoplite*. After scouring through half the deck, he found his deity, *Ares*, Greek god of war. Typical brute force strategy, not his usual play style, but it should do the most damage.

"I'm playing this," Angel said, showing her god card. *Ra*. Egyptian sun god. Yellow heart. Yellow for Egyptian, heart for the Spirit faction.

Well, that anvil dropped outta nowhere. He'd figured Angel ran with an *Ares* deck. He'd take Power over Spirit anytime. And if this really was Dad's game, Dad's rules, then the Egyptian decks would be hard to win with. They weren't as powerful as the original four sets of culture decks Dad had come up with. Shuffle had never been able to pull off a victory with *Ra*.

"Ladies first," Angel said, drawing her opening hand of three cards. She slapped down a card, *War Chariot*. "I attack."

Shuffle smiled as he took the hit, and as the rules came back. Each card had its own abilities, sometimes game-breaking ones. But when it came down to it, the core of the game was simple. *Play a card. Perform its action. Draw a card.*

A long-forgotten feeling returned to his fingers. They tingled and throbbed at the touch of each card in his hand.

The match turned into something more than just the two of them playing. Everything outside of his focus blurred, and everything in front of him changed into a battlefield of clashing swords, snorting horses, flying dirt, and gushing blood. Sparks of magical lightning arced across the sky. The ground shook as the *Minotaur* charged into the fight. A ray of light from *Osiris* bathed the dead, making them rise again.

"I don't know, Pa," Angel said. "I have to defend."

Shuffle looked up. His opponent frowned at her hand and then at the salesman.

He pointed at one of her cards and winked. "Don't fret, you ain't lost yet." The rattlesnake head on his bowler seemed to wink, too.

It didn't matter what she had. Even though the score was still tied thirteen-to-thirteen Belief points, Shuffle knew he had the game nearly won, and victory would come in the form of *Hercules*. He flashed down the card. Dust kicked up from the crate. The rest of the cards and Belief markers nearly fell off from the shock.

The crowd surged forward.

Hercules. Demigod, son of Zeus. A Quest-completer. But in this case, an attacker. Dad had designed *Hercules* to win the game by completing Quests, but sometimes cards had to be played a different way for the win.

Not done with his move, Shuffle added *Giant's Axe*, popping it on top of his hero. "I attack, defeating your hero, *Osiris*, plus you take four hits from *Hercules*, two more with *Axe*, and—"

"Doubled with your god's ability, *Bloodlust*," Angel said, "that's twelve damage."

Shuffle mentally slid the abacus beads to total the hits. "Yeah, you're right. Twelve damage."

"Well, that hurts, folks. My girl is down to one Belief point." The salesman's face twisted with a smile.

Angel's too. They had to be up to something.

"I have to take two hits for using *Ares'* ability. So that drops me to eleven." Shuffle plucked away two clay chips, now unsure if a ten-point lead was enough to win. How could it not be, though? *Ra* didn't have the power to swing for a kill shot. Eleven to one. Victory almost in hand . . . but why were they grinning?

The shadow from above glided closer. Definitely a vulture.

"My turn." Angel snapped a card onto the table. *Horus*. In Egyptian mythology, when Osiris was murdered, Horus was born to get revenge. She tossed down another card with a picture of a lotus-shaped spearhead.

Spear of Vengeance: With a hero in play, damage your opponent's Belief equal to the amount dealt to you from the previous turn.

Shuffle gasped. The battlefield took shape, with *Horus* throwing the gleaming weapon. The spear annihilated everything, leaving a black void.

Angel snapped her fingers. "Twelve damage. You lose."

The crowd fought their way for a better look.

Angel raised her fist as the salesman hoisted her onto his shoulder. The crowd whooped and hollered all around him, begging the salesman to sell them cards. They headed back to the wagon, their new customers at their heels.

The battlefield was a lonely place for the loser. But the defeat didn't even matter. Shuffle had something more important at his fingertips.

Katana climbed onto his lap, her yellow eyes big and shining. Her purring thrummed.

Shuffle picked up *Spear of Vengeance*. It was never in the original pool of cards. It was one Dad created while traveling to Arizona. He'd mailed his notes home for approval. He didn't have them when he disappeared, so the murderer wouldn't have known how to duplicate it.

The picture looked like the drawing he had sent home. Its style was distinctive, and the special ability was worded exactly the same way. Only Dad could've come up with the holy-heifer, sneaky-play, cannon-blast of a special ability.

Dad's ideas hadn't been stolen by some killer. Dad himself was crafting Mythic.

Dad was alive.

CHAPTER 4

MAMA

Shuffle ran, cradling Katana in one hand and clutching the card in the other.

All signs pointed to Dad being alive.

The rules and the game play were the same as Dad's game. The art was his, too. Not as smooth as his normal stuff, but it was close. And nobody but the two of them had known about *Spear of Vengeance* and the other cards Dad created en route to Arizona.

On top of all that, Dad's body was never found. The authorities only discovered a ransacked campsite. No remains. No suspects. After a long search, the lawmen proclaimed Dad dead. They provided a certificate of death and everything. It was an official finality. Shuffle had believed everything proclaimed by that piece of paper with the government-embossed stamp.

Not anymore.

He held onto Katana tighter as he rounded the corner.

But if Dad was alive, why would he create the game

for some stranger in California? Why didn't Dad return? He should be home.

Up ahead was Goldfell's boarding house, where Mama worked. She was out front, sweeping the porch. She needed to know. She'd want Dad back.

"Well, hello." She set the broom aside and grabbed him for a big hug.

Katana jumped off and rubbed on Mama's legs.

"Big news!" Shuffle said, hugging back. "Incredible exciting unbelievable news! I had a battle."

"Battle? You played Mythic?"

"And lost, but that doesn't matter." He took a deep breath and held on to Mama, mostly to steady himself. "Dad's alive."

Mama wrinkled her brow, then her look changed. "You got in a fight, didn't you?"

He showed her *Spear of Vengeance*. "Dad made this, right? Look at the art. He must be alive—held captive and forced to make the game. In San Francisco, where this Slythe character has his business." That's where his gut told him Dad would be at—the same place where Mythic was being created. It was the only thing that made sense.

Mama pored over the card, her evergreen eyes catching the light. She was gonna understand. She had to.

"Jason," she said, "we've prayed for him to come home. We've wished and hoped he was alive." She looked over her shoulder toward the house. "It hasn't been easy."

All the built-up energy seemed to bleed out. This wasn't how she was supposed to react. She was supposed to be excited. "Didn't you hear me? Dad's alive."

"This card has gotten you riled up. Think. Really think." She looked down. "After all this time."

Mama's voice didn't crack or pitch high. It stayed true and cold. And her eyes didn't quiver or moisten with tears. They remained clear.

She hadn't accepted Dad's death right away. After they first got word of his disappearance, she'd argued with her own dad, Captain, begging him to go look for Dad and raging when he'd refused. Most of the time she put on a brave face, but Shuffle often caught her crying when she thought he wasn't watching.

But now it hit Shuffle: she was healed, and he didn't know if he liked that. Nine months ago, she stopped wearing her black mourning dresses. She boxed them up with most of Dad's stuff. Maybe she'd had this look for months, and he just didn't notice. There was no denying it now.

The front door opened, and Peace Officer Bronson stepped out, his boots clomping on the porch. He wiped his hands, getting soot on a towel. "Furnace is fixed."

Mama pulled away from Shuffle, the gap between them seeming a hundred feet wide. "Mrs. Goldfell will be much appreciative."

"Anything for you." Bronson straightened up. "Hey there, Jason."

Ignoring the man, Shuffle turned Mama about-face. "We have to do something. Dad's out there. He's being held prisoner or tortured or brainwashed."

"Honey, you can't do this to yourself. To us," she said. "No need to relive all that heartache."

"But the card." Shuffle avoided the shadow moving in the background.

Mama shook her head. "I don't see it. It just looks any other drawing."

"You're not looking hard enough. Please believe me."

"I believe what you're feeling is genuine, and I love that." She pushed away a strand of her brown hair. "But after everything we've been told. By the Pinkerton detective, the marshals, the rangers. I don't have the strength anymore to believe in the impossible. We have to move on."

Shuffle pocketed the card and hugged Mama back. He wasn't sad, though. He felt sorry for her, because she had given up. Not him. He still had fight in his bones, because he wielded the truth and a dang spear of vengeance.

MOURNING GLORY NEWS

CRIMINALS APPREHENDED; GOLD RECOVERED

Peace Officer Elijah Bronson, 34, single-handedly thwarted Bly Pike, 22, and his compatriots from escaping after they had absconded with gold from National Bank and Trust. On foot, Officer Bronson chased down the gang, who were on horseback. The confrontation ended with very little bloodshed.

"I escaped with a few scratches," Bronson said. "The suspects didn't fare so well."

The gold, a thousand Troy ounces in coins, was worth $19,000.

NOTORIOUS KILLER CAPTURED

DEADWOOD, South Dakota— Jed Smock, alias Jupiter Jed, known in Nebraska and Kansas as the murderer of 33 men, was apprehended at a saloon's outhouse in Deadwood, by a group of bounty hunters with marshal's authority.

"Ain't fair," said Jed Smock, 27, awaiting trial in a jail cell. "There was six of them. And the leader's got to be half rattlesnake. She shot me in the knee, just as I exited the privy. What a mean viper."

CHAPTER 5
THE SUITOR

President Rutherford B. Hayes was useless.

Needing help, Shuffle had sent a letter to the President about Dad being held captive, a national emergency, and got nothing for a reply. Letters to the Arizona rangers and the Cochise County sheriff, pleading with them to reopen Dad's case, hadn't paid off either.

That was nearly two months ago, and after checking the post office every day since, Shuffle was beginning to think there was no one else in the world who would help.

One message that didn't need a response was a letter to Stan Slythe, publisher and printer of dumb dime novels, terrible tarot cards, and frightful photographs. Shuffle couldn't help himself; he had to send the snake a piece of his mind.

> *Stan Slythe,*
>
> *Don't think for a minute you can get away with Mythic. You kidnapped my dad to run your money-grubbing scheme. Needed him because your feeble brain*

can't think past your thick skull. Heck, I bet all your so-called products are stolen ideas and dreams. If I had a dime for every life you've ruined, I'd probably be as rich as King Midas. So, Stan Slythe, I swear on my dad's name, I will burn down your deuce-high paper empire. And then I'm going to take my dad and my card game back, you smelly horsepile.

Worst regards, Shuffle

PS Maybe not me, but the Arizona rangers. Or even the US Army led by President Hayes himself. Bad day to you, sir.

Today, he walked home from the post office empty-handed. The sunset bled into a dark sky. A strong wind punched through town, and the smell of a recent cattle drive stank up the streets.

Two kids played Mythic on the sidewalk of the general store. That was the worst thing about these last six weeks since the wagon arrived in Mourning Glory. The salesman was right; Mythic was wildfire. Shuffle tried to be a part of the hoopla, playing friend or foe. But every time he brought up Dad, he got into arguments, sometimes fisticuffs. At the end, he'd tallied one bloody nose, six bruises, and a record of ten wins, zero losses.

Keeping his head down, Shuffle moved past the gamers.

The days weren't all spent moping around or getting

punched in the face. Just like he'd done when Dad first disappeared, he gathered all the letters Dad had sent him during the expedition, and studied them until his head hurt. He organized Dad's homemade cards and compared them to some of the new ones. Most of them matched, down to the smallest stroke. How could anyone not see it? It was possible the Arizona rangers just weren't clever. Maybe he oughtta hire another Pinkerton. But it would take a dozen years of deliveries to get enough money for a detective. By that time—

"Wait up," called a voice.

Shuffle turned and put his hand up to wave but stopped when he saw it was Bronson—son of a freed slave, Harris-Stowe State University graduate, and volunteer lawman turned office chief.

The officer caught up in two strides. His boots shined from a recent buffing. If there was ever a hometown hero, he would be the one bronzed in the town square with that distinction. He single-handedly saved lives during the Great Circus Elephant Stampede of 1878. His crisp uniform defined broad shoulders and thick arms—easy to see how he could stop a charging pachyderm.

He smiled, wider and brighter than a lemon wedge. "It's getting dark. I'll come with you."

"I can manage." Shuffle walked away.

Bronson strode alongside, grinning like he knew a secret. His trimmed mustache fell neatly just above his lip, and his badge shimmered with a mirror finish. Visiting more often the last few weeks, the lawman clearly had designs on Mama. But now that Shuffle knew Dad was alive, he wished Bronson would back the heck off.

"Have you gotten in any fights lately?"

"No, sir. I don't need for an escort, thanks."

"You oughtta stop challenging those boys," Bronson said. "They're hard as granite, working trails and ranches. Jason, you're . . ."

"Can't wait to hear this one."

"Soft. Hate to say it, but you're like fresh baked bread."

"Great, thanks for the compliment." Shuffle turned onto Main Street, spotting cow dung on the road. Bronson was focused on having a conversation. Maybe he hadn't yet seen the piles of steaming crud. This could get rid of him for the night. Shuffle double-timed it, keeping his eyes on the lawman but staying aware of the trap. "Care to point out any more of my great qualities?"

"You're smart. Smarter than all of them put together. You should know better than to cross them."

Shuffle stepped between two stinking mounds and pointed at the roof of the butcher shop. "What's a cow doing up there?"

Something squished; Bronson groaned.

Feint and Strike: Attack with two units; the stronger unit cannot be defended.

Waving a jaunty good-bye, Shuffle strutted off like a conqueror on parade and stormed up Dove Hill. Bronson should've known better than to cross a battlefield tactician, and with his boots dead center in a dung trap, he oughtta turn tail and retreat.

The moon loomed overhead, big and low and red. Shuffle raced home.

As he opened the door to his house, a waft of rosy perfume hit him in the face. Mama hadn't worn it in a long time. She must've known Bronson was coming over.

Darkness masked the house. No warm welcome? He struck a match and lit a lantern. The light made a yellow shell around him as he followed the perfume to the kitchen.

A rumpled mass lay on the floor. He crept forward and held the lamp to it.

"Mama?"

Her eyes were closed, and blood pooled around her soft, pale cheeks.

CHAPTER 6
A SHOT IN THE DARK

Shuffle dropped the lamp, and the room went dark. The oil's fumes burned his chest from the inside out. He fell to his knees, but he fought past the pain and went to Mama.

"It's Jason. Wake up." He set his head on hers. "God, please. Please wake up. Please."

A weak moan escaped her lips.

Shuffle exhaled, feeling the burn subside. He tried lifting her, but she didn't budge. He couldn't save her alone. "Help! Someone help!"

A creaking sound brought his eyes across the room. The kitchen door opened, and a gun barrel pierced the darkness, gleaming from the moonlight.

Shuffle gasped as a woman stepped into the kitchen, the six-shooter in full view. She turned, facing him, half in light and half in shadow.

The front door swung open, and cow dung stank up the room.

"Jason. It's me," Bronson said.

Click. A sound from the bandit.

Bronson drew his gun and swiveled.

Two flashes. Two bangs. The wall splintered.

Shuffle covered Mama with his body. He cringed as a high-pitched whistle ran past his head. The kitchen door slammed, drawing him to look up. The bandit had gone.

Bronson motioned him to stay put and keep alert. Then he disappeared into the swirling, pungent gun smoke.

The ringing in Shuffle's ears died off, and the room began to take shape in the quiet and stillness.

Holy heck. He'd just lived through a gun battle. Muzzle fire. Gun smoke. Screaming bullets. *Aura of Protection: Prevent damage done to hero.*

Mama moved, thank heaven. Shuffle held her tight, determined not to let her go until they were safe. He supported her head, sliding his hand through a warm, sticky, wet patch of hair.

Please don't die.

Then came more gunshots. Shuffle ducked. Breaking glass, cussing, and another shot sounded from Mama's room. Now was a good time to hightail it out, but if he couldn't get Mama on her feet, then they wouldn't be going anywhere. He'd have to protect her somehow.

"Jason?" Mama's eyes flickered open.

"Yes, it's me." Shuffle tried to control his voice from cracking. "I'm here."

The sound of footsteps drew him to the far door. The smoke dissipated into strange moonlit wisps. Bronson limped back into view, blood trickling from his thigh.

"They're gone." He shambled over and dropped to his knees. "Penny. What happened? Are you okay?"

She reached up.

He took her in his arms.

Shuffle sat back, never so relieved to see Bronson, nor so guilty for ruining the shine on his boots. Things would've been worse if he hadn't shown up.

"Three ladies." Bronson said, checking Mama's head wound. "They got away."

A woman gunfighter? Three of them, even.

Bronson showed a scrap of paper. "I winged one, and she dropped this. Do you know what it means?"

Still trembling, Shuffle took the note, getting blood on it. He tilted it to catch the moonlight.

Cassandra's Warning.

In Dad's handwriting.

CHAPTER 7
GENUINE MYTHIC

Two deputies patrolled outside.

Inside, lanterns and a full candelabra illuminated the house. More light the better. Shuffle had had enough of the dark.

Katana lounged on his lap. Thankfully, she hadn't been taken by the bandits or caught in the crossfire.

After stitching the gash on Mama's head, the doctor checked her eyes and reflexes. She was going to be fine, with maybe a headache to keep her company.

Bronson treated his own wound, swabbing it with iodine and wrapping it up in bandages. The bullet had gone through and missed the vital parts. He was going to be fine, with maybe a limp to keep *him* company.

"The robbers turned your rooms over. Looking for something," Bronson said. "Still no idea what the note means, Penny?"

"Surely they had the wrong house, and they thought I was this Cassandra."

Shuffle traced the C and the W with his finger. He

recognized the delicate curves and bold strokes of the letters from the homemade Mythic cards. Would anybody believe him? He'd shown *Spear of Vengeance* and the other evidence to whoever would listen, and in return, he got shaking heads. The note would likely be no different. Others would choose not to see the similarities of the writing, just like they couldn't see the connection in the cards.

Regardless, Shuffle knew the note was proof that Dad was alive. But why would a bandit have it? Did they take it from Dad, or did he give it to them?

"If you're okay with it, I'll have a few of my boys camp here," Bronson said. "You and Jason will stay with me, just in case they come back."

"Why would they come back?" Mama's voice pitched high.

Bronson put his hand on hers. "Just a precaution."

A deputy knocked at the door. "Sir. Lost the bandits' trail at the bottom of the hill."

Bronson's jaw muscles rippled. "Wake up Douglas, and the both of you find them."

Douglas was a deputy known for his terrible singing of bawdy tunes, but famous for his tracking prowess. He once led Bronson to the Belcher Brothers, who had escaped capture from two Texas rangers and a U.S. Marshal across three states. *Scout Ahead: Quest +1. Opponent cannot play a card on your turn.* Bronson was serious about finding the villains. Good man.

"Jason, pack some clothes for you and your mother," Bronson said. "We'll leave when doc says she's ready."

★ ★ ★

By lantern light, Shuffle sifted through the tornado-tuckered mess that was his room. His newly organized Mythic cards littered the floor. Why would the bandits wreck the place? He didn't have anything that could be Cassandra or her Warning.

Katana climbed up to her perch, a wooden shelf with a wool lining, and watched, her paws and head half hanging off the edge. Had she seen the bandits tear up the room? Would she know what they were after?

Shuffle found that his secret box had been dumped open. His pocket knife and life's savings were in a pile by the lid. A roll of US Legal Tender—seven dollars in greenbacks—plus three dollars in nickels and dimes were untouched. What kind of thieves would pass up free cash and a serviceable folding blade? Apparently, they didn't think any of it was worth the trouble. He pocketed his knife and money, and shoved some clothes, his favorite hat, and Dad's old wool coat into a canvas duffel.

"Come on, kitty. Giddyup."

Katana jumped down and followed him to Mama's room.

A cold wind whistled through the broken window. Dark splotches were everywhere, proof of the night's violence. Hopefully, with the deputies outside, the bandits weren't coming back.

Shuffle scavenged the piles of Mama's clothes for her night robe and a clean work dress.

A lot of Mama's other things were strewn about the floor, including stuff he thought was valuable. It appeared the bandits missed out on a gold and amethyst pendant from England and a jade comb from Japan. Both were gifts from Dad, picked up on his travels. Either the bandits plain didn't see those two items or Bronson thwarted them before they could grab them . . . Or they weren't interested because the jewelry didn't have anything to do with *Cassandra's Warning*.

Near the foot of a toppled dresser, Katana pounced on a length of twine. She bit down on it and tugged, but the twine didn't budge. Shuffle dug away some things covering it and found an opened package wedged between the wall and the dresser. He shoved the cabinet away and picked up the paper- and twine-wrapped bundle.

He unwound the twine and gave it to Katana. She clawed and gnawed at it like it was a rat tail.

The package was addressed to Mama from the station chief of the Arizona rangers, and inside was a list of contents: *1—official declaration of death of Euless Jones, 15—personal correspondences, 1—deck of cards, 1—contraption.*

Shuffle peered inside the package and pulled out the correspondences—Dad's letters to Mama, sent while he was on the expedition. Shuffle remembered when two lawmen had come to the house, asking questions. Mama had turned in her letters and anything else that might have helped as evidence. Apparently, the rangers thought kindly enough to send them back.

He took out the contraption—a small brass rod with a green glass bulb on one end. It was completely foreign but shined of Dad's making. It could be important, but for now he set it down with the letters. If the list was right, there was something else inside that mattered most.

Turning over the package, he shook out a small white carton into his hand. It felt heavier than it looked. Maybe it was filled with gold, or maybe his arm was weak with anticipation. Opening the flip-top lid, he revealed a Mythic deck and plucked out the first card. *Athena.*

Shuffle put his hand on the wall to keep himself from falling. If anything would be considered long-lost treasure, a completely new and different *Athena* deck would be it.

A knock at the door almost made him drop it. Katana arched her back and hissed. He tossed everything into his rucksack.

Bronson came into the room. "Find what you need?"

Shuffle snapped the bag shut. "Sure did."

Bronson lived at the edge of town in a large house with peaked roofs. A lot of space for hide-and-seek, and it was rumored to be haunted by Bronson's ma's ghost. Exploration and poltergeist hunting would have to wait, though. There were Mythic cards to look through.

Shutting himself in one of the guest rooms—hopefully without spirits—Shuffle huddled on the floor with the package.

Out of the fifteen letters, two of them were still in their original envelopes, with arrival postage dating two weeks after Dad's camp was attacked. They were two letters Shuffle had never seen before, and one of them was addressed to him. Mama must've turned it in to the authorities before he had the chance to read it.

Dear Shuffle,

I have a surprise for you. A real Mythic deck as we have imagined it to be. This is one of two I cre-ated with the help of a fine printmaker. He used the best paper and ink to make the decks. If things weren't in pandemonium, I'd have the means to make all our cards. Enough to share our game with the whole world. But in the meantime, the game is for us. I cannot wait for our next duel.

Game on,
Dad

Shuffle gripped the paper like it was a sword hilt. The last four years should've been *game on*. It could've been so much fun. *Our next duel.* It never happened, but there could be a chance to remedy that.

The second letter was for Mama.

Dearest Penny,

Our reunion must wait.

Edward is missing, and I've come to town to meet with the authorities. I want to take the next train home, but I can't. Not with good conscience while he's still gone. Two workers have left us. That makes four hired hands lost. John and Bicker remain but are wavering. Dr. Bloom will stay to the end. I wish I had Apollo's chariot and could return to you this instant. I'd settle for Icarus's wings.

Love always,

Euless

Dad would never stay away from home of his own accord. Not with this kind of feeling in his words. No way. He was out there and being *kept* from coming home. Unfortunately, the letter didn't have any answers about where he might be or who was responsible.

Shuffle inspected the contraption: a brass tube the size of a short candle with a green glass bulb attached to one end. A switch sat below its tapered neck.

Did the contraption have something to do with Dad's idea to keep the cards from being counterfeited?

With a flick of his thumb, Shuffle lit a flame inside the bulb, and an emerald glow blanketed him. He took out *Athena* and held the card up to the bulb. The light brightened the card with a green hue and highlighted a dark band inside of it. Within the band, cutout letters formed words: *GENUINE MYTHIC*.

The light glowed like a blessing from Athena's fingertip.

The next several cards matched the others in style, and their abilities went with the same strategy. Dad had sent a copy of Shuffle's favorite Greek Spirit and Power *Athena* deck. It was a well-rounded kit, and if played with tactical skill, it could be invincible.

On the floor, Shuffle placed *Athena* next to thirteen Belief markers. He stacked his cards and drew a starting hand. But nobody sat across from him to play.

He tossed down *Lone Perseverance: +2 to Quest Strength if using one hero*. He needed Dad home, and he'd bring him back himself if he had to.

Closing his eyes, he wished for Apollo's chariot but decided he would settle for a train to California.

CHAPTER 8
TIME TO ACT

With a candle in hand, Shuffle searched Bronson's house for Mama. She needed to see Dad's final letter, and maybe then, she would believe he was alive.

Strange shapes formed in the dark corridors. The floors creaked with each step, and the air moaned as he opened and closed doors to empty rooms. Eventually, he heard muffled sounds and followed them, keeping the candle low while trying to avoid the potted ferns lining the hallway.

The noises became clearer and the room became brighter. Hiding behind one of the plants, he peeked around the corner.

In the kitchen, Mama sat at the small table. Her hair was down and glistening, and she wore her night robe. Bronson sat across from her with a scattergun across his lap and fresh bandages around his leg. Mama slid a teacup to him. He put his hand on hers.

Shuffle gritted his teeth, keeping himself from busting in and breaking up the tender scene.

"Listen, Penny. I was planning on waiting," Bronson said, "but the incident has given me a sense of urgency."

Mama sat up straight. "Urgency? For what?"

Bronson kept his paw on hers. "I know your son's been talking about this new game and about how Euless might still be alive."

Why was he mentioning Dad?

He took Mama's other hand and clasped them together. "You have to know that I wouldn't do this if it was true. Do you believe it? In your heart, do you feel Euless is alive?"

Shuffle leaned forward, pushing into the fern leaves, hoping she would shoot Bronson down.

Mama didn't say anything. She tilted her head, exposing her neck.

Careful, Mama.

"Please know, I respect his memory and promise—wait, do you smell that?"

The fern lit up in flames. Shuffle dropped the candle and shoved away the burning plant. It smashed across the floor. He crashed into another plant, and it fell on top of him.

* * *

At first, Shuffle moped around, feeling like a fool for killing a plant and getting caught eavesdropping. But the more he thought about it, the less bad he felt, and the more determined he became.

After a bath, he walked down the hallway to what he hoped was his confinement. He needed privacy to plan. Unfortunately, Mama escorted him to the room, trying to figure out what had happened.

"You don't have to be glum," she said. "Bronson's not mad. I'm not mad. It's okay, you can talk."

He should try to convince her, plead with her to forget about Bronson. Sure, the lawman had saved their lives. Sure, he was a paragon of society. Sure, he was handsome and brawny and intelligent.

But he wasn't Dad.

Instead, Shuffle stayed silent. He was done with talking. Done with writing letters. Done with hoping something good would happen. It was time to act.

"Please say something. Anything," she said.

Shuffle looked away and frowned. First things first, he needed to be free of Mama. She couldn't see the truth about Dad, but it wasn't too late to make her realize her mistake. He'd just have to do it on his own. "I don't feel good. Don't think I'll go to school tomorrow."

She knelt and put her hand on his forehead. "Oh heavens, of course." She clasped his cheeks, followed by his neck. "You've had such a night."

Inside the room, Mama tucked him in bed. "I love you."

"Love you, too."

She closed the door, and after a few moments of silence, Shuffle climbed out of the covers and got dressed.

Something had to be done about finding Dad. He had to fix his broken family. Sure, it required him going across the country, alone. It could be dangerous. The chances of success were probably low, but the heroes of legend faced similar odds. He had to dare for that long shot.

The penmanship on the note didn't lie. The art on the cards didn't lie. The spirit behind *Spear of Vengeance* didn't lie. Dad was in San Francisco, making Mythic and, for some dang reason, mixed up with bandits.

Shuffle went over his assets: one canvas bag, one genuine Mythic deck, one authenticator (what he decided to call the contraption), fourteen letters from Dad, an old photograph of Mama, a set of clothes, ten dollars in cash and coin, and one pocket knife. Not a whole lot. To reach California, he'd need more—some food and a canteen of water—but what he had was a start.

The best way to get to California was by locomotive. Unfortunately, the rails didn't run through Mourning Glory, so Shuffle would have to take an old-fashioned stagecoach to Independence, the nearest town with a train station. If he hopped the first morning coach, he'd be on his way before anyone realized he'd gone.

The wind howled as he opened the window. He looked back to the nightstand where the previously unread, fifteenth letter addressed to Mama flickered from the cool breeze. With a deep breath, he climbed out.

CHAPTER 9
RIDING RIFLE

Under the pale red moon, Shuffle sneaked across town to his friend's backyard shed, the one they used as a hideout when they played Pinkertons and train robbers.

He crawled through a loose board and flicked on the authenticator, casting an eerie green light. The shed was roomy enough for a pair of work benches and several equipment racks. Weather vanes in the shapes of roosters, horses, and even flying pigs hung from the rafters. Although he had to dodge sharp edges, he always liked playing with all the metal and tools and what might've been the biggest anvil in Missouri. He pictured Hephaestus's workshop on Mount Olympus to be the same way, just with more armor and weapons.

Shuffle yawned. Sneaking out of Bronson's house was a taxing business. Dad would've gotten a kick out of the secrecy and spycraft. Sometimes he would write coded messages for Shuffle to decipher when they played games or had treasure hunts. Using codes was like having their own special language. Sometimes Dad employed a Caesar cipher, other times a pigpen cipher. The bigger the surprise, the harder the code.

But this whole running-away thing wasn't a game. It was serious. Which why it had to be done in secret.

Yet, he couldn't just leave Mama in the dark and have her imagination whip up terrible reasons of why he'd cut out. He'd have to let her know his mission.

Using his pocket knife, he carved α *FATHER C* into the wall. Alpha and C were clues to use an alphabetic cipher with the keyword FATHER. The coded message . . . well, he'd have to think of one, and he'd have to leave it somewhere else. He didn't want his whereabouts too easy to find. Mama was smart, but she'd surely be too mad and scared to think straight. Bronson had a fair amount of wits, but he was no detective. Somebody would have to be highly clever to put the pieces together. And by the time they did, Shuffle would be well on his way to California.

After a short while, he got comfortable, using his bag of clothes as a pillow and Dad's coat as a blanket. He'd probably freeze his boots off if it weren't for the coat, and thank goodness for wool underwear despite being itchy as a hill of ants. His mind soon drifted off, and he floated to California on a winged hog.

* * *

A low rumbling sound and something sharp clawing at his neck woke Shuffle.

He sat up, still groggy with sleep and feeling as limber as a wooden spoon.

Somehow, Katana had found him. She rubbed her head on his chin, purring. After a moment of nuzzling, she jumped off and stretched in four different ways.

Thankfully, she'd gotten in through the loose board he had used as an entryway—otherwise, she would've been one frozen cat.

✳ ✳ ✳

Shuffle set his new assets on the ground in front of him.

One canteen, dented.

One sausage link, spicy.

One ball of Gouda, encased in red wax.

One vial of Professor Mercury's Wonder Elixir, a cure-all for a hundred ailments, including traveling sickness.

Two jars of marmalade, strawberry and peach.

One loaf of bread, fresh.

The first four items he had bought at the Holland Trading Company. The preserves and the bread he got at the bakery, where he'd had to tender his resignation. Before parting ways, Shuffle left the coded message with the baker.

U IUXX DFGDZ KUFV TUY.

If anyone discovered the key (α *FATHER C*) he had scratched on the wall in the shed, they'd figure out that the message would decode as *I will return with him.* He wanted it cryptic and vague, though Mama should figure out the meaning.

Satisfied with his purchases, he repacked the items, except for the sausage, which he wolfed down. All grand adventures should start with a greasy hot link.

Just as the clock tower struck its seventh chime, he strutted to the Craven Coach building, certain he was going to get the best seat on the stagecoach.

Katana explored the tall weeds around the walkway. Parked out front, the stagecoach looked ready for the long haul, glistening with a coat of green paint, a set of undamaged wheels, and a fresh-looking four-horse team.

Inside, Shuffle nearly keeled over when he saw a long queue at the counter. He brought up the rear behind a married couple wearing rich city duds, a family of six, and two disheveled cowpokes. The ghost of the sausage nearly gurgled up his gullet. He might've gotten there too late.

At a corner table, two older boys were playing Mythic. Seeing them battle it out made Shuffle proud, but it was unfair that Dad wasn't getting credit for making the game. Mythic was never about gaining renown or making money, but Dad deserved some acclaim for creating something that even notorious gunfighters love playing.

Soon, the cowboys left to board the coach, and the line inched up. Above the counter, a clock counted down the seconds. *Tick. Tick. Tick.*

One of the boys playing Mythic slapped his hand down on the table. "Really? You're going to quest with *Sigurd*?" He tilted up his ratty straw hat. "Fine. Go right ahead. I don't care."

"But. I. Wait. Bad move?" A redheaded boy with a cowlick rubbed at his neck.

"Bad like blisters on my butt."

"Let me think." Cowlick's eyes darted to each of his cards.

"Ain't got all morning. I'm riding rifle on the coach." Straw Hat grinned smugly. Made sense that he rode on the stagecoach as one of the protectors. Those guys were generally dumb, brave, or arrogant. Straw Hat was probably two of the three.

The family shambled away, taking a pile of luggage with them. That was a lot of stuff, and the coach was getting full in a hurry. There might not be any more room.

"Then what?" asked Cowlick.

Straw Hat slapped the table. "Attack me, you nincompoop."

"Okay. I attack with *Sigurd*. That is, um—"

"Hold your horses." Straw Hat snapped down a card. "*Blue Blazes*. Three damage to *Sigurd*. Dead. Since he's one of your heroes, two damage to your Belief. You lose."

"Ah, shucks."

The rich couple moved over to a corner, checking their belongings. They had brought a lot of bags, too, for not a whole lotta space.

"Next." The teller pulled down a lever. The counting box rang.

Shuffle took a big step up to the counter. "One ticket to Independence, my good sir."

The teller's eyes narrowed. "One? For you or someone else?"

"Yes, sir, just me. One ticket, please."

"How old are you?"

"Sixteen," Shuffle lied. "Got a growth condition. I can eat all the corn biscuits and pork shanks I want and not gain—"

"Fine, fine, fine. Ticket to Independence will cost . . ." His eyes shifted to a chart. "Five dollars."

Shuffle could've sworn his money just went up in flames. His pocket lint, too. The price would cut into his savings, leaving no cash for a train ticket to California. "Wait a minute. My dad has taken wagons before, and they cost him two dollars at the most. Five is how much train tickets cost."

The teller's eyebrows flared out like white porcupines. "Those are third-class prices. We at Craven Coach run a first-class operation."

"Is there any way you can give me a discount on account of my small size and lack of baggage?"

The teller shook his head. "Next."

Shuffle squeezed his money roll. He'd do no good stuck in Independence. Still, it was better than not going at all. How could he bring Dad back if he couldn't even leave his hometown?

"Wait. Fine. As long as I get to go now," Shuffle said, counting the bills in his hand. "You know, posthaste."

"This one's full. Next stage departs at ten."

Shuffle glanced up to the ticking clock. Ten was almost three hours from now, and he needed to be long gone before Mama caught wind.

The teller tapped at the ticket. "Want this or not?"

Shuffle stuffed the tender back into his pocket and shuddered away from the counter. None of this was going the way he had planned—out of town by breakfast with nothing in front of him but a blue sky and an easy road.

But all great heroes faced challenges on their journeys. It was mishap after mishap, but they persevered. He'd have to find a way. He could—

He bumped into someone.

"Sorry," said Cowlick. "Ain't thinking straight."

"No, my fault."

Cowlick glanced back to the corner table where Straw Hat counted a stack of dimes. "He won my shinies and my best card."

"*Fafnir*, the Norse dragon," Shuffle guessed. It was

a great card, from one of the Norse expansion decks. Powerful and fast.

"That's the one," said Cowlick, snapping his finger.

"Next time, stick to your plan. Quest with *Sigurd*. Attack with *Sigmund* instead. *Odin* is your god, right?"

"How'd you know?"

"You want revenge?" Shuffle pulled out a dollar, coming up with an idea to take Straw Hat's place on the stagecoach. "Take this and challenge him to a rematch. Stick to your strategy, and you'll win."

"Um, I don't want to lose your money."

Shuffle glanced at the wagon. It was almost loaded and ready to go. He handed over the crisp George Washington. "Nope, it's your money now. Have fun."

Cowlick took a deep breath and sauntered over, shaking the greenback like bait.

"Guess I got a few minutes. They won't leave without me," said Straw Hat. The kid rubbed his hands together as though a delicious, fat sausage dangled inches away.

Grinning, Shuffle hurried outside, with his bag tight around his shoulders and his hat tilted over his eyes. His idea might work after all. He grabbed two of the rich lady's flowery-embroidered satchels and loaded them on the back-rack of the coach, hoping they belonged there.

"You the new boy?" the driver asked, fastening luggage to the roof.

Shuffle nodded, keeping his head down.

Another man came around from the front. He held a shotgun in one hand, a carbine in the other. He handed Shuffle the carbine. "Be vigilant, lad. Last orphan got shot in the neck by Black Bart. If a rider comes up to the wagon, shoot first."

Maybe hitching a ride as the rifleman wasn't such a great idea.

Shuffle tried to swallow the heavy lump in his throat, unsure which was worse, the story in his head or the gun in his hands. He would rather jump off a moving stagecoach than shoot the rifle at anyone.

He had fired a gun once. Four years ago, shortly after Dad disappeared, he went hunting with his granddad, Captain. He wanted to prove that he was a man. And he did, until he cried after shooting the pheasant. The kick and the clap of the gun blast had shaken him. The bitter smoke and the way the bird flopped from the air to the ground made him sick.

Sure, he didn't want to get shot, but killing another creature, no matter how small, was a big NO WAY IN HECK. Hoping it wouldn't come to either situation, he clambered up to the rear perch and secured the gun in its rack.

A moment later, the driver finished loading and took his spot at the reins. At the crack of a whip and the driver's call, the stagecoach surged forward.

Katana sprinted from the weeds. She sprang up a

low-hanging footrest and climbed to Shuffle's lap. He eased back in the seat and took a breath.

As for Straw Hat, the kid never came after the stage-coach to reclaim his spot. Maybe he was relieved that he wouldn't have to worry about getting gunned down by Black Bart.

CHAPTER 10
THE RIDER

First-class operation, my boot, Shuffle thought.

His teeth rattled and his back hurt. If the ride was more bearable inside the stagecoach than it was on the back perch, it wasn't by much; there hadn't been any singing or joking from the passengers for a while now. Katana had it best. She was curled around his neck. Her purring hummed against his shoulders. At least the stage-coach hadn't overturned in some ditch or been attacked by bandits . . . yet.

The coach slowed to a stop. Katana slipped down to the seat and watched, alert.

Guessing by the sun, they'd been on the road for three hours. Shuffle wasn't sure how much longer they had left to go. One thing was for certain, the coach shouldn't be stopping in the middle of Nowhere, Missouri.

The driver came around to the back. "Get on that rifle, boy. Keep a lookout."

Shuffle made himself small in the seat. The whole

place—the road, the woods, the sky—seemed to close in on the stagecoach, and it felt like every hidden, dangerous thing could just reach out and get him. "Something wrong?"

"Any riders come charging down that road—shoot 'em. Any riders come out of them trees—shoot 'em." The driver snarled. "Pray you don't have to, but pray with your eyes open."

Shuffle barely managed to nod, but the driver seemed satisfied with the reply and left.

The carbine weighed heavy. The maple stock stung as coldly as its steel trigger. He had gotten over killing that bird four years ago, but he also had vowed never to do it again.

"Why are we stopping?" asked the rich lady passenger.

"Sorry, ma'am. Just a snag on the road. We'll be on our way shortly." The driver tipped his hat and then walked over to the side of the road, where two horses, saddled up but riderless, were grazing.

The other stagecoach man, the one with the shotgun, was there, too, inspecting something in the tall grass. He pointed at the woods and then gestured to the spot on the ground. The driver knelt and put his hand on whatever it was. He shook his head, grimly.

Unwilling to look any longer, Shuffle turned toward the direction they had traveled. The road stretched up an incline. The trees seemed to bend inward from the heavy stillness in the air. Leaves rustled across the dirt, and just over the hill, a dust cloud formed in the distance.

A rider. Closing in fast.

"Someone's coming!" Shuffle's voice cracked. His hands tingled with a buzzing energy.

"Shoot!" shouted the driver, running back toward the wagon. "Now!" The other stagecoach man was nowhere to be seen.

Shuffle's arms trembled as he pressed the gun against his shoulder. It took all his strength to point the barrel straight.

Cresting the hill, the horse seemed to glide. Its muscles rippled with each surge as though its power came from the white blaze on its head. The rider leaned forward. Her braided, dark brown hair whipped backward with the wind, as did a yellow kerchief covering the bottom half of her face. Her eyes, in plain view, shined. She wasn't going to stop, and she wasn't a threat.

Shuffle lowered the gun.

"What are you doing, boy?" The driver slapped the coach. "You got range. Fire."

"No."

"Dang it all." The driver aimed his pistol at the rider. Fifteen yards away and closing.

"Don't. It's a girl!" Shuffle blocked the driver's line of sight with his hand, and the rider raced past in a thunderclap.

"Stupid boy. We could've been dead. Like them two back there." He pulled Shuffle to the ground. Katana growled and hissed. The driver reared back. "What the—? A cat?"

Shotgun came running from the woods, huffing. "What happened?"

"While you were watering the ivies, we almost got attacked by a bandit," the driver said. "Boy here didn't do his job." He kicked Shuffle in the stomach. "A whupping with a good switch oughtta get it in your mind to do as you're told. And no animals allowed."

Shuffle grasped his gut, feeling like he had swallowed a cannonball. "She wasn't a bandit. Just a girl."

Shotgun pushed the driver aside. "The lad's a greenhorn. Give him a break. I told him to be vigilant. Knowing when to pull the trigger is just that." He lifted Shuffle to his feet. "The lad made the right call."

The rich lady stuck her head out the window. "Are we leaving yet?"

The driver faced her, his ears spicy-chili red. "Ma'am. Shut up." He stormed to the front of the stagecoach.

Shuffle dusted himself off, still half-bent from the kick to his gut. "What was that about the other two?"

"Two bodies," Shotgun said. "Two lawmen from Mourning Glory. One of them, I'm guessing, was a tracker. From what I could tell, they came upon a group crossing the woods. There was a gunfight. They lost. The winners, three of them, rode off through the field."

Shuffle moaned. His mouth turned pasty, and a sickening feeling mingled with the pain from being walloped by the driver. The two dead had to be Douglas and the other deputy from Mourning Glory, and that meant the three shooters were the lady bandits from last night.

"I wanted to scare you with the Black Bart story," said Shotgun, with an unconvincing grin. "It's Craven Coach's policy to shoot first and ask questions after. Another rule we have to follow, and I don't like it, is that we have to leave the dead men where we found them. After we get to town, we'll report it."

"Leave them? But—"

"Where're we going to put them? This is no hearse."

"Understood." Shuffle climbed back to his perch and put Katana on his lap. He needed to hold her.

Just because it was policy didn't make it right. It was rotten, but there was nothing he could say or do. He was just a stowaway.

In an unforgiving world, he knew he could end up like the two deputies or, worse, suffer the same fate as Dad. Mama would end up having another funeral with an empty casket.

And that was why he couldn't fail. Mama would do more than tear her hair out. She'd be devastated. When she was young, she lost her mother. Then Dad. Then her father, Captain; Granddad was alive, but he and Mama weren't on speaking terms. Shuffle was all she had left.

He had to make it, not only to save Dad but to make their family whole again.

The stagecoach finally got moving, and soon, they passed the bodies in the tall grass. He said a little prayer for the dead. With his eyes open.

CHAPTER 11
INDEPENDENCE

The remainder of the ride was less than fun. Katana puked up mouse guts. Shuffle dropped the jar of peach preserves. He nearly fell off the perch. Twice. His back throbbed. His butt, too.

But he made it to Independence.

He had no intention of doing that again for a while. The train ride oughtta be much better.

After unloading bags from the stagecoach, Shuffle snuck off to find the train station, with Katana on his shoulders.

People, horses, and wagons crammed the streets. Although busier than Mourning Glory, Independence had the same feel about it. Not quite wild, not quite proper. The smell was most definitely there—cows, dung, and dirt.

Even though he was still in Missouri, he knew a few miles away was a land of frontier homesteads and desert settlements. They were places he'd only read about. It was going to be a different world, and he hoped to see it all. On the way back. With Dad.

Up ahead, in front of the dry meats store, a pack of dogs was fighting. The barking and growling and gnashing of teeth made Katana's ears perk up. Shuffle took a wide path past the scrum along the raised walkways, where instead of cattle and stagecoaches, he dodged people and swinging doors.

Except for one.

The door to Wells Fargo blasted open and struck Shuffle in the head. He fell hard. *Ambush: Attack +1. Opponent's defense is halved.*

Through blurry eyes, he peered up.

A girl stood in eclipse with the afternoon sun. She held out her hand, and for a moment there, he thought he was at the gates of Valhalla, being greeted by a Valkyrie.

"Come on, now. It didn't hit you that hard," she said.

Shuffle grasped her hand; the girl's skin was rough and calloused.

"Pay attention next time so you don't get hurt." She yanked him up, nearly pulling his arm out of its socket.

"How about not kicking the door open so it doesn't catch anybody unaware," he said, rotating his shoulder. Thankfully, it still worked.

She put her arms akimbo and glared. "I've had enough bull for one day. Don't need it from the likes of you." She wore her gray hat at a tilt over her dusty braided hair. A constellation of dark freckles dotted her right cheek. She looked maybe thirteen, tall, and capable.

It had to be so, with a gun at her hip. The only prissy thing about her was a yellow kerchief around her neck.

Then it hit him like the swinging door. "You're the rider from today."

"So," she said, shrugging.

"You almost got shot."

She raised her eyebrows. "You're saying *you* almost shot me?"

"No. I'd never. The driver told me to, but I didn't. He almost did, but I stopped him." His voice went out on a trilly high note.

"Really? So you're my knight in an oversized wool coat?"

"No," he squeaked again. Ugh, how embarrassing.

"Didn't think so," she said, grinning.

"But I *am* on a quest." He crossed his arms, savoring the notion that he was just like Perseus or Telemachus, though he doubted she would want to hear about that stuff.

Katana walked a figure-eight and rubbed her head around the girl's legs.

The girl lifted Katana up to her face. "Tell me, kitty, is this weakling on a great mission?"

He swiped his cat back. "That's plain mean. After I saved your life."

"My apologies, Sir Knight. Don't behead me." She untied her yellow bandana and held it aloft like a delicate flower. "My favor. For luck on your journey."

Shuffle went speechless.

She flicked the bandana over his shoulder. He spun around to catch it, but it disappeared. Or it never left her hand. He turned back around. She had vanished among the throng of people coming and going. *Misdirection: Defending unit loses their action.*

* * *

At the train station, Shuffle went to buy a ticket to California. Instead, he came away with a third-class ticket to Denver. That was all he could afford. Eight dollars bought him a trip to the Rocky Mountains. A dollar and some change (thirty-three cents) remained of his meager life's savings.

The new destination could be a good thing. High up in the mountains, Denver would be the closest thing to Mount Olympus he would ever see. But how could he afford to go from there to San Francisco? Get a job? Rob a bank? Play Mythic for scratch? Any option that occurred to him would either take forever or land him in jail.

With plenty of time to kill before boarding and the musty station smelling like armpits, he went to get his fill of fresh air. According to the ticket teller, the trip would take two and a half days. Long time to be stuck with a bunch of stinkers in a train car.

Outside, Shuffle sat on the edge of a raised porch, his

feet dangling just above the ground. He ate some bread with strawberry jam. They probably didn't serve food in third class, nothing edible anyways. He sipped from the canteen and then poured a trickle of water for Katana to lap up.

A man shouldering a box camera and tripod walked over. "May I take a photograph of you and your cat?"

Shuffle shrugged, figuring there was no harm in it. He closed the canteen and held Katana.

The man set up in front of them and pointed to the lens. "On three," he said before counting down. The box camera clicked. After thanking Shuffle, the man lugged his rig down the street.

"Cute kitty."

Shuffle turned to the voice and peered up at a lady standing on the platform. She wore a big white hat with white feathers.

"Can I pet her?" she asked in a husky voice.

"Sure. But she can be mean sometimes."

"Not this pretty thing," she said, reaching out.

Katana hissed and hunkered down. Her hairs stood in warning.

A handle stuck out of Lady Feather's sleeve. A knife handle?

"Maybe you shouldn't," Shuffle said. "She's had a long day. And I gotta go." Pretty or not, the woman gave off an unsettling aura.

Lady Feather kept pushing her luck, making Katana

growl. This was going to be bad. She was liable to get scratched.

"Don't be like that, kitty. I just want to touch you."

"And hurt your pretty little hand?" Another woman joined them on the platform. She stood a foot shorter than Lady Feather but took up more elbow room like a short stack of pancakes. She wore a green split skirt and vest. Her gray Stetson barely clung to her head of wild red hair. A large satchel draped across her chest, hanging opposite the gun belt at her hip. A sling held up her left arm, which was tightly bandaged.

Shuffle gulped as his throat went dry. Could she be the bandit that Bronson shot? Could the two of them be part of the three bandits the deputies had been chasing when they were killed?

Lady Feather withdrew her hand and rubbed at a silver pendant around her neck. Shortstack had one, too. It was a medallion etched with a skull and surrounded by five arrowheads in a star formation. A sort of badge for outlaws.

"There's something wrong with your kitty. Normal cats love me," Lady Feather said, crossing her arms.

Shortstack laughed. "Guess this fleabag is different."

"That's because my cat's got sense." Shuffle pulled Katana, ready to go wherever the ladies weren't.

"Boy has some gumption," Shortstack said.

Lady Feather raised an eyebrow. "I like that in my men."

Shortstack chuckled, her red hair bouncing. "Watch out, boy. Be glad you ain't shaving age."

A high-pitched whistle cut through the moment.

"Telegraph house is this way." A lady in oxblood leather chaps and black boots with tarnished spurs stood in the middle of the street, causing riders to plow into each other. It appeared she didn't give a dang about causing an accident.

Lady Feather stepped off the platform. "Just wanted to pet the kitty. Good luck to you now."

"A black cat? You got your charms all wrong." Oxblood shook her head. Her wavy, dark brown hair plummeted from underneath a black, wide-brim hat.

"She's lucky for me," mumbled Shuffle, standing up to finally board the train.

"Do I know you?" Oxblood sauntered forward and swiped aside the drape of her red duster jacket, revealing her pair of six shooters and a silver buckle with the skull-and-arrowheads symbol. Was she the leader?

"No, ma'am." He put his head down. Looking in her cold, gray-steel eyes was like staring at both barrels of a sawed-off shotgun. The gunfight at home had been a flash in the dark, but that quick moment was all it took to see the face behind the pistol and muzzle fire.

Oxblood was the same lady bandit who had broken into his house.

CHAPTER 12
ALL ABOARD

Shuffle didn't look back as he cut through the train station. Hopefully, Oxblood didn't recognize him from the break-in. It was dark at the time, and she had to deal with Bronson. Still, the best strategy was to get far away from her and her two bandit friends. No shame in retreating.

The station waiting area filled up with eager passengers, and Shuffle situated himself in the middle of the throng, even though some of the people smelled like a sty.

Katana poked out from his satchel's opening. Shuffle kissed her head, hoping they weren't being followed. Dread gnawed at the back of his mind.

A waft of fruity perfume cut through the stench. A family of three plowed through the crowd, trying to get to the other end of the platform.

"Is that your kitty?" A little girl with ribbon-curly hair wearing a periwinkle dress stopped in her tracks, apparently waiting for an answer.

Her father tugged at her. "Keep moving, my flower."

Shuffle ignored her, hopeful she'd just go away. He didn't need the attention.

"Papa, I want to see the kitty." She pulled back, and he relented.

"Yes, yes, Sweetums. How nice. Now let's go."

Listen to Daddy, Sweetums. Shoo. You're blowing my cover. Perhaps standing in one spot wasn't the best idea.

"Gerald, my skirt hems are getting dirty," the mother said as her eyes darted from one person to another.

"Of course, my love." The father sighed. "Sweetum Flower, please. Time to go."

"I want to touch the kitten," whined Sweetums.

Shuffle frowned. "Just leave us alone."

"That's not how you talk to a lady," she said, turning her nose up. "And I'm a lady of high standing. A boy like you don't get to speak to me like that."

All sorts of prying eyes and ears focused straight at him. Did any of those stares belong to the bandits?

Now on ambush alert, he looked around for the ladies, testing the limits of his eyeballs. He spotted Lady Feather's white plumage swimming among the sea of hats and heads of the crowd. Where there was one, the other two must be near. Time for a tactical withdrawal.

Shuffle skittered away from the little girl and from Lady Feather. He shouldered through the crowd, unsure if the bandit tailed him or where the other two waited. If he kept moving, he could be a harder target to get a bead on, so he zigzagged, side-stepped, and weaved with no rhyme or reason, like a rabbit in survival mode. Or a chicken with its noggin cut off.

The conductor called for first class. A number of fancy folk, including Sweetums, made their way through the crowd and onto the luxury-class car. Thankfully, she would be far from the third-class car, where he would be riding.

The platform remained full. Families, couples, and loners waited their turn, clutching dusty bags, wearing creased shoes. Their eyes looked forward, perhaps to someplace better. Someplace new. Someplace with answers.

A push sent Shuffle into a fellow carrying a pack loaded with mining equipment. That man crashed into the small stick of dynamite that was Shortstack.

"Watch where you're going, leatherface. Can't you see there's a lady standing here?" Shortstack shoved the man backward.

The old miner spat on the ground. "Thought you was a javelina with a wig."

Shortstack reared back and unleashed a right upper cut. The punch lifted that poor sucker off the ground. He fell right on his pack and couldn't get up.

Rising Strike: Attack +1. Opponent damaged cannot attack for one turn.

Instead of watching the rest of the beat-down, Shuffle retreated into the crowd, unnoticed. He circled back and made his way to a hidden corner piled high with crates. Time to formulate another plan.

Scurrying around like a blind mouse perhaps wasn't such a good tactic. Hiding until the time was right, then bolting for the train might be the way to go. No—being stealthy like Katana on the prowl had to be the best maneuver.

Soon, the conductor called for second class. More people boarded the next two cars down the line. This group took longer, and the minutes seemed like hours.

The remaining third-class passengers spread out on the platform. They were the largest group, likely the ones waiting to play out a fresh hand. Maybe there was someone similar to him, searching for some lost truth.

"All aboard," the conductor called out.

The doors on the last three cars opened, and the mass of people surged forward but moved at a turtle's pace. Shuffle left his hiding spot and snuck to the center of the herd, staying alert for any of the three bandits.

At the far end of the platform, Shortstack climbed up on a row of crates, scanning the area. Shuffle sucked in a breath, holding it until he was out of the bandit's view.

Three men stopped to gawk at Lady Feather in her pretty white dress (with hidden knife). Shuffle tiptoed past, using them as a blockade.

Three feet from the entry. Nobody yelled out to stop. One foot away.

Then he hopped up to the door and gave the conductor the ticket.

The conductor punched it, and Shuffle slipped into the train.

CHAPTER 13

UNSCHEDULED STOP

Third class was cowpies. Shuffle reckoned the train car was more fit for livestock than people.

The benches hurt, two unwashed fellows took up most of the seat, the air smelled like armpits, and the noise pounded like artillery in a siege. The walls rattled, and the small window didn't do much in the way of stench removal. The only thing missing was hay on the floor.

Thankfully, Oxblood appeared to be nowhere in the car, left behind in Independence. Shuffle had outwitted her and her bandit friends. Now if only the law would catch her, then it would be game over.

Despite the stifling air and the none-too-comfy confines, he felt a buzz throughout his body. He closed his eyes, wondering if it was what Telemachus felt when he started his search, or what Perseus experienced riding Pegasus.

Shuffle eased into his seat with Katana purring on his lap. He took out his photo of Mama. In the brown-tinted picture, she was young and happy. Captain had just come home from the war. Their reunion had been a joyous occasion. These days, their relations weren't quite so merry. Mama said their bitter falling-out was Captain's fault, that he was a coward because he wouldn't leave the comfort of his ranch to search for Dad. It was hard to believe of a war hero. Chalk up another thing poisoned by Dad's disappearance.

"I promise, Mama. I will find him," whispered Shuffle.

Soon, his eyelids grew heavy, and for the first time since Mourning Glory, he relaxed.

* * *

The shriek of iron on iron woke Shuffle from a nightmare of Mama bleeding on the ground, the jingle of spurs, and the bitter smell of gun smoke.

He lurched forward, but something held him back. Someone had put their arm across his chest before he ate the bench in front of him.

The brakes must've been pulled hard, making the train scream as it slowed.

Shuffle turned to thank whoever had saved him, but he instantly wanted to go back to dreamland, nightmare or not.

The lady in the oxblood chaps.

"Have a good nap, Jones? We're nearing the next stop." Her gun-steel gray eyes flared with a sort of deadly playfulness, like Katana watching a bird unaware of the danger. Except Shuffle knew he was in trouble.

"Sorry, ma'am. Not Jones. The name's Jim Dark-wood. Jimmy, ma'am."

"Darkwood?" She smiled, leaned back. "Is your pa famous? I think I've heard of him. That is, if it's the same Darkwood I'm thinking of."

Shuffle shrugged, playing dumb. Maybe she would think he was the wrong kid. The wrong prey.

"Don't be like that. You can tell me," she said. "You got a famous pa, right? World-renowned?"

Dad, with this Mythic hoopla, could be famous. Instead, Stan Slythe had taken all the credit.

"No, ma'am," Shuffle squeaked. "Daddy's a nobody. He's just a ranch hand."

She looked away, disappointment oozing from her face. Hopefully, she was convinced he wasn't her target.

"Where is your pa?" She rested her elbow on his shoulder. Her long, brown hair seemed to slither toward his neck. "Or are you traveling alone?"

Alone meant vulnerable, which would lead to dead in a ditch for the buzzards and coyotes to pick at his bones.

He hugged his bag, then realized Katana was gone. His gut turned into a butter churn.

"Well?" She leaned in, and the icy smell of mint escaped her teeth. "Where's your pa?"

"I guess he went to the dining car."

"The food car ain't open to third-class dregs."

The train screeched.

"Then he just got up to stretch his legs. He's got bad knees and can't sit for too long."

Oxblood slapped her lap. A cloud of dust popped up from her leathers. "Well, I'm guessing he'd want his seat back?"

"Yes, ma'am. He's rude and unfriendly. Lady or not, he won't like you taking his spot." Shuffle took a breath. It could be his last if she didn't buy what he was selling.

"I better go then." She got up and turned.

Shuffle exhaled, certain he was gonna live.

"So, your pa ain't famous?" asked Oxblood, sitting down again.

Oh, heck. He changed his mind—he was gonna be vulture food.

"I swear the name Darkwood lights my lantern," she said. "Why is that?"

"I don't know, ma'am. It's common around these parts." Shuffle looked for an escape, or for help. The two men across the aisle snored away. The same for the people in front and behind. Would they wake up if he screamed bloody murder? Would they even care? Shuffle glanced up, thinking he could squeeze out the small window.

"Common on the bookshelf. You chose Dash Darkwood from the ten-penny books to be your fake father? Nice try, Jones. I know who you are. First name Jason. Son of Penny and Euless Jones."

The train shuddered, before letting out one last gasp of steam.

Shuffle shrank in his little corner, alone without a play. Game over.

The lady bandit inched closer. "Here we are. Topeka. My stop. Give me the key or it'll be your stop, too."

Key? He knew his assets, and a key wasn't one of them. And Topeka. That was in Kansas, far from Denver. Heck of a lot farther from San Francisco.

"I don't know what you're talking about. I don't have a key."

She stuck a black revolver against his ribs. "Not a peep, or it'll be your last." *The Dark Six: Attack +3. Defender cannot interrupt or counter-attack.*

Shuffle froze. He was gonna get shot. For nothing.

"Does Cassandra's Warning ring your dinner bell, Jones?"

The note Bronson found at the house. The note in Dad's handwriting.

Shuffle shook his head. *Play dumb or die.*

The train car door opened with a bang, making him jump.

She grabbed his arm and dug the barrel in tighter. "You're coming with me after all. You wouldn't be out here on your lonesome if you didn't have it or if you didn't know something. I'm going to get the key. One way or another."

CHAPTER 14
FIRST-CLASS WOES

Maybe being forced off the train at Topeka meant finding a better way to San Francisco. Denver was said to be a mile up in the mountains. Shuffle didn't much like the cold. Or avalanches. Or Sasquatches.

Sure, he'd rather leave on his own than depart with Oxblood and her six-shooter. But hostages couldn't be choosers.

Escape seemed a miracle play, with Oxblood still clamped onto his arm. He didn't know a lick about Cassandra's Warning, Katana was missing, and he was sure as dead.

Until the little girl from the train platform, her yellow hair in ribbon curls, showed up. Sweetums!

"That's him." She thrust a finger at Shuffle. "That's the urchin."

The conductor and a security officer armed with a club stood with her at the open doorway, looking cross.

Shuffle lifted his hat and scratched his head. What did he do to Sweetums to have her pretty dang irate?

"Is that your son, ma'am?" asked the conductor, scowling.

Oxblood pressed her gun deeper. A deadly threat.

But that's all it was. Would she shoot him in front of witnesses? Would she take him and blast her way out? Too risky. Too bloody. He'd have to take a chance with the conductor.

"No, she's not my mama," he said, shutting his eyes and bracing for the bullet.

This time, Oxblood let go and withdrew her gun.

"Come with us, boy," the guard said, tapping the club.

Another threat. But preferring the end of a blackjack to the point of a gun, Shuffle went along with the guard. He felt Oxblood's death stare at the back of his head. She was surely gonna keep hounding him. But now that he was at the mercy of two railroad men and Sweetums, the bandit would have to wait in line.

The conductor led the way through the train, followed by Sweetums, who often turned around to give him ugly looks. The guard brought up the rear. Shuffle wasn't going anywhere but forward.

Stopping in first class, Shuffle breathed in a lungful of crisp, clean air. Big windows brightened the sitting car, which was decked out with plush furniture, velvet curtains, and silver trays of snacks.

"I found the boy. Do I get a prize now?" Sweetums' periwinkle pleated skirt swayed as she ran to her father and mother. They shot Shuffle a scathing look.

The conductor snagged Shuffle's arm. "Son, didn't you know it's against Railroad's policy to bring animals on board?" He pointed to the corner of the car at a floor-to-ceiling cabinet. Shuffle noticed now that his hand was bandaged, blood seeping through the threads. "Behind the console. A black cat. Is it yours?"

Shuffle knelt down at the cabinet. Katana's eyes shone in the dark. "Yes!"

"It pee-peed on my dolly," Sweetums cried.

Everybody piled on: "It scratched the Italian leather chair."

"Pooped in my shoe."

"Hacked a hairball in my hat."

Shuffle blocked out more of their complaints and called for Katana. She chirped back, slinked forward, and entered the bag.

The guard grabbed at it. Shuffle swung away in time.

"Son, for breaking the rules, you are no longer a passenger here," the conductor said. "And for its violent behavior, your cat must be destroyed."

That wasn't going to happen. Shuffle took a big step back. "I'll get off this stinking train. Just leave her alone."

The mother wagged a finger. "That animal must be put down."

The guard swiped at the bag again. Spinning away, Shuffle knocked over a flowery porcelain pitcher from a side table, spilling milk all over a fancy rug.

The far door that led to the next car was still open,

but the cat-haters blocked the escape. Odysseus would instantly have a plan. Shuffle gnashed his teeth and acted like Achilles instead. *Charged with Fury: Attack +2 against all defenders.*

Shuffle kicked the pitcher at the conductor. A wave of white liquid surged out as it flew. The conductor dodged the milk, which soaked Sweetums. But the pitcher hooked and found the conductor's head. It shattered, and he bent over, moaning into his hands. The mother and father backed away to console their crying daughter, but the guard held his ground, raising his club high. As Shuffle dashed toward the exit, he opened the bag and flung Katana at the guard's face. She hit her target, growling and hissing. Shuffle slipped past the guard to the door. Katana dropped to the floor, sprinted between the guard's legs, and leaped back into the bag.

Shuffle darted out of the first open exit and ran. Without looking back, he weaved among passengers coming and going on the boarding platform. He kept his feet moving, matching the heartbeats echoing in his ears. Soon, he made it out of the train station and onto the street. Across the way and catty-corner from the station, he found an alley with three possible escape routes. A decent place to regroup. Finally, hands on knees, he sucked in some air.

"Found you," said a voice, as someone grabbed Shuffle's coat collar and pulled him backward into the shadows.

CHAPTER 15
LIKE AN ARROW

Shuffle released a slow, hissing breath as he stared at the fist clutching his shirt and at the gun inches from his ear.

"Keep quiet or else," said the girl with the yellow kerchief, holstering her pistol. Her pigtails whipped through the air as she took a quick peek around the alley. "You weren't followed, but that don't mean they ain't coming."

He pushed her hand away. "What the heck are you doing?"

She put a finger to his lips. "I said *quiet*."

Shuffle stilled, keeping the contact with the girl's warm body, and whispered, "What are you doing here?"

"Come on, we need to move." She broke away, and it felt like the sudden loss of a hat from a harsh wind gust.

Really, though, he still had his hat, and she was being way too insistent. "Move where?"

"Away from here." The girl grabbed his hand, her grip as strong as a bear claw.

They hurried out of the alley and into a busy street, weaving in and out of people's way. Shuffle bore the pain of the girl's crushing grip for a whole block, until they turned the corner and stopped at a hitching post in front of a boisterous saloon.

Shuffle shook the hurt out of his hand, as casually as possible. "Oh, sure. A watering hole. The perfect place for a kid to hide out. Nice one."

"Close enough to the station to see if anyone's still giving chase. Far enough to give us a chance to bug out to if we get spotted. Besides, this is where my horse is. Unless you want to go back to your dark alley, keep your smart mouth to yourself."

After unhitching the horse, she climbed up and offered her unforgiving hand. "You're not safe in Topeka. Come with me." A scar ran up her forearm and disappeared underneath her rolled-up sleeve. The yellow bandana waved in the wind. Her top lip formed slightly off-set peaks. Freckles guided the way to her eyes. They narrowed. "What you waiting for, Sir Knight? A written invitation?"

Shuffle blinked, refocusing his thoughts. Sure, he needed to get back on track, but accepting aid from this flint-strike of a girl right at this moment would be a dumb move. "But—"

Her eyes focused past him. "Oh, birdshot. Put your head down."

Tired of being told what to do since the second she'd grabbed him unawares, he turned and looked.

A woman wearing buckskins, with a black star dyed

on her tasseled jacket, rode past. A pendant—a skull and five arrowheads within a circle—dangled over her chest. It was similar to what the three bandits were wearing. The ladies were like heads of the same hydra.

Black Star faced him, and he locked eyes with her. Dark, heavy, and focused, her gaze stoned him in place.

Katana called to him from her hiding spot in the bag, but he couldn't look away from the woman.

"Double birdshot. She's spotted you. You're dead," the girl said.

Thankfully, instead of pouncing, Black Star spun toward the sound of some hollering. She urged her horse down the road, toward a ruckus of unruly boys.

The girl offered her hand again. "Lucky fool. She didn't realize who you are. We need to go."

The girl's eyes went up once more, and her face turned grim. Shuffle followed her gaze to Oxblood standing in front of the train station. Black Star moved past the shouting kids and headed straight for Oxblood.

Shuffle didn't wait for the girl to ask again; he grabbed her arm. She pulled him up with a grunt, and he grasped her waist. She smelled like sage.

"Hold the saddle, not me," she said.

Shuffle felt his face flush. "Sorry."

The girl clicked her tongue, and they shot off like an arrow from Artemis's bow.

CHAPTER 16
SIX-PLUM SKYLLA

All Shuffle could do was hold on as the girl in the yellow kerchief sped them along the outskirts of town.

After several seemingly random turns and double-backs, they ended up at the local livery. Apparently, the girl had ridden hard from Independence, fast enough to beat the train, and she needed to get a fresh horse.

The girl went into the office and came out with a canvas satchel and a small parcel under her arm. Shuffle followed her to the stables.

"We get Queen Victoria. Stall three," she said.

Queen V whinnied, and her black mane whipped about as she shook her head. Her brown fur shimmered in the light.

Why did the girl say *we*?

Shuffle raised his open hand, so the horse could get a smell of him. When Queen V didn't chew off his fingers, he turned to the girl. "What's your deal?"

She readied a saddle, strapping her things to it. "What deal?"

"Did you ride from Independence to find me?"

"Yes." She tested the straps and ties of the harness.

Yes? Over seventy miles. On horseback. To find him.

No girl ever chased him across the schoolyard, much less hunted him down across the Missouri-Kansas border.

Shuffle's cheeks warmed. "*Why* did you ride all the way from Independence to find me?"

She shrugged. "I help the weak is all."

"Hold on there. I'm not weak." Shuffle stood a little straighter. "A weakling wouldn't venture out on a quest, you know."

"I'm just ribbing you." She checked her gun's chamber and spun it shut. "I overheard Skylla talking to her gang. She mentioned a boy with a black cat. You. Whenever she puts a name to a list, it's never good."

"Skylla?"

"Yep. Six-Plum Skylla. You've never heard of her?"

"Never that name. I'm guessing she's the lady in the oxblood chaps."

The girl slapped her hands clean. "Six-Plum's a hired gun. Don't know who she's working for right now, but this person wants you bad. Six-Plum and her posse get their man, one-hundred percent."

Shuffle gulped down a lump of spit. Hired killers hunting him down for Cassandra's Warning and a key. He didn't know what those things were, much less have them in his possession. Yet, they were after him. He took off his hat and wiped the sweat from his brow. "Did she say why?"

The girl looked down to her boots. "Nope. I didn't hear a reason, just that they were meeting at Topeka." She glanced up and smiled. "So how did you get away from her up till now? She never comes up empty-handed."

He held Katana close. "See, I'm not so weak after all."

CHAPTER 17

ATALANTA

The girl in the yellow kerchief leaned in against the wind. Her pigtails flickered in Shuffle's face. They smelled like sage.

Despite gaining some distance from danger, Shuffle felt uneasy with his present company. Sure, she was just a girl—a little rough around the knuckles, but not some bandit leader—yet something didn't quite play right. She'd been cagey from the get-go and hadn't said a dang thing since town.

"Thanks for getting me out of there," he called to her as they galloped along. "I'm Jason Jones. Call me Shuffle."

No response.

The Kansas landscape of grass, weeds, and more grass lollygagged for miles and miles and miles. The sun dawdled behind them.

He tapped her on the shoulder. "What do I call the rider who beat the train to Topeka?"

She didn't answer.

He tried again: "What's your name?"

Again, silence.

"I know I'm being chased and, by extension, you're being chased," he said, changing tacks. "Why are you helping me?"

"Told you. That's what I do." She glanced over her shoulder. The color of her eyes hid under the shadow of her hat's wide brim.

The wild landscape looked the same: brown, flat, and wide open. Nothing distinguishing for miles. "Where are we going?"

"Someplace."

"Would this place be anywhere near a train station?"

"No trains. Just Queen Victoria here. Heyaah!"

The horse galloped hard, full speed, turning off the road and onto a field with nothing but grass and sky in front of them. No sign of civilization.

He leaned forward, resting against her back. "Look, thanks for saving me and all, but I need to go where I need to go, and this ain't where I need to go."

She pulled on the reins, bringing Queen V to a stop. An unkindness of ravens cawed from a nearby dead tree. A sharp gust blew the girl's hair from her eyes as she looked back at him. "First, we lose Skylla and her tracker. Second, I need to make a delivery. It was the only way I could get a horse. Then we can continue your quest, Sir Knight."

"We?"

"Well, I think you need my help."

"Not sure I can accept help from someone who won't even tell me her name." He slid off the horse and began unhitching his bag, not intending to really leave. Katana peered up from the bag's opening and yawned.

The girl huffed. "What are you doing? Get back on."

Like a bad lemon, her tone made him cringe. "Thanks for bringing me to nowhere. I can make it the rest of the way on my own, thanks."

"You're not gonna last out here. Six-Plum will find you."

"Why do you even care? Why would you help a stranger being chased by killers?" He stared into her brown eyes. *Don't falter. Don't break.*

Her face softened. "Because I want to be on a quest, too. The bank don't need my delivery service anymore. This is my last job. Without work, how am I supposed to survive? And I sure as heck don't want to die of boredom, neither. So yeah, I have nothing to do and nowhere else to go."

"You don't have anyone to help or any place to stay?" Shuffle asked, curious in spite of himself.

She tilted her hat over her eyes. "I have people, but it ain't the same. I sleep at the livery, or in the storage rooms, sometimes in the stables with the horses. Depends if I get lone—you know what? This is stupid. Just get on."

Shuffle crossed his arms. "We don't know anything

about each other. Why should I accept your help?"

Her eyes narrowed, and her hand drifted toward her pistol, as if she was considering whether maiming him would help her case. Shuffle took Katana out, holding her. It was two against one, now. *Don't back down.*

The girl's cheeks puffed out in a sigh. "Atalanta. My name's Atalanta. Happy now?"

"Atalanta? Your parents named you that? Not the city in Georgia, but *At-uh-lanta*?"

"You gonna give me guff about my name?" Her eyes sharpened to slits like knives. "Maybe I *will* shoot you."

"No, I like it! Atalanta is an Amazon huntress, you know, a lady warrior, in mythology. No man could keep up with her in a race." The girl had proved she could beat a train when on horseback.

"I don't know any of that. My pa didn't read much, just maps and such." Atalanta stared at the space between them, and after a moment, she smiled. "But my ma, she liked books and stories. She was Kaw, and her people are named for the south wind. It kinda makes sense."

"Where are your parents now?" asked Shuffle.

Atalanta holstered her six-shooter. "They're dead."

"I'm sorry." He cleared his throat. "I'm looking for my dad. He's supposed to be dead, but I think he's in San Francisco. That's my quest."

She nodded briskly. "Well, it's none of my business, but I'm game to take a trip to California. You done lollygagging?"

Katana clawed at the bag, apparently wanting back inside. Shuffle guided her into the satchel and rehooked it to the saddle. He climbed up with Atalanta's help. If someone had to aid him on his journey, why not the rider with the name of an Amazon warrior?

She snapped the reins, and Queen V sprang to top speed.

CHAPTER 18
THE KEY AND THE CIPHER

Nearing sundown, Atalanta and Shuffle stopped at a fenced-in hundred-acre homestead, K Midas Ranch. Shuffle stayed with Queen Victoria by the water trough while Atalanta delivered the parcel. Minutes later, she came out with a small roll of money and a shiny, green pear. She fed the fruit to the horse.

"You hungry?" Shuffle rummaged through his bag. "Got bread and cheese."

She motioned to the contraption. "What's that?"

He took it out, the brass cold on his fingers. "I call it an authenticator."

"What does it do?" She stood close, her hair drifting near his face. Sage.

"Put it behind a Mythic card, light it, and it'll reveal a special marking. Counterfeits won't have the mark."

"Show me."

Shuffle pulled out a random card from his deck. He placed the green glass bulb against the card's back and flicked the switch. A spark and a small bit of kerosene produced a flame, and the identifying mark came into view.

She tapped at the bulb. "That's it?"

He shrugged.

"What's special about the game?" she asked.

"It's fun."

Atalanta took a bite of the pear, the clean side. "Fun for idiots eager to lose their shirts. I prefer plinking tin cans. Now *that's* fun, and it hones my skills."

"Those are fighting words." Shuffle wrapped his fingers around the authenticator so hard that he could've choked the cold out of the brass. "My dad made the game, and it's not for idiots."

The girl put her hands at her hips, but after a tense moment, her eyes softened. "I didn't mean it like that. No disrespect to your pa."

"The game just means a lot to me." Relaxing his grip, he put away the authenticator and flipped through the deck, card by card. "Dad originally made it years ago, and when I was old enough, we played it together. Me and him. I even helped make some of the rules and the cards. We had two years of creating and gaming. Dad used to be an antiquities professor back east. I learned mythology from his stories and the game. That was before he left on an expedition. He never came back home and was declared dead. Now, four years later, this game comes out, being sold by snake-oil peddlers." He ran his finger along the curve of the bulb. "If my dad's been missing all this time, how does everyone and their dog get to play the game?"

"Coincidence? Or someone's been using your pa's old stuff?"

"Nope and nope."

"Because he's alive?"

Shuffle nodded.

"My best guess is, he's in California, where Mythic's being made. I have to find him. Bring him back home." Still going through his cards, Shuffle came upon one that wasn't originally in the set—*Trojan Horse*. Like *Spear of Vengeance*, it was a card that they had discussed but never made. *Trojan Horse* made this deck build-out almost unstoppable. Which made sense, since it was Odysseus who came up with the idea. It was unbelievable that the Trojans fell for it. Well, except for two people—a priest (killed by serpents sent by Poseidon before anyone heeded the warning) and a princess of Troy.

A princess of Troy . . .

The thought made his head spin. The ranch lands seemed to blur.

Atalanta nudged him. "What's wrong?"

"The princess . . ."

She spat. "I'm no princess."

"Not you." He snapped up *Trojan Horse*. "The princess was a soothsayer, a fortuneteller, who knew about the Greek soldiers inside the horse."

"Soldiers inside a horse? That's twisted."

"A wooden horse, twenty feet high. Hollow inside, hiding the Greek army." Shuffle told her the rest, how the Greeks used it to infiltrate the city.

She tilted her head. Her eyes caught the light, and Shuffle saw the answer.

"The princess knew about the trick because of her power," he said. "But she was also cursed: no one ever believed her truths. No one believed her warning about the wooden horse. Her name was Cassandra. This card is Cassandra's Warning."

"Wait, so Six-Plum is after that catchpenny?" Atalanta made a face as though a cow had spat cud on her lap.

"This must not be an ordinary card." He flipped it over and back, studying every inch. Just like the legendary horse, nothing appeared different or out of the ordinary. Unless . . .

Atalanta leaned in close. "What?"

Shuffle hit the switch on the authenticator. He handed the brass contraption to her to hold, then he placed the card against the orb.

Something incredible happened, and he couldn't help but suck in a breath.

The key appeared on the card. The key Skylla wanted. It wasn't a physical key that unlocked some box; it was a key that answered a riddle.

Atalanta shook her head. "Those are just stupid letters. Is that even American?"

"Well, no." Shuffle slumped, missing summer. "The word is Latin, from the Greek—"

She stood up, looking unimpressed, and dropped the authenticator in his lap.

He grabbed her wrist. "Hey, sit. Let me tell you about this."

She glared at his hand.

He let go. "Listen, okay. This is important." He lit up the authenticator and placed the card against the glass. The key became visible again.

α *AEGIS C*

"Don't mind the alpha and the C for a sec, okay. The word in the middle is *ee-jis*. Athena's shield."

"Another history lesson?" Atalanta crossed her arms. "What does this have to do with Skylla?"

"She's after a key—a cipher key to a code." Memories of better times filled his head, of days when he and Dad left secret messages for each other. "The alpha symbol means the keyword uses an alphabetic cipher."

She slapped the dust off her gray hat. "Alpha–what?"

"Alphabetic. It's a method that we're supposed to use with the keyword *Aegis*. The keyword will change the alphabet. This new alphabet will be used to create a coded message. Break the code. Answer the riddle. Find out what the heck Skylla wants with Cassandra's Warning. We just need the code."

CHAPTER 19
BECAUSE TREASURE

Shuffle paced along the fence line of the ranch.

The cipher key was useless without the message. Did Skylla or whoever hired her have what was missing? Mama was hurt, Bronson was shot, and two lawmen were dead on account of the darn thing. And for what? What did Dad have that was so important to hide in secrecy and mystery?

Aegis. Athena's shield. It bore Medusa's severed head. It struck fear in men. It even revived a mortally wounded warrior.

It was just a myth.

Except it was also the name of one of the artifacts thought to be in the lost Spanish treasure trove Dad was researching. Two hundred years ago, a royal convoy had headed west on land from Florida to California. The Spaniards were attacked somewhere out west, the treasure lost or stolen.

Six years ago, Dad was approached by his old antiquities mentor, Dr. Bloom, who had discovered the first marker left by the Spanish convoy. Since not all the artifacts and valuables were accounted for, Dr. Bloom hypothesized that the treasure was hidden somewhere in the desert.

A year and a half later, he and Dad organized an expedition to find the cache. After months of searching, Dad had written that they were close. If they found the treasure, Dad was supposed to send for Shuffle and Mama to join him in the desert. But he never did. He never wrote to say they had struck gold. The camp was attacked, and the Arizona rangers never found the bodies, or anything else of value.

Dad must've found something and hidden it before the bandits got there—hence all the secrecy and the need for keys and ciphers.

"I know what they're after." Shuffle took off his hat, his head hurting from excitement, from confusion, from overload.

"Something other than a paperboard card?"

"Treasure," Shuffle said.

Atalanta's face lit up like the evening sky; her freckles were constellations.

He told her what he remembered about Dad's expedition, and she listened without interruption.

"Dad knew something bad was going to happen," he said. "He mailed me the card with the key. The fact that he used a key and cipher means he had hidden something valuable, something that put him in danger."

"Then the money man who hired Skylla must be wise to your pa's treasure." She looked off to the side. "It could be someone your pa's group crossed paths with while on the road."

"Or maybe—"

"A traitor," she said, under a hushed breath.

Shuffle nodded gravely. Whoever put Skylla's gang on their trail had obtained Dad's note somehow. It could've been one of the men from the expedition party, most of them strangers. And there was Dr. Bloom. *He* couldn't have double-crossed Dad. They were more than mentor and apprentice. They were friends. But in dime novels, gold and riches often tore apart even the closest of companions.

"But a note ain't exactly treasure," Atalanta said. "Why hire bounty hunters just to send them after that?"

"The note was just a clue. The gang's searching for the key: Cassandra's Warning. That must mean they have the code."

"And you think this code will lead to treasure?"

"I do."

Atalanta shot at a horse apple thirty yards away. It exploded into green gooey bits. "Well, we have the key and the cipher. Why don't we find the treasure first? That would be a hoot. And it might make whoever's holding your pa captive more keen to bargain with you."

Shuffle nodded slowly. He hadn't planned on this kind of detour, no matter how fun, but it might provide the advantage he needed. Plus, having a centuries-old treasure in his possession would put train fare to California well within his budget. Shoot, he'd have enough gold to ride first class.

"Except we're missing the code," he pointed out. "Without that, we don't have locations or instructions or . . ." More memories of Dad's message game came back to Shuffle with a sudden push of wind. "Whenever he left me a string of codes to break, the first one was always in a letter written as though he was in some far-off land." Dad and his games.

Atalanta spun her revolver, then holstered it. "Do you have any letters from your pa?"

Katana poked her head out of the bag.

CHAPTER 20
ONE OF FOUR

Shuffle and Atalanta took cover under an oak tree. Birds chirped from the branches. Katana went hunting.

Thirsty or just plain dry-mouth excited, Shuffle guzzled from his canteen.

Atalanta grabbed it and took a swig. "Why are you turning red?"

Swapping spit.

"No reason, just hot is all."

"So where do we find the first code?"

He gathered the letters, and the exhilaration made his arms quake just to hold them. Why didn't he think of this before?

"He knew he was in danger," Shuffle said. "He sent the key to me. I think he sent the first message as well."

"You think?"

"I know. I feel it." He handed her half the stack, the ones addressed to Mama. He kept his letters. Private stuff. "The message will look like gibberish."

They read in silence. The first letter almost started a gullywasher, but he held back the tears, not wanting to cry in front of Atalanta.

Dear Shuffle,

The night sky is big and clear out here in the desert. I can almost grab Polaris with my hand, but alas, it is too far. I see the stars of Pegasus. I wish I could take her and fly home. But don't worry, I will return soon, bearing treasures.

Game on,
Dad

Shuffle skimmed through the rest of his stack, looking just for the code and not for any sentimental memories. No need for all that heartache.

"He was in danger, all right. Read this." Atalanta scooted closer, shoulder to shoulder, sharing a letter.

Penny,

Things just got worse. One of our workers, Iowa Pete, was found dead. Got drunk and broke his neck falling off his horse coming back from town after we sent him out for supplies. I don't believe it. He was a good rider and a teetotaler. Bicker is on high alert now. Our backers are getting restless. Even if the money runs dry, we'll be okay. It's just the other stuff that is happening. Dr. Bloom won't give up, though. Please, don't worry.

This will be worth it all. The trouble, the sorrow, the time lost. Hold on to hope. I'm nearly there.

    Love always,

    Euless

The rangers had seen Mama's letters, including this one shouting with evidence of something rotten, but for some reason, they didn't see the proof in the words.

Dr. Bloom seemed determined to continue despite the terrible accident. It was possible he would stop at nothing to get the treasure, even if it meant backstabbing Dad.

Then there were the backers. The men who financed most of the expedition. Dad wasn't rich, nor was Dr. Bloom, so they'd had to convince men of deeper pockets to pay for the workers, horses, and equipment. Maybe one of these rich men had decided not to share the fruits of the investment.

Or the explanation could be as simple as greedy bandits. The Arizona rangers and the local lawmen had subscribed to that theory since the beginning, but they didn't have the key and the cipher to consider as evidence of a greater conspiracy.

Shuffle continued with his set. Letters he knew frontwards and backwards. If there was a code, he would've known it. He had read them all a thousand times.

Except for the one Mama turned in to the rangers before he got the chance to read it. The one that came with the prototype deck. Dad's final letter.

He flipped over the paper. Scribbled on the back:

TKTG UABEWL LD LVDKS W LJMKL

"I found it!"

She nudged him. "You can figure that out?"

"Gimme something to write with, and I'll show you."

Atalanta fished out a charcoal stick and some butcher paper from her pack. Shuffle wrote everything down as he explained how the keyword modified the alphabetic cipher. Below it, he jotted the normal alphabet, followed by Dad's coded message.

AEGISTUVWXYZBCDFHJKLMNOPQR
ABCDEFGHIJKLMNOPQRSTUVWXYZ
TKTG UABEWL LD LVDKS W LJMKL

Using the cipher alphabet, he started the first letter of the keyword message, T, and translated it to F. He decoded the next letter, K, to S. He did this until he cracked the code.

For the second time, Atalanta paid attention. No one could resist mysteries and treasure, not even a cool-as-gun-steel rider.

"This is it," Shuffle said, showing her what he'd figured out.

FSFC GAMBIT TO THOSE I TRUST

She frowned. "What in cannon smoke does that mean?"

For a moment, he couldn't make sense of the words, imagining artillery fire, explosions, and clouds of chaos swallowing him whole.

But after a moment of feeling dumb, he realized what it all meant.

"FSFC Gambit is a Mythic strategy. Four-suit, four-color gambit." He showed her *Athena*, his deck's god, as an example, pointing out Black for Greek, Spade for the Power faction, and Heart for the Spirit faction. One color, two suits. "All decks are a single color, because there wasn't a deity that represented more than one culture. And most deities didn't support more than two suits or factions, because that would be too powerful."

By the look on her face, Atalanta appeared to be dumbfounded by the barrage of cannons, too.

"But there's one god card that allows four colors and four factions. And it's one that I made up. *Cihtym*." Shuffle grinned as the memory of him drawing an all-powerful bearded fella wearing a dragon skull for a helmet and holding a giant fire-sword flickered in his mind. "Mythic spelled backwards. It was a joke."

Atalanta's face unfroze. "You're saying this stupid thing can lead us to the treasure?"

Shuffle thought hard about the four-suit, four-color gambit, digging into his memory for all the key parts to the strategy. One god—*Cihtym*. All four suits (spade, diamond, clover, and heart), and the four original colors—black for Greek, red for Japanese, white for Chinese, and green for Aztec. The exact cards came to life as he remembered them. The green diamond

Huehuecoyotl danced in celebration. The white heart *Monkey King* leapt over a mountain. The red clover *Musashi Miyamoto* drew his two swords. The black spade *Odysseus* . . .

His *Odysseus*.

Shuffle frantically flipped through his deck.

Atalanta leaned in close. "What are you doing?"

He found Odysseus and shined the authenticator on its back. The hidden strip revealed the normal marking, Genuine Mythic. He tried it in reverse, and something different happened. The card appeared to have veins like a leaf with the sun behind it. There was a slight crease near one of the corners. He picked at it until the corner peeled back. He froze, his fingers trembling. There it was, a hidden layer. Taking a deep breath, he pulled the false backing. It peeled away.

The hidden layer, the true backing of the card, depicted boundary lines, terrain, and landmarks. Dad and his games. This one, though, was serious. It was a game that called for secrecy and complication. He had given up a whole year of his life to hunt for Aegis. It and the rest of the treasure had to be worth millions. When he knew it was in jeopardy, he must have done everything possible to keep it safe. Unfortunately, he didn't save himself or the rest of his expedition.

"What is it?" Atalanta tugged at Shuffle's sleeve.

"It's part of a map."

"A treasure map?" Her voice drifted off her lips.

"I bet so. Part of a larger whole. It's one of four cards that will fit together to make a complete map."

"Four?"

"There are four important cards in the gambit. This card," Shuffle said, handing over *Odysseus*, "and three others that work together to be unbeatable."

She kept her eyes trained on the map, studying it, maybe figuring out what corner of the West it was supposed to be. "Looks like the desert—the Mojave. Never been there, but that's the California line. Do you have the others?"

He knew he didn't have any of the cards; they didn't fit his *Athena* deck. He had left a whole cache of cards at home, scattered on the floor. But his gut feeling told him none of those contained the other map pieces. The other cards were going to be special ones, prototype cards Dad made during the expedition.

"The second part of the coded message," Shuffle said. "The part that says *To those I trust*. It means he trusted people with the treasure cards. Probably three other people. They have what we need."

"Did he write about them in these letters?" Atalanta began reading the next one in her hand.

"You're on to something." Dad liked most people he met, especially the ones who earned his trust. No matter if they didn't see eye to eye, as long as they were honest.

Shuffle dove back into his stack of letters. Page after page, he didn't find any clues. He only came upon memory after memory. The letter where Dad mentioned seeing a mountain lion brought Shuffle back to when he first read it. He had swallowed a tooth by accident that day and wondered if big cats ever swallowed their own teeth when they were kittens.

Eventually, Atalanta found a possibility in one of the letters mentioning a woman who had saved Dr. Bloom from a mysterious illness the local physician couldn't figure out. *I trusted her when no one else in Santa Fe did, and she saved Dr. Bloom's life with medicine no one else believed in.* Her name was Cici Nightshade. Current whereabouts— Santa Fe, New Mexico.

Soon, they discovered two more whom Dad "trusted" while on his journey.

The second one was a traveling gunfighter who reclaimed Dad's money purse from a thief. *A man of dash and style, he refused a cash reward, but asked to playtest prototype Mythic decks. I trust his judgment and instinct, and we got along famously.* His name was John Henry Holliday. Current whereabouts—unknown.

The third was a former soldier who served under Granddad's command. The ex-soldier traveled with the expedition and protected them from bandits on a few occasions, even suffering a gunshot wound. *A trustworthy fellow, although still haunted by demons, he returns home knowing he has done us well and has made his captain, our Captain, proud.* His name was Alec Sterling. Current whereabouts—Dodge City, Kansas.

"Long shots," Atalanta said, handing over Mama's letters. "You think your pa sent them the other map pieces? Before his camp was attacked? Before he disappeared?"

"I have to believe it." He repeated his dad's words in his head: *To those I trust. I trusted her. I trust his judgment. A trustworthy fellow.* Dad's puzzles and riddles meant something. They were a part of him, not just some idle hobby. He took honesty and honor seriously, and in a serious situation, he wouldn't turn to anybody else. "Why he didn't send *me* all the cards, I don't know. But he meant for me to have the main clue. The key. The message."

Atalanta relaxed her stance, her hips cocked to one side. She rested her hands on her gun belt. "Then you can trust me to help you find the treasure."

"And find him."

Her freckled cheeks lifted as she unraveled a smile.

Shuffle looked back and forth at each letter. "Who do we start with?"

"Easy," she said. "The ex-soldier guy. Dodge City is about sixty miles away."

CHAPTER 21

DODGE CITY BLUES

The Arkansas River led to Dodge City. It had been a day and a half of hard riding, back-watching, and barely sleeping, but Shuffle could feel the second map piece was close.

He and Atalanta entered town by way of Front Street. Stores advertised goods from guns to groceries, and the farther down the road they went, the rowdier the saloons became.

She pulled up to the Siren's Grasp Saloon. "This place is your best bet. Ask around. I'm going to take Queen V to the livery. She's had a long ride."

The voices and tone beyond the saloon's swinging doors didn't suit him fine. They were loud, low, and lewd. Not his kind of establishment.

"How about we check elsewhere? The barbershop would be a good place to start."

She puffed out a laugh. "Waste your time then. I'll meet you here when you're done tiptoeing around the campfire."

"There are only two places every civilized man will eventually visit," he said, sliding off the horse. "The barbershop and the grave. I bet the barber will know where Alec is."

"Good luck," she said as she rode off down the street toward the stables.

With Katana curled around his shoulders, Shuffle tested his fate with the barber. Then the dry goods store. The pharmacy. And finally, the cobbler. Nobody knew of Alec Sterling, former sergeant in the 1st Missouri. Shuffle gave up on the easy way, and met Atalanta outside Siren's Grasp.

He pointed to the Long Branch Saloon down the road. "How about that one?"

"Nah, it's too respectable." She spat. "This here watering hole is a shining beacon for those with personal demons."

Admitting she was right, Shuffle pulled up the old bootstraps, not knowing if they were allowed inside, and went through the front doors.

Atalanta followed. "Don't worry. It'll be fun."

Music from a player piano filled the first floor as a sooty mist crept through the air. Betting chips clinked from busy game tables, and the pop-crack of an eight-ball break resounded from a game of billiards in the far corner. Hard-looking men hunched over glasses of libation, and soft-skinned women drifted among them like ghosts.

Atalanta handed over a dollar bill. "Get us some chow and drink. I'll claim a table."

Shuffle weaved through a crowd to the bar. A bison skull with an eyepatch hung on the wall over the shelves of bottles and mugs. He climbed up to an open spot, setting one foot on the brass rail below like it was second nature, except it wasn't. He had no clue how to order food and drink from the saloon keeper.

"Beat it. We don't offer charity to street urchins," the bartender said, serving up a frothy mug to a customer. "And no animals."

On cue, Katana leapt off Shuffle's shoulder and disappeared into the crowd. Heads turned as she padded through the saloon and out the door.

Shuffle slapped down the money. "Two lunches. Two lemonades."

"We got firewater and the like. Go across the street to Long Branch for something fancy."

"I think the kid means that old bottle of snake pee," said the wrinkled man to Shuffle's right. He peered up from under a ratty mop of hair.

"Is that what you're drinking?" Shuffle sniffed and frowned. "Then no thanks. I've smelled better cow dung."

Old Wrinkle Face flashed a jagged, rusty blade. "Don't judge me, street rat. I happen to like my drink."

"Leave the kid alone," said the curvy saloon-lady, wearing a corseted dress. She shoved Old Wrinkle Face out of his spot and took his place. "We serve sarsaparilla.

Our own flavors. Thirsty cowboys and the like make their way here to satisfy their thirst." She lifted her chin just so, exposing a beauty mark that looked like a star. "And for one reason or another, they keep coming back."

"I can see why," Shuffle said, taking off his hat.

"Would you like a sample?"

"No thanks, ma'am. Just lemonades."

"Fix him up a couple cold plates and waters with lemon," she said with a wink.

"Yes, Caly." The bartender snapped his towel and then wiped the space in front of Shuffle clean. He swiped the dollar before fixing up the food and drinks.

"Thanks, ma'am." Shuffle tipped his hat, trying hard not to stare. *Distracting Allure: Opponent's hero cannot use abilities this turn.*

"What brings you to brave the Siren's Call?" She crept closer.

Shuffle slid his hand for a drink that wasn't there. "I'm looking for a fellow by the name of Alec Sterling. Gun for hire. Ex-soldier for the—"

Caly inched closer. "May I ask why?"

"Because he has something of mine." He smacked his dry lips. *Barkeep, where's that lemonade?!*

"I'm not surprised. He owed many people, including me, a thing or two. Earned enough to gamble, lost enough to be in debt."

Something was odd about what she was saying or, rather, how she was saying it.

Shuffle pulled his hat to his chest. "Um, you're speaking as though he was—"

"He used to love the house sarsaparilla, Three-Headed Dog. But when times got tough, he turned back to the firewater and got himself into some trouble his trigger finger couldn't get him out of." She leaned in, her lips radiating warmth across his cheek. "The poor fella is dead."

* * *

Shuffle had only been to a graveyard once before, and he hoped to never visit another one for a long dang time.

The too-quiet stillness. The crooked headstones. The emotionless angel statues. All of it sent a chill to his teeth. Worst of all was Alec's grave marker: a rough-shaped rock with just his name chiseled by what might've been a chicken.

Atalanta joined him at the foot of Alec's plot. "Caly said Alec lost everything to a local gambler before he was killed by criminals."

How could Dad have been so wrong about Alec? The man was a wagerer who dealt with criminals. He lost the card and his life. Maybe simply he wanted to take a chance at bettering his life—and failed. Perhaps being flawed didn't make Alec untrustworthy. It just made him a risk.

A crow cawed from a skeletal tree.

"If we find the other cards, we'll still be able to search for the treasure." Shuffle tried to sound confident, but he knew a puzzle with a missing piece would lead to nothing but more problems.

"Or we could find the gambler."

"Did Caly give you a name?"

Atalanta flicked a bug off a moss-covered tombstone. "Paul Femus."

"Did she tell you where we can find him?"

"Didn't have to. I know where he is."

CHAPTER 22
PAUL FEMUS

After a few hours of riding south from Dodge City, Shuffle and Atalanta entered an area of rolling hills and dense gray woods. Dead leaves littered the ground. The knock of a woodpecker echoed through the trees.

They came to a stop near a stream where the smell of roasting meat hovered in the air.

"We're close." Atalanta checked her pistol. "Be on the ready."

On the ready? Did she expect trouble?

She clicked her tongue and popped the reins. Queen V obliged, and they continued toward the aroma.

The stream turned into a creek. Granite shards stuck out from the ground, possibly hiding copperheads and water moccasins. Poison ivy wrapped around skinny trees. An owl swooped across the branches.

After a while of weaving through the shadows, they crossed the creek at a shallow spot and climbed up a slope. Atalanta pulled the hammer back on her revolver. How could she hold that thing with one hand? He doubted he could lift it with two hands, much less point it at anyone.

The woods opened into a field. Atalanta set the pistol on her lap, and she urged the horse into a trot to a fenced area that spread out for acres where sheep were grazing, with a llama milling about the herd.

Atalanta steered along the fence line.

"Went the back way," she said. "We're coming up to the front of the place."

A large, shabby barn came into view, and the meaty aroma got stronger. Two men, one short with a scruffy beard, the other tall with a sunburned bald head, roasted an animal carcass on a nearby spit. They watched Atalanta and Shuffle ride past. Scruffy spat into the fire, getting most of it on his large, ratty beard; Baldy picked his nose.

Shuffle avoided their stares. "What is this place?"

"It's a trading post for cattle drivers. The Shawnee Trail is only half a mile away."

A large sign Swiss-cheesed with bullet holes swung above the door. *FEMUS FOODS AND WOOL GOODS.*

Attached to the riddled advertisement, a second, newer sign reflected the light. *MYTHIC SOLD HERE.*

* * *

The plan was to buy the prototype card, if this Femus fella had actually won it from Alec. Hopefully, he hadn't realized how valuable the card really was, and the price for it would be low.

Shuffle held the door open for Atalanta. She smirked and pulled him inside.

The place smelled like a barn, no doubt due to the wool sweaters and blankets.

From behind a glass-topped counter, a tremendously girthy man greeted them with a snort and a nod. "You got coin. I got goods."

Reflected light flared from a large ruby on the man's leather eyepatch.

Shuffle stayed rooted by the door. Not even the rack of dime novels and penny dreadfuls could draw him any farther.

"Don't be chicken," Atalanta said, nudging him forward.

"Come on, boy. I know what you're here for. And it ain't for the Dash Darkwood books."

In the glass case, Mythic cards filled the counter in rows, sorted by culture and faction. Rarer ones at the top. A *Beowulf* caught his eye. Norse hero, Power and People factions. Beside it was *Grendel*. Norse monster, Power and Spirit factions.

"I knew it. You're a player. I'm one, too." The man leaned in close, and somehow the glass countertop didn't break. "You looking at *Beowulf*? I run a Norse deck. What about you?"

"Greek."

The man rolled his eye. "Let me guess. *Zeus* with *Hercules*. No, you seem like a *Perseus* kinda player."

So the one-eyed man was the gambler, and he seemed to know his stuff. This wasn't going to be an easy barter.

Atalanta came up from behind. "Got any real good cards, Femus?"

"Ponygirl. Didn't see you there." Femus pointed at his patch and bellowed out a laugh. "Got one eye, you know."

"Where are the real treasures?" She side-glanced at Shuffle and winked. He felt his legs go jelly. Then again, she was overplaying their hand, asking for valuables they might not have the tender to pay for.

Femus stood and crossed his arms. "You saying I just sell junk?"

"I don't know," she said. "Shuffle here has come a long way to buy the best."

"See anything that fancies you?" Femus's voice dropped to serious depths. "I got a rare *Silver Glaive*. Perfect for *Perseus*."

Shuffle scanned the cards. All of them, not just the rare ones, were special. Dad had made the lot, and Shuffle wasn't going to take any for granted. But he was there for one of the four prototypes that surely contained the other map pieces. None of them seemed to be under the counter. "I'm looking for a card made before these ones came out. Still genuine, but one of a kind."

Femus took a deep breath, his cavernous, hairy nostrils flaring. "You heard about that?"

Shuffle nodded. He was at the right place at least.

"A kid like you can't afford it," Femus said.

Atalanta elbowed Shuffle. "Please, how much could a piece of cardboard be worth?"

"More than the flea-bitten skag you rode on." From a high shelf behind him, Femus pulled down a card encased in a glass sleeve and set it on the counter. "Is this what you're after?"

Monkey King. Hero, Chinese Spirit.

A gasp escaped Shuffle's lips as he pored over the intricate picture of the *Monkey King* wielding his staff while flying on a spiraled, magic cloud. Dad was in rare form when he did the artwork on this one—not a stray line.

"You're right," Femus said. "Only one like it. Worth hundreds. You got that kind of scratch or did you just want to look at it?" He smiled, revealing a red-enameled tooth.

"Hundreds?" Atalanta scoffed. "Come on, Shuffle. He's trying to rip you off. Can't be worth more than five."

It appeared Atalanta wanted to try the back-up plan, which was to leave, come back later in the middle of the night, and steal the card. He didn't like that idea. It reminded him of the three lady bandits scrounging through his house and Mama lying unconscious on the floor.

"Stick to riding ponies." Femus's hand swallowed

the treasure card as he swiped it away. Never to be seen again, unless—

"Wait." Shuffle dropped his deck on the counter. "I'll play you for it."

"I doubt you got anything to ante up to match its worth."

He showed the gambler *Odysseus*. "One of a kind, too."

Femus sucked in his breath. "A Maker's card."

Atalanta hid her face under the brim of her hat, furiously shaking her head.

Shuffle focused on the ruby. "Well, you up for a game?"

CHAPTER 23
RAGNAROK

A cloud of dust dispersed to every corner of the shop as Femus cleared off a table with a swipe of his big arm.

Bands of light from nearby windows highlighted the battlefield, revealing nicks and scuffs and even a few big gashes.

Baldy, one of the men from outside, sat down next to Femus and handed him a small burlap sack.

"Normally, I play for dollar coins and trophies, but the Maker's card will do." Femus removed bullets shaped like mushrooms from the bag and lined them up as his Belief markers. A few of them looked speckled with dried blood.

"It ain't too late to back out," Atalanta whispered, leaning over Shuffle's shoulder. "We have Plan B."

"No. I got this." He showed Femus his *Odysseus*. "It's part of my deck, so know that I'm not holding out."

"Oh, don't worry. I got my eye on it." He smirked, then glanced over at Baldy, whose chin quivered.

"Bet you do." Atalanta swung her chair around and

straddled it like a saddle, sitting even closer. "Careful, Shuffle. He's more crooked than a dog's leg."

Shuffle turned toward the scent of sage in her hair. It was a comfort compared to the barnyard smell. "Don't worry. I got two eyes on him."

"Now that you and Ponygirl are done whispering sweet nothings, how about we play?" Femus tossed down his god card, *Loki*. Norse Wealth and People factions. The ruby on his eyepatch glimmered. "You first."

As Shuffle set aside his Belief markers and drew his opening hand, Femus vanished, the room lost its animal smell and drab color, and he imagined *Athena* scanning the battlefield—a peaceful plain of green grass and wildflowers. The late morning sun cast long shadows off the thirteen shrines behind her. Across the way, *Loki* sat on a throne of rune-carved stone, in front of his thirteen shrines.

In Norse mythology, Loki, the trickster god, caused a world-shattering event called Ragnarok that killed all the gods. In Mythic, *Ragnarok* was a unique Quest that required several events to happen. Dad had made it special by making it the only Quest (not three) for *Loki* to win the game. That meant Femus would surely be packing some serious tricks to pull it off.

But to win the game, a player needed more than tricks. *Athena* and *Odysseus* had them, plus defense and offense, recovery and destruction.

Memories of past games faded in and out, as Dad's

shadow whispered ideas and secrets only Shuffle could hear. *Defend and trap.*

Across the battlefield, *Balder*, the Norse hero, stood tall, gleaming in gold armor. Nearly invincible, he'd have to be defeated with the right tactical play.

"Wait to strike," the shadow said. "Draw him in."

Shuffle played *Telemachus*, Odysseus's son, and armed him with the shield *Aegis*. "I defend."

"Playing it safe?" Femus hacked out a laugh. "Can't win by being safe. You need to get dangerous." He slammed down two *Valkyrie Warriors*, and along with *Balder*, he pushed the cards forward to attack.

Shuffle looked deep into the art of the cards, the battlefield shaking as they charged. *Balder* slashed at *Telemachus*, and the *Valkyries* trampled over four shrines. Four Belief points gone.

Soon, monsters and gladiators peppered the ground with arrows and blood. *Typhon*, the five-headed beast who fought Zeus. *Skeleton Warriors* and *Fire Imps*. *Skoll* and *Hati*, two Norse wolves who hunted the sun and the moon. Godly spells—*Luring Song* and *True Aim*—zipped through the air.

"Come on, Shuffle," Atalanta said. "Why aren't you winning?"

"My turn." Femus leaned back, his chair creaking under the slow push of his confident girth. His hand moved strangely, and his thumb and middle finger snapped as he drew his next card. He slammed it down without looking. *Fenris*, the wolf who killed the god Odin during Ragnarok. "To play it, I have to sacrifice *Balder*. But it brings me closer to completing my Quest."

Atalanta flung down her chair. Baldy whistled and hollered. Femus traced his finger around the eyepatch ruby.

The game's end loomed, in favor of Femus and his tricks. Drawing him in was a risk with a high chance of failure. Shuffle wiped the sweat pooling under the brim of his hat. Katana slept inside his satchel. He hugged it tighter. The duel appeared doomed.

"Spring the trap," the shadow said.

But with what?

His hand didn't offer any answers. He picked out *Little Owl* and focused on Dad's graceful artwork. The owl's big eyes peered back, offering no kind of helpful wisdom.

Except—Shuffle reread the card's special ability: *Draw two cards, keep one and return the other to the bottom of your deck.*

It wasn't the trap he needed, but it did shed some crucial information on his opponent.

Femus was drawing his cards from the bottom of his deck. The strange sound his fingers made was a telltale sign of his cheating. He had to know what was on the bottom because he'd stacked it that way, and if it was true, he'd have something there that would win the game.

CHAPTER 24
SMITE TO TARTARUS

Dust flitted through the light. The woolly smell of the room made Shuffle's nose itch.

Femus drummed his fingers, pointer to pinky, against the table. "You giving up?"

Shuffle sat up, certain the match for the *Monkey King* card was near its end. And he'd be the one to finish it.

Inside the satchel, Katana began to stir. Shuffle patted it for luck as he looked over his hand.

"Why would I give up when I'm having so much fun?" He played *Odysseus* followed by *True Aim*.

Femus shrugged. "That doesn't kill my wolves, and it only does two damage." He pulled away the Belief markers, bullets with specks of blood.

"I'm not done." Shuffle tossed down *Smite to Tartarus*.

A bead of sweat trickled around the gambler's eye. "So? What does it do?"

"It sends any unit not killed to the bottom of your deck." *Spring the trap.*

"Bottom?" Femus's lip quivered.

"Yep. Banished to the abyss."

Femus hammered his fist on the table, shaking everything not bolted down. "I don't believe you!" He clawed the card off the table and read it, then roared as he slammed the card back down.

Baldy, one of Femus's thugs, picked his ear. "Why you angry, boss? The boy ain't won yet."

"Shut up." Femus scratched at a spot under his ruby-studded eye patch as he gritted his teeth.

Shuffle hid a smile, certain that Femus could no longer cheat and win.

The battle continued with more monsters, warriors, and divine magic hitting the fray. The clash of swords and thunder rumbled. The cries and screams of the fallen rang out. *Defend, attack, draw in, and trap.*

Shuffle played his turn. With *Distracting Maneuver,* *Odysseus* slipped through defenses and destroyed *Loki's* remaining Belief.

He had won, and winning against a cheater made the victory extra sweet.

Surprisingly, Femus didn't fling his cards to the floor. He extended his bear paw of a hand for a good-game shake.

Not only was the gambler's grip probably capable of crushing rock; he was a dishonest player, drawing from the bottom of a stacked deck. Yet, good sportsmanship should never be tossed aside for fear of the loser and his retaliation.

They shook hands, and after a long, awkward moment, Shuffle tried to pull away, but Femus didn't let go.

Dang it. So much for trusting a fellow gamer.

"I want that card. Actually, your whole deck." Femus's eye glazed over with a feral look. "I'll pay you in California gold. Even throw in a wool blanket."

Atalanta unsnapped the buckle of her holster. "You tried to hornswoggle Shuffle, but you still lost. Now you have to give up your card."

"It's between me and him, Ponygirl," growled Femus through his teeth. "Stay out of our business."

"Let go." Shuffle yanked back, but Femus held strong. "I don't want your gold, and your blankets stink."

Baldy reached for a shotgun in a dark corner, and a shadow came over them from behind, the wood floors creaking. Great. Plan A was going to heck in a handbasket.

With the barrel of her pistol in her hand, Atalanta whipped around and smacked the thug sneaking up on them. He fell as Atalanta spun the revolver to shooting position and aimed it at Baldy. "Lose the scattergun," she said, popping the hammer back with her thumb.

Great Hermes, she lived up to her Amazon name and moved faster than lightning. *Bolt from Heaven: Attack +2. Attack twice; the first cannot be prevented.*

Baldy dropped the shotgun, but Femus wrapped his arm around Shuffle's neck.

CHAPTER 25

RIPPER AND JUDITH

Despite being choked, Shuffle forced his eyes open to show no fear. He wanted Atalanta to think he was brave.

But it was hard to do with his throat in the crook of a tree-trunk-sized arm. He could hardly breathe! And now, Femus held a knife. The blade looked like it could slice right through bone.

"Ponygirl, acting before thinking," Femus said. "It was going to be a generous offer." The stink of his breath, up close and personal, made Shuffle sick.

Atalanta peered up from the shadow of her hat, no doubt calculating the time, angle, and air speed needed to snap off a shot. She stood very still, but Shuffle imagined that a fire coursed through her veins, ready to power up her special attack. Could she change aim from Baldy to Femus and shoot with pinpoint accuracy before he used his knife?

A bead of sweat snaked down Baldy's head. Femus squeezed tighter. Atalanta adjusted her back foot. *Cowpies*. This was it. The moment of death.

Ting-ting.

A crusty old man walked into the store, dusting his hat on his leg. "Supper smells good."

Femus's arm relaxed.

Shuffle bit it hard, his teeth sinking into skin and muscle. He tasted dirt and salt.

Femus grunted and shoved Shuffle at Atalanta. She caught him before he fell.

Baldy charged and tackled them, causing Atalanta's gun to slide across the floor. Shuffle backed into a shelf, while Atalanta and the thug tussled, fists swinging. She kicked Baldy, but he fought back, pulling her hair. What a dirty move!

Still in the fight, Shuffle grabbed a jar and smashed it against the glistening target that was the thug's bald head. Pickles: *Defeat non-hero, non-monster unit.*

Ca-click. It was the now all-too-familiar sound of a hammer being cocked back. In one hand, Femus had Atalanta's revolver aimed right at her. In the other, he held Shuffle's bag.

The other thug who had tried to sneak up on them, Scruffy, had come to and armed himself with the double-barrel. The scatter-shot blast up close would rip them in half.

"Well, now. Let's have that deck of yours," Femus said, grinning. He opened the bag.

Katana sprang out, all wild and hissing, claws out.

"Caaaat!" Femus yelped, dropping the bag.

After a few good swipes, Katana jumped to the floor. *Blam!* Femus took a pot shot at her.

"No!" Shuffle lurched at Femus, but Atalanta grabbed him. He fought against her grip, but she held on strong. Even if he was in the crossfire, he couldn't let his cat get killed.

Another shot, but Katana zigged.

Two more gun blasts. Smoke filled the room. A black blur zipped straight out the door. She had made it.

The crusty old man looked at the bullet holes near his feet. "Not for sale, then?"

"Get out of here, geezer," Femus yelled. Blood ran down his cheek where Katana had sunk her claws. He picked Baldy up and shoved him. "Find that cat and bring it to me. I'm gonna skin it alive." His eye flashed redder than the ruby on his patch.

"The heck you are!" Shuffle pulled free from Atalanta and reared back to punch Femus. No one was going to hurt Katana.

Femus pointed the pistol. "Worry about your own hide."

"Be smart about this, Femus," Atalanta said.

"Didn't get to where I am by being smart."

Shuffle and Atalanta shared a look, shaking their heads.

Femus opened the deck box and smelled the cards. "Take these two to the barn. Feed them to the beasts."

Ca-click, ca-click. Two hammers, two barrels. "Ripper

and Judith are gonna love you," said Scruffy, smiling from underneath his greasy, matted beard.

Atalanta put her hands up. Shuffle did too, plastering on his best brave face.

* * *

As expected, the barn stank of animals and hay. Maybe even of death.

Shuffle sat on the floor, back to back with Atalanta, with their hands tied to the same post.

"Ripper just killed a coyote. Her blood's up." Scruffy shined the lantern light on his pockmarked face. "Judith—well, her blood's always up."

"You guys are scum," Atalanta said. "This is a new low. I mean, are your brains full of gunpowder? If you don't let us go, the law will hang you for sure."

Scruffy sneered and pulled the rope hard, cutting skin.

"What she means to say is, if you let us go, we won't tell the marshal," Shuffle said. "We'll just be on our way and forget this ever happened." As much as he wanted to reclaim his deck and the treasure cards, he'd rather leave without them if it meant their lives. He was after Dad, not gold and artifacts.

"The law ain't gonna know. How could they when they won't even have your bones to find?" With a snort and a spit, Scruffy tromped out of the barn, shutting the door.

Dying in the dark, tied up to a post and never to be seen again, was not a heroic way to go. And why did it have to be animals? Teeth and claws and slobber. Attack dogs, most likely, whipped and beaten to make them killers. *Abyssal Hounds: Attack +2. If Abyssal Hounds damage opponent's Belief, opponent discards two cards.* Or kids.

No way it was gonna happen.

Shuffle thought of his assets. "We can get out of here. I have a pocket knife."

Atalanta shifted, inching closer. "Great. Can you get it?"

Wriggling his hands, he barely budged. He yanked and tugged, but the rope cut into his skin, burning his wrists. "No, I can't."

"The idiot didn't take my blade neither," she said. "It's on my belt. Can you reach it?"

"Which side?"

"My right, and be careful. It ain't a folding knife."

Ignoring the pain in his arms, Shuffle fought against the binding. He had to find Katana and escape. Closing his eyes, he focused past the bite of the rope and stretched his fingers like vines growing past thorns and rocks for sunlight. He found something cold—the knife handle. He clawed at it, and the sheath's buckle snapped. He pinched and pulled the handle, inch by inch, until he freed the knife.

"Got it!" He clung to it as if it was Excalibur.

"Great, but we're not out yet. Cut the rope. Careful, the blade is sharp."

The celebration march turned into a battle cadence. Shuffle focused again, feeling the steel edge press up against the rope. Steadying himself with a deep breath, he sawed at the bindings. His wrists, elbows, and shoulders hurt like heck, but he didn't care.

Atalanta clicked her tongue. "Are you cutting it?"

"I don't know." All he felt was the searing pain that ran from his hand all the way to his shoulder.

Then the rope loosened.

"You're doing it! Keep it up," she said.

Her words spurred him on. There was no way he could lose his nerve now.

The binds slackened. Nearly there.

Shuffle imagined drums beating, accompanied by trumpets and cheers. And kisses.

The last cord of rope fell.

"You did it!"

Shuffle howled.

"Them idiots are gonna regret messing with us."

"Here." Shuffle found Atalanta's hand and placed her knife in it, handle first. Her skin against his fingers made him pause. The shadow of the room became less cold and dangerous, turning into the warmth of a blanket.

After taking the knife, she stepped away, and Shuffle returned to the real world—a dim, dank barn.

Not a second later, the lock on the door clicked.

Atalanta sat back down, against the post. "Pretend we're still tied up, then we'll jump 'em."

Shuffle took his position just as the door slid open. The flare of two lantern lights cut into the darkness. Strange shapes shambled in.

"Here they come, kiddies," Scruffy hollered. He shut the door, laughing on the way out.

Shuffle imagined two salivating, hundred-toothed monsters hungry for blood and guts. Heroes confronted those kinds of beasts all the time. Maybe it was his turn to face one in battle.

"Get up," Atalanta said, standing.

He tried but couldn't, as his legs went jelly. Being a friend to all animals, he never thought he would have to fight one, or be eaten by one.

"Come on, Shuffle. Move it."

The beast snorted, then the other animal answered with a grunt. Their feet—no, claws—scraped on the wood floor as they stalked forward.

Nope, not gonna be mongrel food. He forced himself to stand.

Atalanta nudged him. "Get your weapon ready."

"I'm not killing anything. Let's just get out of here." He grabbed her arm and backed away. She came along without resistance.

They retreated faster as the strange animal shapes scuffled closer.

Shuffle stumbled over a hay bale. He fell, losing Atalanta. The scraping of claws drew near. He scrambled up but slammed into something, crashing down again.

The beast growled, gurgled, and gagged, and then it threw up.

Ooze slid down Shuffle's arm. The bulk of it stuck to his sleeve, smelling like grass and puke. It had to be making room in its stomach! He raised his fist to fight it off.

The sizzle and flash of a match turned into a bright light.

"Are you okay?" Atalanta held up a lantern.

Shuffle froze as a woolly, long-necked animal lowered its head and slurped up the stinky mass on his sleeve. The creature chewed as if the cud was as delicious as pie.

Atalanta brandished her knife.

"Don't hurt it," Shuffle said. "I have a feeling we're not going to be eaten."

"What in Buzzard's Peak is it?" She sheathed her blade.

Shuffle had heard llamas were pretty docile, except when it came to coyotes or wolves. They'd probably fight off those predators with their powerful legs and solid hooves.

"They're llamas. Sort of camel. From South America. I bet Femus trained them to protect his sheep herd. He probably thought they'd see us as a threat and kick the heck out of us."

"Femus is an idiot." Atalanta waved the lantern closer to the other one. "Ugly beasts."

The llama hissed and then spat in her face.

"Ugh! You're lucky I don't have my gun." She found a stack of wool blankets, using one to wipe herself clean.

Shuffle rubbed his hand down the chewing llama's thick fur. It wore a harness with an iron tag engraved with a name. "This here is Ripper. That one must be Judith."

"Well, Judith needs to learn some manners." Atalanta spat on the floor. "Anyway, we need to ditch this place."

The lock clicked. Raised voices at the door.

"Ready for a scuffle?" Atalanta turned the knife in her hand so the blunt part of the blade rested on her wrist while the sharp part was facing outward.

"I'd rather not." Shuffle grabbed the wool blankets. "I have an idea."

CHAPTER 26
ESCAPE

The two thugs, Scruffy and Baldy, crept into the barn with lanterns.

Atalanta and Shuffle hid. *Unmatched Guile: Cancel opponent's action card.*

Scruffy whistled. "You kiddies still kicking?"

"Think the old gals got 'em good?" Baldy's voice wavered. "Not sure about killing kids."

"Reckon so. Too bad they was trespassing. The animals was just protecting our territory."

The two goons tromped forward.

"Look. A hat. And what is that?" Baldy hustled over. "It's sticky. It's blood."

Shuffle's hat, but not his blood. He'd used Professor Mercury's Wonder Elixir—good for travel sickness and faking out fools.

Scruffy spun around, his boots scraping hard against the wood floor. The lantern swung about, causing waves of light and shadow. "Don't see no other remains."

Shuffle held his breath and hung on to Ripper's chest

harness for dear life. He couldn't see much, inches off the floor and hanging upside down under the belly of a llama. Atalanta was doing the same underneath Judith. Wool blankets also helped conceal them. Dad would be proud. Odysseus, too.

"What's this on your mouth?" Baldy asked Ripper, maybe half expecting the llama to answer. He stood on his tiptoes.

Scruffy crept over to Judith. "Well, what is it?"

"More blood!" Baldy's voice wavered. "I don't believe it. Ripper ate the kids. We're gonna hang for sure."

Again, Wonder Elixir. And the woolly, cud-chewing llama loved every slurp.

Scruffy shook his partner. "Settle down. No one's going to find out. I bet they were orphans. Why else would they be out on their lonesome? No one cares."

Mama would care. She'd be angry and devastated. That was why he needed to find Dad and get home safe. He'd hate to hurt Mama any more than he had already.

"Come on," Scruffy continued. "Let's get the girls out to the field. We need to help Boss with the new customers. We'll tell him about the kiddies after."

Baldy grabbed the harness, his hand inches away from Shuffle's head, and led Ripper out the barn's rear door. Scruffy and Judith (with Atalanta) followed close behind.

Shuffle stifled a laugh. The two goons fell for it, and they were gonna set him and Atalanta free.

They came to the pasture, where a breeze swept underneath Ripper and cooled Shuffle's back, the first sign of freedom.

"You don't need this, girl," Baldy said, pulling the wool blanket off.

Now exposed for all to see, Shuffle gripped the harness even tighter, clinging to the llama as his muscles burned. It was dark, but anybody looking at the spot would notice something wasn't right with the llama's belly. *Hey, a boy-sized lump!*

Baldy turned and took the blanket off Judith. Atalanta hung on with one hand. In the other, she readied her knife. At least she'd be able to fight.

"Boss is going to skin us alive if we're late," Scruffy said, walking away while scratching his beard.

Baldy hurried to catch up, and a moment later they were gone.

With a gasp, Shuffle dropped to the soft, cold earth and rolled out from under Ripper. He rose to his feet and stretched out his arms high in a V. It was the second time he had escaped capture. Second time he bested the villains—granted, these two were buffoons.

Atalanta joined him. She straightened her kerchief and dusted herself off. "Great plan. Worked like a Winchester."

Shuffle stood to his full measure. Maybe Bronson was right about him being smart enough to handle the world.

"Still, this ain't over," she said.

"Right. I need to get my stuff and find Katana."

She tilted her head, her pigtails swaying to one side. The moonlight formed an aura around her, and her eyes reflected the pale shine. She balanced her knife on her finger, blade point down, then spun it in her palm. "All right, it's time for Plan B, which is two twigs short of a brushfire. That's why I like it."

"Good. I'm not leaving my cat to that card swindler."

After a deep breath, Shuffle ran toward the barn, with Atalanta following. He hunched down low as he crossed the open, moonlit field. He climbed over the fence and hit the east side of the barn, his back flat against the wall. Atalanta claimed a spot right there with him.

Laughing, cussing, and singing filled the air.

Atalanta peeked around the corner. "There's six trail hands at the tables by the spit. Femus and his two men are over there, too. Whooping and hollering." She looked to the right. "It's dark, but there's enough moonlight. They may see our movement. Let's circle those trees and double back to the store. We'll be far enough way to get Queen V, if she's still hitched."

Shuffle couldn't help but smile at the way she was talking like a field commander.

She frowned at him. "What?"

"Nothing." He gestured toward the stand of trees. "Ladies first."

She pushed off, running. He followed her to the trees, where an outhouse stunk up the place. Not wanting to linger, he hoofed it to the store.

Eight horses were tied to the hitching posts, with Queen Victoria among them. They had a ride out.

Atalanta surveyed the surrounding area. Shuffle followed her eyes the best he could.

"It's safe," she said, carefully walking onto the porch. She coaxed the front door open, the bell clinking slightly, and then glanced inside. "I'll wait for you in the woods on the other side of the road. Don't dawdle."

"If I get caught, you have my permission to go." Shuffle didn't know why he said it. To sound brave, or to say it before she did, because he didn't want it to come from her.

She shook her head. "No matter what dumb decisions you make, I won't leave you to those loose cannons."

* * *

Inside the store, the moonlight made strange shadows of the things on the shelves, the books on the racks, and the wool sweaters in the corner. The cards all looked the same in the dark.

Shuffle climbed over the counter to the other side, landing on top of his bag on the floor. Rifling through it, he found that most of his stuff was still inside, except for his deck and authenticator. He checked the shelf where Femus kept *Monkey King*. It wasn't there; neither was *Odysseus* or the rest of the deck.

While quietly calling out for Katana, Shuffle searched the rest of the store. No luck. He tried the rear door. It opened to a bedroom. Stupidly or, he'd rather believe, bravely, he slipped in.

The noises of revelry from outside made their way into the room. By the sounds of it, the trail hands were getting mighty drunk. Shuffle would bet that Femus and his crew were going to cheat them out of a thing or two.

Antlers and skulls hung on the walls. Taxidermied animals topped shelves and tables, including the biggest cat (dead or alive) Shuffle had ever seen. The animal bared its fangs and claws. An attached engraved plate read: *Half lynx, all wild. She took my eye; I took her hide.*

No way was he going to let Katana be turned into a trophy. He checked under the bed. He called out. Nothing.

He opened the drawer of the bedside table. She wouldn't be in there, but he looked anyway. Good thing, though. He found his deck, Atalanta's revolver, and both the treasure cards: *Monkey King* and *Odysseus*. He peeled off the false back of *Monkey King*, uncloaking the second treasure map piece. He sighed as he glanced at the lines and landmarks on the card. Where was all this going to lead? What was going to be under the X? Hopefully, when he had the pieces, he would be able to put them together and solve all of Dad's mysteries.

He pocketed the cards and stowed the pistol in his bag. The gun was even heavier than he'd expected. Atalanta had to be stronger than half the boys from Mourning Glory.

As for Katana, maybe she would never be found. She could be free, living and hunting in the woods. Anything was better than being Femus's stuffed trophy.

A flicker of light shined through the window. Femus and Scruffy were heading toward the building.

Not wanting his head mounted on the wall, Shuffle hurried out of the bedroom. He had made it halfway through the store when the side door began to open. He ducked behind a rack of wool sweaters.

Lantern light filled the room, accompanied by the heavy footfalls of a big man wearing boots. The footsteps stopped in front of the rack. Shuffle held his breath, able to see Femus and his glimmering ruby-studded eyepatch. A creaking sound came from the bedroom where he had left the door open.

Femus drew his giant Bowie knife. It shimmered like a grease slick.

"What's the hold-up?" asked Scruffy, trailing behind.

"Heard a sound." Femus crept forward, blade at the ready.

Shuffle bit his lip, feeling his face and chest about to explode from the lack of air. If Femus realized the stuff was gone, he would probably tear the place down to search for them. Then there would be nothing but a whirlwind of trouble.

Scruffy picked a cockroach out of his beard. "Well? Anybody there?"

"Nobody." Femus lowered the lantern and sheathed his knife. "Come on. Get the pickled peppers. I'll get the moonshine."

Once the two goons had gone, Shuffle gasped, gulping air. That was a close call, and without Atalanta and her quick-strike ability, he wasn't sure if he could've gotten out of a scuffle.

Katana was still missing, but Shuffle knew he couldn't stay to search for her any longer. Without her, his shoulders felt cold and his bag felt empty. He looked back one last time as he dashed out of the store. He crossed the road and slipped into the woods. Fallen leaves and broken twigs crunched under his feet. He reminded himself that Katana being gone was better than her being a trophy on the wall. She was capable of taking care of herself. She would be okay. He had to believe it.

"Psst, over here," Atalanta called out in a hushed tone.

Shuffle froze. His eyes weren't adjusted to the dark, but he badly wanted to see her face.

"To your right."

He turned and followed her voice. After nearly getting his eye gouged out by a branch, tripping over a tree root, and ripping into low-hanging, thorny vines, he found her.

"Look who came to me." She handed over Katana. The lucky cat purred as she wrapped herself around his shoulders. He sighed at her warmth.

"Have something of yours as well." He presented her with the revolver in a stupidly fancy way. "Plan B accomplished. I scored the cards."

She opened the chamber, checked the rounds, and spun it shut. "Let's put this place in our dust."

"Giddyup."

Atalanta smirked, then frowned. Ducking down, she pointed toward the east end of the road. "Look. There."

Three dots of light broke the darkness. They got bigger, and in moments, the lights turned into lanterns held by three riders. Females, armed to the hilt: Skylla, Black Star, and another bandit. The third one held a rifle the size of a long spear, no doubt an elephant gun. And that wasn't the only enormous thing. The bandit's curly hair, easy to discern even in the dark, had to be five times the size of her head.

"Be still," Atlanta said. "When the time is right, we run."

Of course, the escape couldn't be too easy. Skylla and her gang had to show up to make a game of it. What a pile of cow patties.

The three bounty hunters rode up to Femus and the group having their nighttime barbecue. The laughing, singing, and cursing stopped, and a quiet chill filled the air. Femus rose to meet them, and despite his large size, he was dwarfed by Skylla on her horse. Even from far away, Shuffle noticed the way Femus sagged his shoulders and kept his head down.

After a brief conversation, Femus grabbed Scruffy and lifted him off his seat. The thug stood in front of Skylla with his hat in his hands. He spoke, then jabbed a finger at Baldy. They yelled and slapped at each other.

A thunderous boom sent the two bickering fools to the ground. The third bandit, Big Hair, had fired her elephant gun to the sky, smoke pluming from its long barrel. *Destructive Force: Opponent's units of power 2 and under are destroyed.*

Femus picked up his goons, and the three nincompoops led Skylla and her two bandits to the barn. Hopefully, it would take them longer than a minute to figure out the blood was only Wonder Elixir.

Atalanta sprang to her feet. "Let's go. Now."

Shuffle followed her to a small clearing further into the woods. Queen Victoria and another horse, white with gray spots, grazed on grass at the base of a tree.

"Got you one," Atalanta said. "He's gentle."

Riding a strange horse, at night of all times, was a bad idea. It had been a while since he last rode one solo, and that was just a trot around Captain's farm, not hightailing out of the woods.

"I don't know." Shuffle approached the horse with his hand out. It took a big whiff, then snorted.

"You'll slow Queen V down, not good when we have Six-Plum on our tail."

He frowned. "So I'm going to be a horse thief now?"

"Better than a corpse."

She had a point, so he climbed up into the saddle and gripped the reins like he was boss. Raising and lowering its head, the colt snorted again and stamped an eager rhythm on a small patch of ground.

When he was confident he wouldn't be thrown off, he followed Atalanta as silently as he could out of the brush and bramble. Once they hit the main highway, they rode as the crow flies.

CHAPTER 27

LONG GONE, NOW MYTHICAL

Waking up came too early. The sun agreed—it hadn't shown up yet. With three bandits on your tail, a decent stretch of sleep was no longer a luxury. A nightmare of being chased by three diamondback rattlesnakes didn't help, nor did getting nudged in the shoulder by Atalanta's crusty boot.

"Sleepy time is over," she said. "My secret path gives us a bigger lead. Best we take advantage."

Shuffle shrugged off her rude awakening and stretched, purposely long and slow. She looked blue in the fading shadow of his dream. Everything did, in various shades. The trees and shrubs, darker. The sky and her eyes, lighter.

Queen V and Shuffle's horse snorted and huffed from a nearby tree. It seemed they were eager to go as well.

"Don't dawdle," she snapped.

After packing up and finding Katana as she returned from her nightly hunt with a field mouse in her mouth, Shuffle rode after Atalanta, who'd decided to leave him behind. He didn't panic. Not at all. She was just his guide through an unforgiving wilderness. No big deal.

Soon, he caught up to her as the blue transformed into gold, the sun finally rising over the flat horizon at his back.

"Finally," she said. "I was beginning to think you'd gotten caught by Skylla."

Shuffle patted his horse's white neck. "Yeah? Well, you oughtta remember I escaped from her once before." One of his finest moments.

Without even the slightest acknowledgment, she clicked her tongue and sped off across the dusty, brown grassland dotted by pale green shrubs with sharply pointed leaves.

When they came across a wooded creek, Atalanta slowed down, and together they carefully followed the water for a mile, until the going got too rocky.

"Another secret path," she said, as she took a barely noticeable trail south by southwest. "It'll get us to the Cimarron Cutoff quick enough."

On the other side of the creek, the landscape turned into wide swaths of welcoming turf, its tall, thin blades parting kindly as they rode through and reforming almost perfectly behind them.

Shuffle neared a large bald spot in the grass where an animal's horned skull and bones lay sun-bleached and hollow.

"Was that a buffalo?" he asked. He'd read about the

majestic animals that roamed the prairies in thunderous herds. Big, furry beasts with stout shoulders and fierce horns.

"That's right," she said. "They used to be everywhere."

"Used to be?" Shuffle now caught up to her, riding side by side, as she seemed to drift.

"Yeah, they'd come and go, depending on the season, from the rolling hills of Texas past Montana to Peace River and Misery Mountain in Canada. Millions of them. Now there are barely any." Atalanta tugged at her yellow kerchief.

"What happened?"

"Hunters," she said, her voice heavy and grating. "White men. They slaughtered the buffalo, hundreds a day, for their hides, for a profit, and for the killing."

The word *slaughter* sent an ill wave down Shuffle's gut as if it were a curse that affected anyone who happened to be nearby, even the innocent and the ignorant.

"The Indians hunted the buffalo, too, right?"

She shot him a sundering glare. "Don't you know anything, Shuffle? The Plains peoples depended on the buffalo. Yes, they hunted them, but they did it with reverence. They used all of the animal, not just the skins, because their livelihood depended on it." Atalanta's voice softened without losing its gravity. "It was more than survival. It was spiritual."

"I didn't know."

Another pile of bones came into view.

"The land's important, too, you know." The sharp edge came back to her voice. "I guess they didn't teach you at school that all this land—the land Femus has his store on, the land Dodge City is on, the land of Independence and of your hometown—it all belonged to the Indians. Now they're in the Territory, a patch of land that don't compare."

Shuffle shook his head. He knew that Mourning Glory was founded before he was born and that settlers had been there for years. He knew about the Indian Territory, an area wedged in between Kansas and Arkansas and Texas. To think of it now, it seemed extremely small compared to the spread of land Atalanta said was their original home. He'd hate to move from his house to just his room.

She continued, "The Indians only agreed to relocate if the government stopped the white hunters from killing the buffalo. It was a treaty—supposed to be fair, right? But it wasn't, because the government lied."

Shuffle took a deep breath. "You're saying the government didn't stop . . . the slaughter, and they shrank the size of the allotted land?" That would be going from living in a small room with a plate of food to surviving in a closet with just a slice of bread.

"You're catching on," Atalanta said. "White hunters went on wiping out the buffalo, didn't even bother with the hides. Like I said, they did it for the killing. They'd just leave carcasses like those to rot. And the Indians suffered. When they fought to keep their land, they suffered more."

"That's terrible."

"Now you know something," she said, her face in an unrecognizable twist. Maybe she was holding back tears, or a barrage of cussing.

It would've been a mythical sight to see: the buffalo roaming the land in thunderous herds and the Indians in their ritual hunts. But those Indians weren't just some myth to stock his daydreams. They were people, treated unfairly, and he was able to be born and to grow up as he had because of that.

He figured all he could do now was to treat the animal and the man with respect wherever and whenever he might come across them. That, and not get lost in Atalanta's dust.

DODGE CITY DISPATCH

GAME STORE ROBBED

Local game store owner, sheep rancher, and wool goods tycoon Paul Femus, 47, claims a boy and his cat stole a horse and a valuable playing card for the game Mythic.

"The stinking tumbleweed and his demon cat snuck into the store while I was entertaining cowpunchers at my barbecue pit," said Femus. "Made off with my prized possession worth a hundred greenbacks." Although most cards are valued at less than a penny, the card taken, Monkey King, is one of the rare Maker's cards of a game called Mythic. The horse was a three-year-old white colt.

The alleged thief is described as a short, wiry boy with brown hair wearing an oversized duster coat. The cat has all black fur and yellow eyes.

MYTHIC: Deputy Bat Masterson plays Mythic. Do you?

THREE-HEADED DOG SARSAPARILLA: It's so good, you'll stay for more.

EAGLE OR LEGEND?

Witnesses said a giant bird, an eagle twice the size of a bull, flew across the sky at various times on Friday. One witness, Jimbo Masters, 19, saw the bird at night.

"It was this big ol' thing, at first like a shadow in the dark before sparking like steel on rock. It screeched, then flashed like lightning. I thought it got struck by a bolt, but there wasn't a cloud in the sky."

Could this be the Thunderbird, a Lakota legend of a benevolent spirit who governs the weather, guards the truth, and protects man—or a conspired hoax?

CHAPTER 28
SANTA FE

Shuffle didn't ache anymore.

The last two weeks had delivered some rough times: evading Six-Plum Skylla through the Cimarron Cutoff, sleeping in the bushes during a rainstorm, and falling off his horse—twice.

But the saddle sores had calloused, his back and legs felt stronger, and his hands controlled the reins without a problem.

"If only you could see me now," he said to the photo of Mama. It had a few rips and some bent edges, kinda like his scars.

"She's pretty," Atalanta said.

He passed over the photo. "Yeah. She was young then. Now, well, she's just as bonny, but she doesn't smile near as often."

Atalanta looked at it for a long moment before passing it back. "Well, you're right about another thing. She'd be surprised by how much you've changed."

Shuffle looked away to hide his surely blushing face.

A lot of the credit for his survival had to go to Atalanta. She'd taught him how to ride like a true horseman, how to build a campfire, and how to swing a weapon. In return, he'd taught her how to play Mythic. Even trade.

Stowing away the picture, Shuffle wondered if Mama had changed, too. He remembered how different and grim she looked after first hearing about Dad. That was one thing Shuffle hated about leaving—the pain and worry he had to be causing from being gone. But he couldn't return home, no matter how much he wanted to. He needed to keep heading west to find Dad.

Soon, the road through the red rock of the Sangre de Cristo Mountains opened into a wide landscape of shrubs and cacti. Santa Fe shimmered in the horizon like lost treasure, wondrous and inviting under the setting sun.

Shuffle coaxed Katana out of her comfy spot. She climbed up onto his shoulders and curled around his neck, gripping his jacket.

Atalanta raised her hat, her face catching the warm light. "What if Cici isn't there?"

Cici Nightshade was one of the people Dad might have entrusted with a treasure card.

"She will be."

"What if she don't have the card?" Her eyes narrowed.

Shuffle had to hope it was in Cici's possession. If the belief wasn't there, then the game was over. They'd have to make their way to California empty-handed, without a bargaining chip to secure Dad's freedom. Shuffle would abandon the search if he had to, but they'd already risked so much to get this map—he hated to think it would be a waste.

"She has it. I can feel it—here." He stood up on the stirrups and pointed at his butt.

"Why, you—"

He spurred his horse into a gallop and left Atalanta in the dust, shouting curses.

Katana dug in her claws, but Shuffle didn't even wince.

Atalanta caught up fast, her yellow bandana whipping about. She made a gun-hand and pulled her mock trigger before charging away like Odin's spear.

✳ ✳ ✳

Atalanta waited by a trough outside a saddle shop. "Too slow."

Queen V lapped up the water, almost nonstop.

"But I didn't nearly kill my horse. Isn't that right, boy?" Shuffle patted the colt, who snorted a reply.

"Queenie can take it. Besides, here we are, before dark."

Boxy, flat-roofed adobe buildings hunched along the street like tired workers squatting in the shade. Spiky thistle branches jutted out of the trees and shrubs.

"It's different around here," Shuffle said, climbing

down from the saddle. His pants nearly slipped down his hips, despite his belt being tightened to the last hole. Katana jumped off his back and stretched.

"Looks like you need some new boots," Atalanta said, circling.

Shuffle glanced down. Wrinkles and rips streaked across the leather. The laces hung by their last thread. "Maybe." His voice didn't crack, like it normally did when he felt a little flush. He guessed that was a good thing.

"Hey, I have an idea." Atalanta flipped a quarter in the air, then caught it. "Let's do some shopping before we meet this Cici lady."

Let's—meaning *together*? Interesting. "We need food and supplies, right?" he said.

"New duds," said Atalanta.

He tugged at his sleeves. They were short and frayed, lining up just below his wrist. "How about some lemonade?"

"You've got the dimes. And while you're at it, you can ask around for Cici." She flicked him the quarter.

He cleared his throat, not wanting to sound too desperate about wanting to hang out with her. "Just me?"

"Have fun, and in a couple hours, meet me at the cathedral." Atalanta tipped her hat and strode away.

Sometimes it was hard to have fun alone. Katana agreed, meowing a long, tongue-stretching, whisker-flaring, drawn-out cry.

"Looks like it's just us two," he said, watching Atalanta disappear around the corner.

* * *

A steaming tub of hot water, a bar of soap, and a boar-hair bristle brush—everything a dirt-crusted, bandit-evading adventurer needed.

While soaking in the copper tub, Shuffle perused the local newspaper for something interesting, but found nothing worth musing over except for the date. Being on the trail through Indian Territory had made him lose track of time. According to the newspaper, the day was May 7, 1881. He'd turned thirteen six days ago.

To think, it'd been about three weeks since the night he climbed out of Bronson's window.

He missed Mama and the Shaker lemon pie she'd make to celebrate his birthday. Now that he was no longer a boy—at least not feeling like one—he couldn't cry home about it. He rose up for a breath, feeling the cool air on his face. The day he and Mama and Dad were together again would be the better occasion to celebrate.

Now in clean duds that fit and in boots that didn't crush his toes, Shuffle strutted out of the bath house, feeling like a new shield forged by Hephaestus.

Freshly brushed and fed, Katana purred.

After a short walk to the saloon, Shuffle sauntered to the bar. Instead of the usual deer antlers or longhorn skull, a portrait of a Spanish conquistador hung above the glassware and beverage cabinet. His face was ghostly and distorted, almost comical. His small hands were scarlet. Shuffle shrugged off the way the painting seemed to stare at him and slapped down a dollar. "Lemonade and a plate of chicken, good sir. And some information."

"Sure thing, *muchacho*," the bartender said, smiling under a black chevron mustache. He chiseled an ice block, using a steel pick to make chips for the drink. He served it up quick and cold.

Shuffle took a sip. Tart and sweet, the best combo.

Minutes later, the bartender brought out dinner: a chicken leg and thigh, topped with a green chili sauce, and with a side of black beans. Shuffle took a bite of the juicy meat and crunchy skin. Mama roasted chicken with carrots and onions. This one was almost as tasty. Katana agreed; she devoured her share in a hurry.

"What do you need to know?" The bartender poured a refill. Beads of water formed on the outside of the glass.

"Do you know a lady by the name of Cici Nightshade? A healer, maybe? She helped my dad's friend when he was sick."

"Cici?" His tanned face paled like sun-bleached bone.

"Yes, sir. My dad mentioned she used medicine no one thought would work."

"It's best you forget about Señora Nightshade."

"Why?" He hadn't traveled a thousand miles just to forget.

"I don't want to tell you, because I don't want to be responsible. If you please, finish your meal and forget."

"Responsible for what?" Shuffle looked down at his plate. The chicken quarter looked like carrion—mostly bones and cartilage remained. Thankfully, no maggots.

"I don't want to say, but I will. To save a life. *Mi buena acción.* My good deed. Yeah, that's it." The bartender furiously wiped at the space between them.

"Not following, sir." Shuffle stood, his knees a little wobbly now.

"I'll tell you. Listen, and mind my warning. The woman you're looking for is not a healer."

Shuffle tilted his glass of lemonade for one last drink. It was empty.

The bartender's eyes widened. "She's *una hechicera,* a witch."

CHAPTER 29

CAPTAIN

The round eyes of the conquistador in the painting seemed to stare right at Shuffle.

Unnoticed before, the smell of tobacco and stale cactus juice burned at his nose. The conversation of the room melded together into a mash-up of noise.

"Witches don't scare me." Shuffle took a dry gulp, wishing for a refill. Back home, the older kids at the schoolhouse told lots of horror stories. He knew it was just to keep the younger kids afraid. This was not the time to be soft. "Let me guess, she's some old lady who lures children into her gingerbread house and eats them for dinner."

The bartender frowned, his face as serious as a fresh deck of cards. "She turns travelers and trespassers into pigs. *Se los come para el desayuno.* She eats them for breakfast."

Dad had survived his encounter with Cici and had come away from it trusting her. That was a good enough reason not to worry about becoming a ham steak. But then again, he'd trusted Alec Sterling, who gambled the card away. Dad's judgment of character failed him out here in the desert. Maybe before turning Dad into a pig, Cici created a doppelganger, an evil replica. That would explain why he was making Mythic for Slythe.

There were truths in some of those myths. Maybe not about monsters with a hundred arms, but about real people. Imperfect people who made mistakes. Alec. Cici. Even Dad. He left, never to be seen again. But if he trusted Cici, he would've sent her the card. Witch or not. With his family on the line, Shuffle had to try.

"I'd appreciate it if you'd kindly give me directions." He slid a dime to the barkeeper.

"You don't believe in witches?"

"I do." He slid over another shiny ten-cent piece. "I'm just not scared, and I like bacon."

* * *

Shuffle walked out of the saloon with directions to Cici's ranch memorized. Katana padded out of a dark corner on the wraparound porch and rubbed herself against his legs. He picked her up and placed her around his shoulders.

"Witch, my boot," he said. "She turns trespassers into pigs. Riiight. If Dad trusted Cici, then I trust her. Besides, I have you. A witch's best friend." He patted Katana's head. "First, we need to meet up with Atalanta."

The sun sank under the horizon, painting the sky in bands of pink, purple, and blue. The adobe buildings looked blood red in the dying light. He left the busy streets behind him as he ventured deeper into town, where every dark corner made a sound.

At the plaza, the cathedral appeared ghostly orange in the lamplight. The center stained-glass window glistened like an eye.

The front yard of the church was empty of people, and he didn't feel like waiting outside. Alone. Maybe Atalanta was in the sanctuary.

Inside, lanterns and wall torches lit the church, but the air was cold and musty. Tall columns rose up to the vaulted ceiling. Two rows of pews filled the chapel's nave. Shuffle walked down the center aisle, his footsteps echoing in the quiet hall. A family kneeling in prayer got up and left their pew, passing him on the way out. The main doors slammed shut, resounding throughout the cathedral. The quiet was almost as bad as being in the dark.

He sat down, and Katana explored the length of the pew. If the stained-glass window was the eye of the church, the chapel was the stomach. Hollow, big, and damp. The cathedral had to be five times the size of Mourning Glory's church. Five times creepier, for sure. The statues seemed alive but cold. And the shadows. Shadows everywhere.

The door banged open. Katana jumped straight up,

and her ears pointed in fifty different directions in the span of a second.

Footfalls echoed through the nave. Shuffle turned around, hoping it was Atalanta.

A tall, broad-shouldered man broke the shadow of the foyer and strode down the aisle, his spurs rattling.

Shuffle gulped.

The man kept his head down, his charcoal hat brim obscuring his face. The veins on his hands spread out like spider webs around prominent knuckles. His long, bony fingers hovered around twin revolvers at his hips. *Dual Iron Sixes, Attack +6.*

Shuffle faced the front and gathered Katana to his lap, feeling her tense muscles and raised hairs.

Ka-chunk-chink. Ka-chunk-chink. The man closed in. Shuffle sank lower, hoping the man was going to the front row to pray.

Ka-chunk-chink. Ka-chunk-chink. The man stopped. He put his hand on the back of Shuffle's seat, a choke-hold away.

"You've changed," said a familiar voice. "Not just from the last time I saw you, but from the time since this picture."

Shuffle looked up.

Captain held a photo between his fingers like a rare prize. His chiseled face, bushy beard, and green eyes with copper flecks like Mama's verified it.

Shuffle shot up—Katana jumping to the floor—and

was about to embrace his granddad when he remembered he was supposed to be angry at Captain for his refusal to look for Dad. For his cowardice, as Mama had called it.

He paused a few feet from Captain. "What are you doing here?"

Captain handed over the photo.

Shuffle plucked it, sensing a sneaky card play. The picture on matte paper was of him holding Katana just outside the train station in Independence. The memories of that day flashed before him: the photographer and his boxy camera, Skylla and the two other bandits, and on the train, vengeful little Sweetums.

"I figured this out, too, using the cipher key you left in the shed." Captain handed over the message Shuffle had written in code: *I will return with him.*

Shuffle inched away, beginning to feel the phantom clench of shackles around his wrists. "Mama wrote you, didn't she?"

"I received a telegram."

"Thought you didn't speak to each other."

Captain rested his hands on his gun belt. "Officer Bronson told me what happened."

Bronson, of course, Mama's knight with a shiny badge.

"You came a long way to track me down, but you wouldn't even leave your front porch when Mama asked you to find Dad. Are you trying to make it up to us? I'd say you're a little late for that. Three years late."

Captain tilted his head, his neck making a cracking sound. "You've caused a lot of grief for a lot of folks."

"If Mama's worried, you can tell her that I'm fine, that I'm safer than a Wells Fargo lockbox."

"You can tell her yourself."

Shuffle glanced down at the picture and cringed at his past self—a soft and scared boy. He handed the photo over. "I'm not going home. Not without Dad."

Captain smiled, which was a rare thing. The only other time Shuffle had seen him crack a grin was when he shot a coyote from two hundred yards.

"I made a promise." He clamped down on Shuffle's arm.

"You should've made that promise three years ago." Shuffle tried pulling free, but he only felt his shoulder stretch away from his body as his arm was wrenched behind his back.

"Don't fight, Jason, and we'll do it the easy way. We'll be on the next train home."

"This don't seem easy to me." Shuffle cringed as a sharp pull of pain slashed up his neck.

Katana growled. Her ears lay flat and her hairs spiked along her back. She surged at Captain, wrapped her claws around his leg, and bit. He didn't budge.

Thunk.

Captain's hold loosened. Shuffle strained to look over his free shoulder.

Atalanta stood there, gripping her pistol by the barrel

like a club. Not good. She'd just prodded a grizzly bear with a blunt stick.

Captain rubbed at the back of his head. "Little miss, this is none of your—"

Atalanta swung her weapon.

Captain caught her wrist, and she dropped her gun. With her other hand, she punched him across the chin. Captain frowned. She attacked again, but he let go of Shuffle and caught her by both wrists.

Now free of Captain's grip, Shuffle slipped both of Captain's pistols out of the holsters and cocked the hammers back with his thumbs. He pointed the six-shooters at his granddad. His arms quivered from the weight of the steel, and of his choice. He steadied his aim. No turning back now.

"Captain! Let her go." Shuffle took two backward steps down the pew row. In dime novels, villains always made the mistake of sticking the barrel into the hero's back or chest. Dash Darkwood always swiped the gun away and punched the fool cold with his signature move. *Diamondback Strike: Attack +2. Opponent discards a card.* Captain was no fictional character—he was a real hero, and a real killer. The Hornet of Shiloh. *1000 Stings of Fury: Attack +4. Destroy opponent's units that attacked the previous turn.*

"I'm sorry, Captain. Even though you're my grand-dad, I'll shoot you in the leg if I have to. In front of God and everyone." The dangerous bluff began to make him feel sick. He clenched his jaw, keeping himself from throwing up.

Captain released Atalanta and put his hands up. "I know you think your father is alive, and you want to find him. That's commendable, Jason. You've made it far. Not just anyone has the fortitude—"

Thunk.

This time, Captain dropped like a sack of crooked horseshoes.

CHAPTER 30
THROUGH THE RAIN

Atalanta spun her revolver, then slid it in and out of her holster. "Dang. My grip is bent."

Katana jumped on Captain's back, a warrior triumphant.

Sucking in long, calming breaths, Shuffle laid down the heavy guns. He wasn't going to get dragged home, and nothing else mattered, not even Captain waking up with a headache.

"What is going on here?" An old priest in a red robe came out from the shadows of the altar, rubbing a long loop of rosary beads. Two younger priests in black followed close behind.

Atalanta covered her gun with her coat. "This man attacked my friend."

Shuffle sensed a golden opportunity to get Captain off his back. "That's right. Raving about some money I owed him. But I don't know this old coot from Adam. I think he's drunk."

"Is he injured?" The priest hurried to Captain's side.

"Just a small bump," Atalanta said, shrugging like being knocked out cold wasn't a big deal.

The old priest felt Captain's neck and back. "He's breathing, but he needs a doctor."

"No way, mister—I mean, Father. He needs to be in jail." Shuffle tried to make his best vulnerable and scared victim face. "This crazy cowpuncher needs to be off the streets. He's dangerous. He tried to hurt me. What if he tries to hurt another kid he thinks has his money?" *Clever Words: Opponent cannot attack this turn.*

"Think of all the helpless orphans," added Atalanta.

The three priests spoke in Spanish. One young priest glanced over at Shuffle, his eyes narrow. The other shook his head and made sharp hand gestures at Captain. The old priest nodded, his face worn with concern.

"Okay, we will hold him here, but you will fetch a lawman."

"Yes, will do. Right away," Shuffle said, with no intention to do so. He wanted Captain hindered, not thrown in a hoosegow, or at least not permanently.

The two young priests carefully lifted Captain off the ground and carried him away.

"Father, if I were you, I would keep him far from his guns." Shuffle nodded toward the iron. "And don't forget to lock the door."

The old priest stared at the revolvers, the rosary slipping out of his hands. If only he knew the half of it.

Shuffle hooked Atalanta by the arm and headed for the door.

She looked at him, her eyes reflecting the hundred lights from the candle station. "That really your grandpa?"

"I'll explain when we get to Cici's," he whispered. "Let's get the heck out of here before he wakes."

✳ ✳ ✳

Shuffle and Atalanta hurtled through the dark streets on horseback, guided by a thousand stars. Once they hit the outskirts of Santa Fe, he slowed his horse. She matched his speed, riding beside him.

"Where were you?" he asked, peering at her shadowy silhouette.

"Scouting."

Shuffle snorted. "Scouting ahead for what? And don't give me a horsepile answer. I almost got busted because you weren't around."

"I like how you took care of the situation back there." Too dark to tell if she was smiling, but she sure sounded impressed.

"Yeah, well, that wasn't the first time I handled a problem. Won't be the last. But don't change the subject."

She laughed. "I wasn't at the cathedral because I was looking out for one of Six-Plum's gang," she said. "Making sure we didn't have another bounty hunter on our trail."

"Another one?" Remembering the badge Skylla and the other members wore, he began to understand what it symbolized. Five arrows encircling a skull. Five soldiers with one leader. "Fantastic. Captain shows up, and now there's a sixth bandit."

"You call your grandpa Captain?"

"I call him that because my mother calls him that. She's done it since I was little. Heck, since she was a girl." He sighed, remembering Mama, angry and in tears, pulling him away from the ranch while Captain sat on his porch, silent as a gravestone. Mama had called him a coward for refusing to go look for Dad. When Dad was declared dead, she grew even angrier at Captain—hadn't uttered his name since. "Never mind that, though. Will we ever shake Skylla and her gang?"

Atalanta made a dismissive noise in her throat. "They're part of the landscape—the Wild West, as you townies call it. They're everywhere, until they're not. Like them clouds heading our way."

Lightning flashes lit the underbelly of a deep, dark storm front hidden in the night sky.

A strong blast of cool wind swept through the dry plain. Shuffle shivered as the gang ran through his mind: Skylla, Shortstack, Lady Feather, Black Star, and Big Hair. "Did you find her? The sixth bandit?"

"No one's seen her for days."

"Good. Maybe we'll make it to Cici's without a run-in with another tracker who wants my hide."

Atalanta nodded. "Which way now?"

He recalled the directions. "It's supposed to be a few miles out of town. North by northwest, a small road off Beggar's Trail, marked by a stone border wall and a sign with a pig on it."

"A pig?"

"That's her thing." Shuffle imagined it hurt being transformed into a hog. Eating slop couldn't be too pleasant either. He shook away the worst possibility: being slaughtered for his tenderloin.

"North by northwest, huh? You got us in the right direction. You're learning."

He sat up tall in the saddle. Catching on at the schoolhouse was one thing. Picking up survival skills seemed a whole lot more substantial. "Yeah?"

"Yeah, except we gotta go through that." She pointed toward the storm.

* * *

Blades of rain fell out of the sky, coldly cutting to the bone. The wind howled.

Everything but the rain seemed to disappear in the dark.

A bright blue flash and booming thunderclap blasted through the night. The air was charged with danger. He could feel it crackle on his skin.

The colt reared. Shuffle held on, using every muscle,

every surface of his body to grip the saddle, the ropes, and the horse. Gaining control, he followed the road the best he could, finally finding Atalanta waiting near the stone wall and the pig-shaped road marker for Cici's ranch.

They hurried up the trail. *Crash-boom.* He leaned against his colt, clinging to a fleeting warmth. The horse's muscles rippled with each long stride.

Crash-boom. Crash-boom. With each flash of lightning, skeletal trees and spear-tipped cacti looked like undead warriors from Tartarus. Atalanta disappeared into the abyss and reappeared farther away with each blue burst of light.

Crash-boom. The horse snorted and whinnied. His hooves pounded the ground, gravel and dirt crunching under the force.

Crash-boom. Shuffle tasted blood and rain. He bit down harder on his lip until he felt pain.

Two lights appeared in the distance. Eyes in the dark. He kept his head up, focusing on the glow. It was either a beacon to safety or a lure to even more danger. He had to gamble to find Cici; otherwise he could get bucked off the horse, drowned in a flash flood, or struck by lightning.

Thankfully, a house came into view, where a pair of lanterns hung under the awning. Witch's hut or not, it would be safer than being out in the open during a lightning storm.

Making it to shelter first, Atalanta slid off her saddle. Queen V galloped away.

Crash-boom. Shuffle tilted as his horse flailed back on its hind legs. The reins slipped through his hands. He tipped backward, feeling weightless, then heavy as he fell.

He hit something hard.

CHAPTER 31
THE PIG

Shuffle opened his eyes to shadows dancing on the wall like revelers around a fire.

Morning light crept through the long gash between the curtains of a small window.

A heavy wool blanket covered him from chest to feet. He sat up on the bed, pain flaring at the back of his head. He rubbed at his neck, looking around the room. Tattered books lined a shelf on the opposite wall. A crate on the floor was filled with wooden toys, plus a stuffed doll with busted seams and a missing eye.

The pain wrenched, now at his temples, and he gripped the sheets, bracing against each pulse. He closed his eyes and focused on the darkness until his head stopped pounding. His thoughts became clearer: the storm, Cici's house, his horse rearing back, the fall. When the pain became tolerable, he opened his eyes. A mobile hung from the ceiling, made of what looked like bat wings. He was definitely not home, and the clothes he wore weren't his—too short in the shirt sleeves and trouser legs. He ran his fingers through his damp hair, missing his hat. His new goose egg throbbed as he touched it. At least he didn't have hooves or a curly tail.

After a moment, the quiet of the room caught up to him.

"Hello?" He patted around the bed for Katana. She wasn't curled up in the blankets, on the small side table, or on the floor.

The door creaked ajar, before swinging open.

"Atalanta?"

No one came in that he could see, but footfalls scraped at the floor. He leaned forward to take a better look.

A small pig, pale with brown splotches, snorted at him. It wore a yellow bandana. Atalanta's bandana!

Shuffle rolled backward off the bed and hit the floor as though taking cover from incoming gunfire. He peeked around the foot of the bed. "Atalanta, is that you?"

The pig made eye contact, blinked once, and waddled forward. Shuffle braced against the floor, unable to move away. The pig stopped short of biting his face off and oinked, even sounding like Atalanta when she'd grunt.

"I can't believe it. What happened?" He held her, inspecting every angle. "You're so round and smelly."

She blinked a reply.

He gritted his teeth, thinking she would never shoot, fight, or ride again. "We're going to find that witch, and she better turn you back." He tucked her under his arm.

A small hallway opened into a den—the witch's sacrificial chamber, no doubt. He took out his authenticator to use as a weapon. Its small glass orb probably wouldn't do much damage, but it was better than nothing. *Bludgeoning Club: Attack +1.* Prepared for battle, he ventured out, the floorboards creaking with each step.

Wide, dusty bands of light cut into the room. The smell of a forest after rain drifted throughout. A table and two rocking chairs with knitted seat cushions were arranged for ritual. A painting of a prize pig hung above a long bench. Two doors faced opposite each other. Windows flanked the door to the right.

"That one leads to the outside," he whispered. "Should we escape?"

Atalanta squirmed, almost slipping free.

"Yeah, you're right. We should fight. Cowardice is for chickens."

The other sinister door, likely leading to the torture chamber, beckoned to be opened.

He looked into Atalanta's magic marble eyes. "If I end up being turned into a pig, too, and we both lose our tails, I want you to know I would've never made it this far without you. I'd be buzzard food in Kansas. I would've never had the guts to face Femus. I'm ready. Are you?"

She scrunched her snout.

"Of course you are. You're the toughest, meanest knuckle duster I know. Pig or not."

He crept to the lonely door. The brass knob chilled his fingers. He turned it, inch by inch, until it clicked. He nudged the door open a sliver. Inside, a long table with six chairs filled the room—a dining room of death.

Singing, or chanting, came from an adjacent, unseen room. Armed with the authenticator, he eased through the door.

The death chamber connected to a kitchen with a potbelly stove-oven in one corner, an icebox in another, and a large counter in the center. A woman, her back to him, hummed a tune as she prepared something undoubtedly pernicious. A wooden spoon pierced her gray hair knotted in a bun. *Ladle of Curses: Opponent discards 2 cards.*

Katana popped up on the counter. She rubbed her head against the woman's arm.

The woman petted Katana, gliding her hand from head to tail, then placed a small plate of food on the counter. She was going to poison his cat!

CHAPTER 32

CICI NIGHTSHADE

"Bad girl, Katana!" yelled Shuffle. Raising the authenticator above his head, he charged at the old crone. "Stay away from my cat!"

Katana arched her back and took a defensive hop, her ears pinned back. The woman glanced over her shoulder.

Someone grabbed his weapon. Shuffle held on, and his top half stopped while his feet kept going, slipping forward. He let go and braced Atalanta against his chest as he crashed to the floor, landing on his butt.

"Ow," he said, collapsing onto his back. Atalanta snorted.

A shadowy figure towered over him. He blinked, his eyes adjusting.

A girl looked down at him, the authenticator in her hand. She wore a yellow farm dress with billowed shoulders, high collar, and pleated skirt. Her hair tumbled in dark waves.

He groaned. "Look, minion. Tell your mistress to change my friend back or I'm gonna—"

"Birdshot. You lose your mind?"

He gasped, peering harder at the girl's details: scar along the arm, freckles on her cheeks, and a mean-as-viper stare. "Wait a sec. Atalanta? You're not a pig?"

"You must've hit your head harder than I thought."

He looked down at the little porker. It nuzzled his chin.

"Did you think . . . ?" Atalanta laughed. "Your wagon's short a wheel, tough guy. I thought you'd get a chuckle out of her wearing my bandana, not go loony."

He shoved the hog off his chest. "Funny. What did you do to your hair?"

She tilted her head down and away and drifted her hand to the end of a long curl. "It's different, right?"

"I think I like you better as a pig."

Her eyes narrowed. "Yeah? I liked you better uncon-scious." She jabbed him in the stomach with the brass end of the authenticator.

"Oh, help him up. He's had it rough." The woman came into view. Dry, dark mud plastered her face. Her eyes gleamed with mismatched color, one brown, the other blue. She held out her thin, knobby hand.

The two ladies pulled him to his feet; Atalanta tugged extra hard.

He rubbed at the twinge of pain in his shoulder. "I'm sorry for acting like a rabid bobcat. I thought . . ."

The woman smiled, the cracks at the corners of her eyes and mouth splitting out like tributaries of the

Mississippi. "Seeds of lies grow crooked trees with rotten fruit. Sometimes, the unknowing eat the fruit anyway. You took quite the spill. How are you feeling?" She reached out to touch his head.

He flinched away. "It still hurts. But I'll be fine."

She pulled out a chair. "Please. I was just fixing you a healing drink."

"You're Cici, right?" Shuffle sat down, almost crumbling into the chair, feeling suddenly drained of energy. Katana jumped to his lap and curled into a ball.

"That's correct. Cici Nightshade." She handed him a steaming cup of a greenish-brown liquid. "Drink. This will help with the pain."

It smelled like a graveyard. He leaned away from the unholy stench.

"Not the most pleasant of aromas," she said, "but it works wonders."

Keeping his head down, he strained to glance upward, wondering if the mud on her face was hiding hideous burns or grotesque tumors.

"You don't have to be afraid. I won't transform you into a pig." Grinning, she added a dollop of honey and stirred. "Trust me. Your father did."

"I'm guessing Atalanta told you my story."

She nodded. "Please, while it's hot."

Shuffle sat up and took the cup. He blew on the steaming liquid and sipped, bracing for the worst. *Please, don't let it be poison.* Instead of a rotting corpse, he tasted grassy herbs with a tang of spiciness, better than any snake-oil cure-alls he'd ever dared to drink.

"Thank you," he said, taking a big slurp. "Atalanta, you should try a cup. It's really . . ." She was gone.

"You're a long way from home." Cici sat next to him. "But so was your father when I first met him."

He grasped the warm cup like a memory he didn't want to lose. "Dad was on a mission. As am I."

"You're convinced he's alive."

He nodded, though he wasn't sure it was a question.

"And you've come here to get something he sent me."

"A special card for a game. Do you have it?" His stomach rumbled.

"Is that what it is?" She rose from the chair. "But first, breakfast."

CHAPTER 33
OLD COYOTE

Shuffle sat up, feeling his strength returning and his headache subsiding. He wore his own clothes, and a clean shirt felt like a fresh start.

The squatty pig roamed the dining room floor, and Katana kept watch from the top of a tall cabinet.

The aroma coming from the kitchen smelled like mornings at home. He eased back in the seat and closed his eyes, missing Mama's cooking. There was only so much nuts and cheese he could take.

Cici came into the dining room, balancing three full, steaming plates of scrambled eggs, potato hash, and biscuits. She smiled, her face clean of the mud mask. Her smooth skin seemed to glow.

Her mismatched eyes sparkled at him. The food looked delicious, but he could hardly eat, distracted by how young Cici looked compared to her wrinkled neck and bony hands.

Atalanta kicked him in the shin, then turned to Cici. "Thanks for breakfast."

"Absolutely. Please, enjoy."

Unable to resist, Shuffle gorged his food in record time. He sighed, patting his belly.

After breakfast, Atalanta took it upon herself to wash the dishes. She kept having to nudge the little porker away with her foot, but the pig would just go right back to bothering her. Meanwhile, Cici went into another room and then returned with a small box ornamented with gemstones and tiny bones.

Unlocking the box, Cici revealed jewelry, paper mementos, and small wooden animal figurines. She plucked out a card and set it face down in front of her. "You still wish to continue down this path?"

"Yes, ma'am."

"You may not like what you uncover. Do you have the strength to face what has been buried all this time?"

Dad in a shallow desert grave was an old fear. Now, after surviving Skylla, Femus, and the thunderstorm, Shuffle knew he wasn't the same boy he'd been back in Mourning Glory. If there were worse things to come, he would take them on.

"I've made it this far. I'm not turning back."

She slid him the card.

He took it: *Huehuecoyotl, green diamond, Aztec Wealth faction.* According to Dad, Huehuecoyotl, or Old Coyote, was a trickster god who loved a good story and a good party. Shuffle felt like revelry as he peeled the false backing and uncovered the third map piece. He was one step closer to Dad and the treasure.

Cici set her hand on his shoulder. "You still hunt another, yes?"

He nodded, not surprised she knew. "Yeah, a man named John Henry Holliday has a card."

"Seek where the living roll bones and the dead wear boots."

He loved puzzles and riddles, but with the hard road ahead, some easy info would've been much appreciated. "That's great, ma'am, but if you know where I need to go—"

"Y'all gotta see this." Atalanta ripped off the apron. With her eyes trained out the window, she drew her revolver, holding it up at the ready.

Nothing like a quick draw to signal urgency. Shuffle dashed to the kitchen, stowing the card in his shirt pocket.

Outside, a hundred yards beyond the pig corral and boundary fencing, Big Hair had taken up position behind an oak tree, her elephant gun sticking out like one of the branches.

Atalanta ran off, and he followed, cutting into a side room. She leaned against the wall and peeked out the window. "Dang. Just like I figured. Over there by the boulder."

Black Star nestled a long rifle against the big rock, eighty yards away.

"Come on." Atalanta nudged Shuffle, and they both hustled to the opposite room.

Sixty yards away, Lady Feather dug at a fence post with her jagged knife. Shortstack hiked a shotgun on her shoulder.

Shuffle banged his fist against the wall. "How did they find us?"

They hurried to the den and scanned out front for more enemies.

Fifty yards from the house, Skylla perched on a warhorse that stalked back and forth along the locked gate. And the sixth bandit of the gang—a woman wearing an old Army jacket and a blue headscarf over frizzy black hair—was arming a wagon-set Gatling gun. *Typhon's Hundred Flames: Attack +3. Destroy opponent's units of power 2 or less.*

Skylla wasn't gonna stop coming after him, unleashing her whole gang. Apparently, the promise of treasure clung to him like honey on hushpuppies.

"What'll it take to lose these ladies?"

"We been doing our darndest, but this is their livelihood," Atalanta murmured. "No doubt the bounty is high, but really, they're just surviving. That ain't easy for women, you know, and all they have is each other."

"Well, it seems like they're in it for the fun, and I think—" Shuffle gulped hard as Gatling Gal loaded a magazine of what looked like an infinite number of bullets into her shining brass machine gun of destruction.

CHAPTER 34
GODLESS HAIL OF BULLETS

Surrounded—four out back, two out front.

From the saddle of her warhorse, Skylla shot the lock off the gate and clopped toward the house. Her chaps looked particularly ruddy in the dawn's luster.

"There's no escaping. We're gonna have to fight." Atalanta checked her revolver's chamber.

Cici went out to the porch, armed with a wooden spoon. Nothing like a ladle to ward off an enemy attack.

The bandit stopped short, freezing as if Cici had stepped out for a high-noon draw.

Hold the reins! The spoon worked. There had to be something strange about the old wood and about Cici's old hands and mismatched eyes. Or Skylla just believed the rumors.

"No harm will come to you. If you give up the boy."

Cici crossed her arms. "Why threaten a child? What is it you fear?"

"Stay away from me, witch." Skylla pulled back the hammer of her black steel pistol.

Shuffle held his breath. A spoon couldn't possibly deflect bullets.

"The boy's got something we want. If he hands it over, he will be unharmed."

Shuffle pressed his hand against his deck, knowing she was here for the treasure cards and likely for some payback for all the trouble. She seemed like the sort who'd keep a grudge.

"I suggest you leave." Cici waved her spoon above her head in circles, then pointed it at Skylla.

The bandit's warhorse snorted and reared back, kicking up a fury of dust. Once she got the steed under control, Skylla glared at Cici before turning back to the gate.

"I don't think she liked that," Shuffle said to Cici as she returned to the house. Maybe the townies were right to be scared. She radiated an unseen power that even Skylla seemed to fear.

"You need to leave. Remember what I told you," Cici said.

A strange whirring noise, followed by thunderous bangs, resounded in the house. Atalanta pulled Shuffle down.

The doors splintered. The glass shattered. Debris cut through the air, whizzing by like a hundred angry bees. Bullets screamed overhead, ricocheting off walls. One lead plum drilled a spot barely a foot away. Shuffle gasped, staring at the tongue of smoke coming from the hole.

Atalanta crawled toward the rear of the house. "Let's go. Stay down."

"I can't." The hole looked deep, like the bullet had drilled itself to the underworld.

The barrage kept coming, destroying almost everything in the house. The hornet's nest of Shiloh must've been like this, only with a hundred more bullets, and a hundred more dead bodies.

The rapid fire and ricochets turned into one long thunderclap.

"Come on, Shuffle!" Atalanta began to turn back, but shrapnel cut off her path.

A flash of movement cut across the room, not bullets or splinters, but a black blur. Katana dodged whistling death as she scrambled toward Shuffle. Her fur spiked up, her ears down, but instead of running scared, she buried herself against him. Feeling her heartbeat gallop, he scooped her up and stowed her in his pack where it was safer.

He reeled in a breath. "Okay, let's run!"

"Go to your horses. In the barn." Cici drifted to the couch under the pig painting. Closing her eyes, she sat very still.

"What's she doing?" Despite the bullets flying everywhere, he didn't want to abandon her.

Atalanta pulled at the tail of his coat. "Let her be. We need to get out."

Shuffle shook his head, uncertain how Cici was

going to fend off the bandits long enough for him and Atalanta to escape. Superstitions couldn't possibly protect her against gold fever and guns.

The shooting stopped, filling the dusty air with silence. The bandits were probably reloading.

Atalanta opened the back door. "We gotta fly."

"I'm fine. Thanks for asking. How're you?"

"Angry." She cocked the hammer of her pistol.

He glanced over his shoulder for one last look at Cici. With the piglet nestled in her lap, she remained as calm as a summer cloud. What was she doing? Conjuring a spell? There was no such thing.

Atalanta tightened her yellow kerchief and adjusted her hat. "Ready? Now." She hotfooted out the door.

Shuffle followed, hunched low, into a dense fog.

The morning had been clear as crystal, but now, the place was like Niflheim, the world of mist. The Norse land of the dead. Maybe the tales had some truth in them after all. Maybe Cici was more than a pig farmer.

Gunfire blazed. Bullets zipped through the mist, making ghostly bursts in their wake. Keeping his head down, Shuffle ran for his life.

The fog covered the ranch grounds, making good cover, except he couldn't see more than two feet away, and he tripped on a spiny cactus. He hit the ground, which was muddy from last night's downpour. He grabbed his shin, feeling it throb. Gritting his teeth, he forced himself to stand. "Atalanta, where are you?"

When he didn't get an answer, he limped through the muck. Staying put wasn't a good idea.

Soon, the air thickened with the stink of manure and the sound of snorting pigs. Certain he was lost, he followed the pen's fencing. It could lead to the barn. Instead, following the fence brought him close to someone partly covered by the misty veil.

It wasn't Atalanta.

The person had her back to him and was scanning the fog with a shotgun. Curly hair and a green vest came into full view. Shortstack, her arm still in a sling. She pivoted, now facing him. Her eyes widened, and she smiled.

"Well, well. Look what I found."

Atalanta burst out of the fog and grabbed for the shotgun.

Even one-handed, Shortstack fought back. She crashed her shoulder into Atalanta, sending her into the mud. She stepped on Atalanta's hand and aimed the shotgun.

Shuffle grabbed a heavy rock with both hands and rushed at Shortstack, raising it over his head. He closed his eyes and smashed the rock into something hard. The jolt juddered up his arms.

He opened his eyes to the bandit lying crumpled on the ground. One down, five more on his tail. With the fog dying out, it was gonna be hard to stay hidden.

"Don't worry. She's got a skull like a ram." Atalanta unloaded the shells out of Shortstack's shotgun.

She tossed them away in opposite directions. "Come on. It's this way."

A *pop* and a *zing* cut through the air, and a bullet hit a nearby fencepost. A bandit yelled at them to stop.

Without the fog for cover, Shuffle crouched low as he ran, fighting his painful ankle. A post shattered into splinters, and he stumbled. The blast must've been from the elephant gun.

"Why are they shooting at us? We're just kids."

"Just trying to scare us. Otherwise, we'd be buzzard food. Get down." Atalanta hurled a canister nearly a hundred feet toward the two shooters hiding behind the fencing. She aimed and fired.

The bottle exploded. The bandits blasted backward and landed in twisted heaps, writhing in the mud. A wave of heat and stink spread through the air.

Amazing shot, amazing explosion. Not so amazing smell.

Shuffle climbed to his feet. "What the heck was that?"

Atalanta holstered her revolver. "Methane."

Gas from pig dung. *Devil Pig's Unholy Blast: Attack +1. Opponent returns two battlefield cards, of power 2 or less, to their deck.*

After a second of being in awe of the carnage, they hustled to the barn, where their horses were waiting.

Saddled up, they took off, heading west, with clear air ahead and a cloud of dust behind. No stopping now. Hopefully, Cici and her little porker were okay.

Beyond the fence line, Shuffle and Atalanta cut between two ridges, but as they sped through the other side, another rider came flying out from cover.

Black Star stormed up to Atalanta and pulled her off the saddle. Shuffle yanked hard on the reins. He circled back to help and, if he must, to fight.

A lasso flew overhead and landed on his lap. It tightened before he could even say "horsepile." He couldn't aid anyone tied up like a rodeo cow. Black Star prowled closer, holding the lariat and brandishing a long, jagged stone knife.

Pop. Zing. Thwap.

A wet, warm spray hit Shuffle in the face.

CHAPTER 35

THE THREE AND THE HANGING TREE

Holy horsepile! What just happened? Shuffle blinked away the warm splatter on his eyelashes.

Black Star gripped her hand, gaping from a bullet wound.

It was blood, sticky yet dripping down his face.

"Leave him, or I leave you dead."

Shuffle recognized Captain's voice and calmed.

"Leave him!" Captain's shadowy figure stood on the high ridge fifteen yards away, obscured by the sun's blinding light.

Black Star released the rope and sped down the trail toward Cici's. Four bandits nixed.

Spitting the gore from his lips, Shuffle wriggled free of the lasso and climbed down. He rushed to Atalanta's side. "Hey, are you all right?"

Atalanta rose to her knees, arching her back and grimacing. "Just got the wind knocked out of me."

She grabbed his forearm; he grabbed hers, feeling the jagged scar, and pulled her to her feet. She dusted off her hat. "Oh, birdshot. Him again?"

Captain rode up on his favorite horse, and he'd probably brought his favorite rifle, too. Shuffle supposed it was only a matter of time before he caught up to them.

Shuffle faced his granddad, primed to take the fight to him. "Listen, Captain. Thanks for saving us, but I'm not going home with you. I'm going to find Dad. If you don't want to face Mama empty-handed, you can come with us."

"What? No." Atalanta pulled him to her and whispered. "We're not taking the old bullet. He'll slow us down. And he probably hates me for cracking his skull."

"He hates everybody." Shuffle yanked free and faced his granddad, toe to toe. "Captain, we have two more trigger-happy ladies on our tail, and I can't stay around reliving family squabbles. What will it be? Are you gonna ride with us, or you gonna return home and deliver some disappointing news?"

Captain lifted his hat, and from under the shadow, something akin to a smile stretched along his craggy face. But his look turned sour, and he drew out his repeater. "They're advancing! Follow the road. Turn at the goat path and ride up the hill. Go! I'll catch up." He began shooting down the trail.

Shuffle got back on his horse as return fire zipped past. Great. Couldn't he get through the rest of this day without facing a rain of gunfire? A bullet buzzed right by his ear, giving him his answer.

Down the road, Skylla charged forward, her dark six-shooter blazing.

Then a red mist popped at her chest, and she fell off her horse. Granddad must've landed a shot. Maybe her dangerous hunt had finally ended.

But no, it wasn't over. Gatling Gal fired her weapon, spitting flying death from the wagon being pulled by a team of horses.

Shuffle spurred his horse into a sprint. He rode hard even long after the gunshots stopped. He didn't know how far he had gone when Atalanta caught up to him.

"That goat path is just ahead," she said. "We can take it or keep going straight and lose him. Your call."

Shuffle knew Captain wouldn't stop hunting him, so might as well have a war hero by his side. Though they'd been ice cold for the last few years, Captain was still his granddad. That had to stand for something.

"We're turning." Shuffle urged his horse faster, the wind rushing against his face.

After taking the winding goat path, they stopped at the top of the steep hill. A lone tree stood sentry, with a frayed rope hanging on its highest, thickest branch. A cottonwood blossom.

They took cover behind a rock at the end of the trail and waited, ready to ambush any bounty hunter hot on their tails.

Soon, Captain rode up the hill. When Shuffle popped out from behind cover, Captain leaned back in his saddle. "They're regrouping. We got an hour on them." Captain reloaded his repeater. "Where to now, Jason?"

"I'm not sure. I need to find a man named John Henry Holliday. Cici said we should go 'where the living roll bones and the dead wear boots,' or something like that. Sounds like nonsense, but I think she's serious, and I've got a feeling she's right."

"If this is all you're going on, Jason, you should reconsider." Captain ratcheted the lever action of his rifle. "You seemed so sure of yourself, I figured you had the tactical information to find your father. But now, it appears you're headed toward a crossfire of false hopes and outlaws."

"Easy there, old bullet." Atalanta climbed up on her horse and circled around Captain. "The old lady might have a wagon wheel loose, but I know the place she means. Shuffle, if you're willing to trust her, we should go."

Shuffle climbed back into the saddle, ready for the next move. "Let's do it."

She turned to Captain with a smirk. "We're headed to Tombstone."

SILVER CITY SENTINEL

OGAR GANG CAUGHT; SHERIFF SAVED BY BOY

Sheriff Daniels and his deputies apprehended the Ogar Gang late Monday night.

After a boy won the Mythic tournament at the Crazy Eye Saloon, a scuffle broke out which escalated into a shoot-out, followed by an uncontrollable fire. The drinking establishment burned down, leaving it a charred tangle.

"Silas Ogar was cheating," said witness Jack Goodson, 15, of Bisbee. "But the boy still played great. When Silas lost, he flipped the table and drew his pistol. The boy stared down Silas, cold as Pike's Peak. Then *bang*. Chaos."

"During the melee, one of the Ogar boys had a bead on me," said Daniels, "but the boy broke a chair over my would-be shooter's head before he got off a shot." The boy and his compatriots—a black cat, a young girl wearing a yellow bandana, and an older man in a long, black coat—survived the shootout and immediately left town. Their whereabouts are unknown.

STRANGE WEATHER

The recent mix of heavy thunderstorms and unbearable heat waves has locals in a tizzy.

"This weather's confounding," said Bob Leeman, teacher, 44. "It's supposed to be a dry heat, but all this flooding then drought then flooding then drought makes me wanna pound rocks with a hammer."

"The end is near. Repent, heathens," said Eve Drownage, seamstress, 38.

Are recent storms an omen of doom?

BANDIT ATTACKS ON THE RISE

Three weeks ago and for reasons unknown, bandits destroyed the home of a pig rancher. Property damage was extensive, but no one was hurt.

"Fear makes the fearful into irrational animals," said rancher Cici Nightshade of Santa Fe. "But calmness and tranquility triumph."

Last week, reports of wagon train attacks along Southwest Passage brought concern of a new group of highwaymen.

And on Monday night, twenty miles out of town, a family of three were accosted by a heavily armed posse. Their leader was described as a woman wearing blood-red chaps.

STAR DRAGONS PERFORMANCE

TUSCON, Ariz.— A traveling circus of Chinese acrobats will perform for one night only before heading to California.

CHAPTER 36
TOMBSTONE

They drove the horses hard all morning, finally getting to town with enough daylight left for a long search. Dust kicked up from the parched ground even as they slowed to a trot. Hopefully, Cici had clued them in to the right town for the final map piece.

Folks hustled about, not paying too much attention to them. The women hid under parasols and the men sported wide-brim hats to keep themselves shaded from the unrelenting sun.

"Is this a friendly place?" Shuffle asked Atalanta.

Her yellow kerchief flickered in the dry wind. "I think you'll like it. It's a gaming town. The cemetery's named Boot Hill because the buried gunslingers are still wearing their boots," she said.

"Should we look there first?" Shuffle closed his eyes, regretting what he'd just said. It wasn't long ago when they searched for Alec Sterling only to find the man's sad, faded gravestone.

"Better place than any, especially better than the

gaming tables," Captain said.

Atalanta chuckled. "What are you afraid of, you old bullet? A little dust-up over a hand of cards?"

Captain kept his eyes forward. "Gaming's changed out here in the West. The stakes are higher than just a handful of nickels."

Shuffle rode closer to his granddad. He needed Captain believing that they could find Dad. He needed the war hero focused on the quest. "We just need to find John Henry Holliday. He'll have the card."

Atalanta suggested they try the barbershop.

"There are only two places every civilized man will eventually visit. The barbershop and the grave," she said.

Shuffle smiled, remembering the time he had told her that very thing.

"Dad put in his letters that John Henry Holliday was a man of dash and style. So, I guess this might work." Boot Hill Cemetery would have to wait.

They strolled into the barbershop, and the bell hanging at the door chimed. Talc and dust hung in the sunlight coming in through the windows.

"Looking for a cut?" asked the barber, sweeping the floor around a leather and iron chair.

Shuffle touched the back of his head, his hair curling at the nape of his neck. "No, sir. I need help finding someone."

The barber looked up into a wide, brass-framed mirror hanging on the wall. Off the reflection, his eyes met

Shuffle's, and he stopped mid-sweep. He put aside the broom and came into full view, along with his two holstered guns, one under his left arm and the other at his right hip. A barber armed with dual sixes. Only in a town called Tombstone.

Atalanta crept to the far corner of the room. Captain slid aside the drape of his long coat.

Shuffle took Katana off his back and carried her against his body. *Enough with the fighting already.*

The barber's eyes narrowed. "You . . . the boy with a black cat . . . you're looking for someone?"

"Um, yeah. Is that a problem?" Something about the barber wasn't quite right. Did he hate cats like Femus had?

"No, no problem. So long the cat don't pee on anything."

Shuffle smirked, thinking about Sweetums and the train. "She won't."

"I know a lot of people and I like to help, but I only extend that courtesy to those in the chair." The barber winked, his curled mustache tilting.

Maybe, just this one time, there wasn't going to be a shootout, and all it would take to get some information was a trim. And it had been a long time since his last haircut.

Shuffle set Katana down and took off his hat. "Sure, okay. I'd like a haircut."

"Your friends can sit." The barber gestured to the bench along the opposite wall. "They're making me nervous."

Shuffle crossed his arms. "I should say the same thing about you."

The barber looked a bit confused for a moment, before he remembered he was packing steel. "Rough town. Have to be prepared."

Really? Who'd want to rob a barber? The tips couldn't be that good.

Shuffle slid into the leather and iron chair. The barber reclined the seat and slapped a hot towel around Shuffle's face.

"I only want a trim. My head hair, not a shave."

"It's complimentary for first-time costumers. It'll make you a new man."

Atalanta broke her silence from her dark corner. "Don't do it. You'll look like a baby without the peach fuzz."

A smile almost broke across Captain's stony face.

"Shut up." Shuffle felt the hair above his top lip. *Peach fuzz, my boot.* Katana jumped on his lap, making him sink into the cushion. "Fine. Do it."

The barber finished pasting on the towel, the heat almost burning.

A new man. Riiight. He'd been through enough rites of passage to know that he was no longer just a small-town kid. Letting the warmth take him, he closed his eyes.

∗ ∗ ∗

Shuffle opened his eyes as a cool lather was slapped across his face. The soap smelled like pine trees. He looked around the room.

"Where's Atalanta?"

"Getting supplies," Captain said, snapping the pages of a newspaper. "Cat's with her."

The barber stropped a pearl-handled straight razor. Its blade gleamed. "It's so sharp you won't even notice. Relax."

Shuffle gripped the arm rests as the razor neared. Relax? Impossible to do with a knife at your face. What a stupid tactical decision—leaving defenses open to a killing blow.

The barber slid the blade upward. Shuffle imagined the sharp edge a breath away. Up and up it went. Close to drawing blood.

With a smooth flick, the barber lifted the razor. "See. I bet you didn't feel a thing."

Wrong. He felt the icy danger of standing at a cliff's hundred-foot drop, and it was great. To think, the boy he was before would've keeled over from fear. Dad would've been proud. Too bad he wasn't the one to do the shaving. With all the time apart, they'd missed out on a lot of important moments.

The barber continued, sliding the blade down

Shuffle's cheek. "I take it you've been traveling far and wide, stopping here, like you said, to search for someone?"

"Far and wide don't even begin to describe it."

"So I've heard." He held the razor at Shuffle's neck. *Knife.*

The barber pressed the blade to skin. "Well, I know every man in town worth their salt."

Air. Breathe. Please, let it be painless.

"Oh, sorry." The barber lifted the razor away.

Shuffle gasped.

Captain stood, his hands inching toward his guns. "Jason. Are you okay?"

"I'm fine." Shuffle glared at the barber. "Are you done now?"

"My apologies." The bartender handed him a towel. "So, who are you searching for?"

Shuffle wiped his face clean. That'd be the last shave he'd need or want for a long while. "A man by the name of John Henry Holliday."

The barber's blue eyes dilated. He took a step back and smiled. "I thought so. The moment you walked in, my gut told me you were here for me."

"You're John Henry?"

"Call me Doc, and I know you're here for a fight."

CHAPTER 37

DOC HOLLIDAY

Captain swung his hands to his pistols.

Doc drew and trained his guns on Captain, faster than a rattlesnake on a mouse. Truth of the matter was, Captain was a soldier, not a gunslinger. Quick draws probably weren't essential on the battlefield, with there being cannons and all. Besides, he was old.

Shuffle sat up. "Hey, put your guns down. I'm *not* here for a fight."

"Oh, I meant an entirely different kind of scrap," Doc said. "My reflexes just kick in. Useful to have in my line of work."

"Haircutting?"

"Dentistry."

The door chimed, and a skinny old man wearing a bow tie and a white smock walked in. "Thanks for minding the store, Doc. Did you have to turn anybody away?" The old man froze when he noticed the hold-up.

Doc nodded. "Don't mind us."

Shuffle flung the towel to the floor. "So, barber isn't a side job?"

"Nope. After my trim, I stayed to watch the store while he had to step out. Good thing you started with the shave. I don't know a lick about cutting hair." Doc spun his revolvers and slid them in the holsters. "Well, I'm starved. How about you folks join me for a meal and we can talk more then?"

Shuffle was at a loss. One minute Doc was drawing his shooters on them, the next he was inviting them to dinner. It seemed they'd have to go along with it if they wanted that Mythic card.

Later, Shuffle and Captain met up with Atalanta and Katana at the Orient, the saloon where Doc apparently worked on occasion as a Faro dealer. According to him, he'd also won a fair number of Mythic games.

Doc let them have a private back room to eat dinner: overcooked game hens, burnt potatoes, and sour lemonade. It was better than nothing, and everyone had seconds. Except for Doc. Seemed he was the wiser.

After the food was taken away, Shuffle tried to get this encounter back on track. "Look, Doc, we got off on the wrong foot. We haven't even been properly introduced."

"I know who you are. The boy and his black cat. Demon of Dodge City. Cavalier of the Cimarron. Savior of Silver City. The boy with the Maker's deck, and the Maker's *Odysseus*."

Everything sounded like ridiculous horsepile, except the last part. Titles belonged to heroes of great stature. He wasn't anything until he found Dad. Regarding the Maker's deck, maybe all the run-ins with Femus and the other gamblers had started rumors about the priceless cards. That kind of fame would attract every thieving gambler out there. "I'm not looking for trouble."

"But you *are* here to challenge me to a Mythic duel."

Doc placed a fitted felt cover over the table. Perfect for gaming.

"Hate to disappoint you, but I'm not here to play," Shuffle said, stroking Katana's dusty fur. Though she hated getting wet, she'd need a bath. They all did, but it appeared cleanliness would have to wait.

"I'm the only one who's beat Billy the Kid," Doc said, with an upswing of his chin, "even though he still gets all the recognition. But there's something about your tale that is much more special. I have to be a part of it. No money involved. Just a friendly game."

"You are part of my story. Five years ago, you saved my dad from bandits and gained his trust. He sent you a card, a Maker's card, before he died."

Doc grew pale and coughed hard into a handkerchief. "You're Euless Jones's son? I heard rumors, but I thought since Mythic was around, he and his family . . . you were now living the high life somewhere. I'm sorry."

"That's right. I'm Jason. His company was attacked here in Arizona."

"I should've been there." The flickering lamplight made shapes in the shadow of Doc's face. "In the letter with the card, he mentioned coming across some trouble. He had other security, so I thought nothing more of it."

"You're not at any fault," Shuffle said. "But you can help."

"Anything."

Shuffle leaned forward. "I've got clues, and a gut feeling he's alive in California. To get to him, I need the card he sent you."

Doc pushed back against his chair, sitting upright like an obelisk. "Again, I have to apologize, but you can't have it."

Atalanta slapped the table and shot to her feet. "You dirty skunk. Your kindness and crying is an act. A lie. The card belongs to Shuffle."

"No, little daisy. The card is mine. His father sent it to me. Not him. It would be dishonorable to give it up easily."

There had to be some way to get Doc to give up the card without resorting to violence. Maybe offer up something he'd been clamoring for. Something too good to pass up.

Shuffle removed the deck from his pocket. "You're a gambler, right?"

"That's what I live for. The risk and the reward."

"Then we'll have that battle you want, and I'll prove to you I can handle whatever waits at the end. Handle whatever took Dad away from me. I challenge you, Doc. For the card."

"You need something on the line." Doc stroked his mustache. "Do you have the guts to put up your *Odysseus*?"

Atalanta snarled and shook her head. "Not again."

She was right. This was like the confrontation with Femus. One map card for another. No longer playing for nickels. But the way Doc's cobalt blues gleamed, he appeared to be a more capable opponent than the cat-hating, stacked-deck, one-eyed cheater.

Shuffle slammed his deck on the table. "I'm your huckleberry. We've got a deal."

CHAPTER 38

THE LONE JOURNEY HOME

Sweat beaded on Shuffle's head. His shirt stuck to his back and under his arms. He licked his lips, in dire need of some lemonade, preferably with ice chips. He didn't know which was more taxing: the heat of the room or the challenge in front of him.

After setting up small pieces of purple quartz for his Belief markers, Doc spun a silver dollar high in the air. It shined from the lantern light. He caught it and flipped it over like a flapjack on the table, his hand still covering the coin. "Call it."

"Tails," Shuffle said, petting Katana, who was curled up in his lap.

Doc revealed it, showing the profile portrait of Liberty. "Heads. Guess I have the honor of starting the duel."

Sometimes the first player had the advantage, depending on the deck. Sometimes it was better for the second player to adapt and counterattack.

Doc laid down his deity card, *Amaterasu*, the sun

goddess, representing the Japanese Spirit and People factions. Red heart and clover.

Shuffle looked deep into the bold lines of the art. The deck would have defensive strategy, leaning heavily on special items and gaining twenty-one Belief points to win. A difficult strategy to pull off, but a cardsharp like Doc might be able to do it.

Katana purred, and the edges of the room softened. Atalanta and Captain turned into shades blending into the background, with Dad's shadow joining them.

"I'm ready," Doc said as he played his first card, *Whispering Forest.*

The strokes of black print dissolved into the shapes of cherry blossom trees. The wind rustled pink and white leaves into the air. *Amaterasu* hovered high above the earth, sitting in the midst of swirling clouds. From the edges of the goddess's robes, rays of light shined down on her thirteen temples.

Athena peered up to the sky, shield and spear raised for war.

Soon, the battlefield rumbled with *Oni*, trickster demons, and *Winged Horses*. Clashes between *Hoplites* and *Samurai* sent sparks and blood everywhere. But despite the violence and destruction, *Amaterasu* built more temples.

"What's happening?" Atalanta asked.

Shuffle blinked and looked away from the table. "No matter what I throw at him, Doc's adding to his Belief. If he gets to twenty-one, he wins."

"The secret's out," Doc said, grinning.

From the back corner of the room, Captain grumbled as he rubbed a shine into the steel of his repeater. He cocked the lever, loading the round into the chamber. Hopefully, it wouldn't come to that.

Atalanta fanned her face with her hat. "Got a decent play?"

"Always." Shuffle caught his voice wavering a bit. He hoped no one else got wise of his false bravado. Thankfully, everyone probably thought he was sweating on account of the heat, not because of shot nerves.

Atalanta leaned in close. "I think you got the sucker right where you want him. Now crush him, and we can leave this oven."

Shuffle sat up straight like a real battlefield commander. Katana stretched, arching her back before leaping off his lap. Good, more room to maneuver.

He scanned the situation once more. The shadow in the wind whispered. *The spear strikes, while the glove takes.* A two-prong strategy might work: delay the sun goddess's ability to raise Belief temples with attacks, and complete three quests to win.

Athena summoned *Typhon,* the winged giant with snake coils for legs and fire in its eyes. It rampaged across the battlefield, tearing down cherry blossom trees and enemies. The Japanese warrior *Yorimitsu,* armed with the *Sword of Valor,* stood in its way. The fight between them ripped gashes in the earth and toppled mountains.

All that violence to sneak *Odysseus* past his opponent's guards and *Slay the Nemean Lion*, a Quest card, now completed.

Card after card, battles raged. The dead pile grew high, and *Amaterasu's* Belief temples rose in number. Every so often Doc would hack up a terrible cough, but the state of his lungs never seemed to interfere with his focus.

At last he played *Jewel of Benevolence*, bringing his Belief total to twenty—one point away from winning.

Captain put his gun down and surveyed the table. Katana watched from a high shelf on the wall, her tail hanging like a meat hook ready for a carcass.

Shuffle had just scored *Calydonian Boar Hunt*, his second Quest. And it was his turn now. His last chance to win.

Shuffle focused on his hero, *Odysseus*, standing alone on the battlefield. A wind rushed through the wrecked trees and fallen foes. A weapon materialized in his hand, a gift from *Athena*, the *Bow of Odysseus*. It filled him with enough power to finish.

Distract and sneak. Sneak and win, said the shadow of memory, drifting at the edge of his vision.

Shuffle laid down the third Quest card, *Lone Journey Home*, for the victory. "Can you stop me?"

CHAPTER 39
BOOT HILL

Shuffle leaned back into his seat, the heat of the room sticky on his neck. *Odysseus* stood out from the rest of the cards, a champion above all others.

Digging his elbows into the table, Doc perched over the battlefield like a vulture. He wiped away the sweat bleeding down his forehead. His blue eyes darted, perhaps scanning the survivors and the carrion for something that would change the outcome. He smiled wryly. "Looks like I'm no daisy. You win."

Atalanta swept her arm around Shuffle and pressed against him, the scent of sage on her skin. "I can't believe you didn't mess up!" She clamped down on his shoulders and gave him a savage shake.

"You deserve this." Doc held the *Miyamoto Musashi* card between his pointer and middle fingers, giving it one last look. With a flick, he spun it through the air to Shuffle's pile.

The fourth card—the final piece of the map. Now all they had to do was find the treasure, get to San

Francisco, and barter for Dad's freedom—no Sunday stroll in the garden, that's for sure. Shuffle sank in his seat as the effects of traveling over a thousand miles caught up to him. Everything hurt, and the thought of another thousand miles of hard riding began to drain the excitement of winning.

"Your maneuvers were . . . well executed," Captain said, patting Shuffle on the back.

Not since the fight with Mama had he shown that much affection. Memories of better days, when the whole family was together, came to life in zoetrope. But flickering images weren't good enough, especially when he was close to finding Dad. "I can teach you to play. You'll be great."

Captain gave him another pat. "Doubt it."

"Oh, lighten up. If I could stand to play, you could, too." Atalanta held Katana up to her face. "Ain't that right, kitty? The old bullet needs to relax."

Doc gathered his cards into a neat stack. "Stay the night on my account, and tomorrow, I'll introduce you to a man who can get you to California."

Shuffle tucked in the *Musashi* card with the rest of his deck, careful not to look too eager. "Why would he help us?"

"He knew your father."

∗ ∗ ∗

Doc holed up Shuffle, Atalanta, and Captain at a nearby boarding house, similar to the one Mama worked at back home. Except the place lacked a certain warmth, and the complimentary lemonade didn't taste as good.

Captain had left without a word, maybe thirsting for something stronger. Katana had gone, too, out to hunt.

Shuffle pressed his face with the glass of lemonade, its ice chips melting. He'd won the last treasure card, bringing him closer to his real prize.

He peeled off the false back of the *Miyamoto Musashi* card, revealing the map piece. It had landmarks: a large tree and a three-peaked rock or mountain. But there was no X for the hidden treasure. Dad had always used an X in their hunts.

Atalanta sat across from him, her hair up in a tight bun. Her long, slender neck exposed a contingent of freckles normally hidden by her braids and yellow bandana.

"Do they match up?" she asked, dabbing at her face with the kerchief.

He drew back from his pinpoint focus. "Match up? Oh, right." He took a deep breath, calming his heartbeat.

There wasn't a windrose on any of the cards, so he simply arranged them in order of when he got them: *Odysseus, Monkey King, Huehuecoyotl,* and *Musashi.* None of the path lines matched up. It looked like a puzzle badly put together. "There's no connection, but it doesn't even matter without the X. I could be wrong about these cards." He tried another arrangement. It didn't work either.

Atalanta looked the new card over. "None of these landmarks are familiar, but look, this plateau goes with the mountain range on your card."

The two cards didn't line up perfectly, offset by just a little, but the drawings connected. Shuffle continued with the other cards until he connected them all into a cross. Except there was a small gap, not large enough for another card. Unless . . . the four cards overlapped a fifth card.

"Wait a sec," Atalanta said, "that landmark. It's a bird."

"You're right."

Atalanta tapped at the picture. "Some riders say the thunderbird roosts in the desert mountains. I know which range that is. Never been, but I could find it."

A crackle of energy surged through Shuffle. "What about the gap? I bet that's where the treasure is hidden."

"Your pa didn't mention another card, another person he gave it to, right?"

"Not in his letters. And having a fifth card, a fifth faction, doesn't fit the four-color strategy."

"I bet I can find the site without the missing piece," she said.

"Risky. We could be wandering the desert 'til we're Captain's age."

She shrugged. "I like our chances."

Shuffle thought combing the desert with a big chunk of the map missing was a bad idea. There had to be something that put it all together. As he closed his eyes, fishing for the answer, an image of cards being dealt, face up, flashed in his mind. The fifth card shined. "Of course. The deity card that goes with the four-color strategy. *Cihtym*."

"Go on," she said.

"It's the card I made up." He traced the edges of the gap in the map. The emptiness pulled him in like the darkness at the bottom of a lake. "It's the only one that could use the different factions. And Dad must have it."

Atalanta scowled. "Well, that's no good. You need the treasure to get to your dad, and you need your dad to get to the treasure."

Shuffle swept the four cards back into a stack. "Maybe the cards themselves will be enough to trade for Dad's freedom. Maybe we don't need to get the treasure."

Atalanta chewed on her lower lip. "But what if your dad's—"

"He's not dead. And I'm going to find him."

✳ ✳ ✳

Morning came, and the heat took a turn for the worse, now humid with wet dog smell.

Shuffle rolled up his sleeves. Atalanta fanned at her face with her hat. Katana stretched out on the stone floor, her little tongue sticking out as she panted.

"I'll get the horses ready," said Captain, wearing his long coat despite the weather.

Meanwhile Shuffle and Atalanta met Doc at the

front of the boarding house. He was coughing into a handkerchief. "I came out to the desert for the dry heat. My constitution isn't agreeing with the weather."

"Mine neither," Shuffle said.

On foot, Doc led them to Boot Hill Cemetery, a gravelly patch of land dotted with cacti and spiny shrubs. Rocky piles with headstones marked burial spots.

Atalanta carried Katana on her shoulders. "Are we meeting the undertaker?"

"No, but someone who's buried just as many people." Doc winked. "Don't worry, he's on your side."

Shuffle tugged at his collar. "If you say so, Doc, but I ain't trusting no one just yet."

"Smart," he said with a laugh that turned into a violent coughing spell.

When they reached the top of the hill, Doc pointed to a well-dressed, squatty man standing under a skeletal tree, charred and gashed as though it had been struck by lightning. "That's Edward Eight."

They approached the man, slow and wary. After a silent moment, the man turned and nodded. A smile drew across his round face. "Perfect timing."

"Showing up late is disrespectful," Doc said. "Well, except to one's own funeral." The two men laughed.

Shuffle didn't think he'd ever get used to gallows humor.

"You're Professor Jones's son, Jason." Mr. Eight's eyes hid behind the glare of his glasses.

Mr. Eight had the upper hand in knowledge, and that didn't sit well. Shuffle put on his most businesslike tone. "Doc says you can help me. But what will it cost?"

The diamond pin on Mr. Eight's necktie sparkled. "Sharp boy."

"None craftier," Doc said.

Mr. Eight took off his felt bowler and put it to his chest. "And the young lady with the feline?"

Atalanta eyed him with her sniper's stare. "I'm Shuffle's right hand of vengeance. Don't try to pull one over on us."

Surprisingly, Mr. Eight grinned. "Why, Doc, what have you told them about me?"

"Just that you're a snappy dresser," Shuffle said.

"Alas, my part in our little repartee must end," Doc said. "I've got to meet the deputy marshal. Something to do with undesirables causing a ruckus at the O.K. Corral. Good luck, Jason. I'm highly impressed, and I don't doubt that you will find your father." He tipped his hat to Atalanta and left.

All in all, the gunfighting dentist seemed to be a decent man. Shuffle had to hand it to Dad: he hadn't misplaced his trust.

"Well then, you want to know what I can do for you?" Mr. Eight dabbed at his face with a silk cloth. "I can—no, I *will* help you get to California."

"San Francisco?" Shuffle asked.

"Certainly."

Atalanta dragged Shuffle away by the arm. "What about the Mojave? What about, you know, *it*?"

"It can wait. I'm out here for my dad. That's the only thing that matters." Pulling free, he returned to Mr. Eight. "You say you'll help us, but how exactly? We already have horses."

"Well, I have a train."

CHAPTER 40
ROUGH RIDE IN LUXURY

Mr. Eight needed a few hours for his men to get the locomotive ready, more than enough time to send a telegram to Mama.

Shuffle ran to the Western Union and sent a message to the Mourning Glory Post Office.

C3 KDOIZDB WKHUH

Translation using the Caesar cipher with a three-letter shift: *Halfway there.*

Hopefully, the letter would put her at ease, since Captain hadn't reported back. If anything, it should get her excited; the hard half was over, and he should be home soon.

Back at the station, Shuffle met with Mr. Eight on the boarding deck while Atalanta and Captain waited with the horses.

The train hissed, raring to charge out of the gates. Its engine glistened with a painting of a woman in a golden chariot pulled by two flying serpents, Drakones, one slithering along the cattle-catcher and the other rearing up along the funnel-shaped chimney.

Shuffle took a deep breath of the smoky, sticky air, as an odd feeling curled in his gut. "Medea?"

The woman in the painting, Medea, was a sorceress and daughter of the sun god, Helios. She had also murdered her children, the ones she had with Jason of the Argonauts. Whether the train was an omen or a coincidence, he shrugged off the happenstance. It wasn't like he and Mr. Eight were married.

Mr. Eight leaned on a walking stick with a golden handle in the shape of a big-horn ram's head. "Isn't she a beauty?"

"I'm more interested in the fare," Shuffle said. "I'm sure the ticket is more than a couple silver dollars."

"Allow me to tell you how I know your father. His mentor, Dr. Bloom, and I were good friends. We shared a love of antiquities. Hence, the mural on the engine. When he mentioned the expedition to me, I agreed to help finance the trip."

Money. That was almost always the bottom line. *Wealth Beyond Belief: Double hand limit. Draw four cards.*

Shuffle stared Mr. Eight down, unsure if he should trust someone so rich. He couldn't help remembering Dad's letter. Someone associated with the expedition could've double-crossed them. Someone who wanted the treasure for themselves. Maybe it had been this fellow.

And even if it hadn't been, what could such a man, a

man who had practically everything, want in return for his help now?

"I sense you don't trust me," the rail baron said, tapping a rhythm on his cane, "but you have no other choice if you want to get to California as fast and as safe as possible. The Southern Pacific isn't finished; it only goes to Yuma. My private line goes all the way to Los Angeles. Otherwise, you have to gallop back to Santa Fe to catch the Atchison rail."

"I know the way." Shuffle shrugged, pretending not to care. He needed to toughen up the negotiation and not be hoodwinked. Really, though, a train ride sounded mighty appealing at almost any cost.

Mr. Eight put his hand on Shuffle's shoulder. "That's a long, difficult road. You won't have to suffer it if you trust me. I don't want nor need the riches. I want to be part of the discovery and have my name inked alongside Dr. Bloom's and your father's. But I will admit to you, under the stipulations of their contract for my monetary backing, I am owed two artifacts as repayment."

"So that's the price for your help? You want some of the treasure?"

"I'm *owed* two pieces. No more, no less."

Men like Mr. Eight didn't get rich by getting what they asked for. They got rich by taking what they wanted, and Shuffle had a feeling the rail baron wanted more than two pieces. "I'm going to find my dad first. The dig will have to wait."

"Naturally." Mr. Eight rubbed a shine on the gold ram head.

"If Dad decides to finish the excavation, he and I will choose the treasure to give you." And one of them sure as heck wouldn't be Athena's Aegis—the main artifact Dad had been hunting. The main reason why he left home.

"Fair enough." Mr. Eight held out his hand, a silver ring shining on his pinky.

For the moment, Shuffle kept his distance. "You'll get me to San Francisco?"

"A boat from Los Angeles will be required, but I can arrange that."

"Okay, deal." Shuffle shook on it. The rail baron's hand was plump, but smooth and cold like porcelain.

Mr. Eight smiled. "All aboard."

* * *

Atalanta and Captain loaded up the horses in the stable car. Shuffle carried Katana while Mr. Eight gave the ten-penny tour of his private locomotive.

After going through the passenger and dining cars, Mr. Eight showed Shuffle the treasure car—a spacious trailer decked out with more luxury than first class. There was no trace of coal smoke or humid stink, only the cloying smell of roses. Damask rose, just like Mama's perfume, except a hundred times richer. A round table and four chairs with claw and ball feet stood in the center of the car. Oil paintings graced the walls. Built-in shelves displayed artifacts from different times and places. Mr. Eight pointed out a bronze mirror from Egypt, a copper helmet from Crete, and an onyx lion from Mesopotamia.

"But this is my favorite," Mr. Eight said, gesturing to an artifact on a pedestal. "The Mask of Agamemnon."

Shuffle drifted forward, drawn in by the shining golden face. It had closed eyes and a straight mouth. "The king of Argos. He commanded the Greek army in the Trojan War."

"Your father taught you well. Heinrich Schliemann, one of Dr. Bloom's rivals, discovered it just a few years ago. But I was able to procure it for my collection." He unraveled a grin.

Shuffle found himself wondering about the true cost of this ride. Dad had kept most of the expedition a secret. Something as legendary as the Aegis would've attracted too much attention. Did the backers know? Did Mr. Eight expect to get the shield?

Shuffle looked out the windows, wondering when Atalanta and Captain would come aboard. Being alone with this sharp suit was beginning to twang his nerves.

On the other side of the car, two large steamer trunks made of wood and metal nestled in opposite corners. They looked more secure than JP Morgan safes. Shuffle knocked on one of the lids. Yep, solid like a cannonball. And there weren't any padlocks.

"Ah, those are my Pandora's Boxes. Redwood construction with iron bands riveted with steel. And they're bolted to the floor of the car. But inside . . . inside are the true treasures." Mr. Eight pressed two places, hidden pressure plates along the side, and the lid unlocked with a resounding clang. He heaved it open. A pair of blue and white porcelain vases, the size of bread loaves, nestled inside a velvet mold. He leaned in, tracing his fingers over the blue dragon detail. "Chinese pottery. Exquisite and priceless."

Shuffle didn't like the glint in Mr. Eight's eyes. Maybe the deal for the fast and easy way hadn't been such a good idea.

"Even if robbers tried breaking into the chests, which would be futile, the vases would be safe from harm. Beyond the redwood and iron, inside is technology developed by one of the brightest minds of our age. A protective measure called impact-weave, a woven lattice of bamboo and silk. Ingenious, really. Someone could try to break in with a cannon, and the blast will not damage the valuables inside." He shut the lid and pressed the panels, locking the trunk. "The precious treasures are safe, and these are going to my home collection in California. You see, our little trip isn't an inconvenience for me."

Captain and Atalanta came in, escorted by the steward. Thank goodness they weren't going to be *accidentally* left behind.

Mr. Eight lowered a transmitting cone from a nearby panel. He pulled on a lever and spoke into the transmitter. "Engineer. We're ready to go."

The engine's steam horn blasted out a reply, and the train began to roll toward an overcast horizon.

CHAPTER 41
BOARDED

The train hurtled west. Its lazy sway belied its great speed, as the world just beyond the tracks flew by in a blur. The farther away things were, the clearer yet more unmoving they appeared, like a goal just out of reach.

Shuffle leaned against the window, wondering if Dad had seen the same red rock plateaus and cacti-covered mountains. The colors ran deeper, less washed out, under a skyfield of dark clouds.

"I'm going to stretch my legs." Captain got up from the bunk and left the passenger car.

Atalanta sat across from Shuffle, cleaning her gun. She'd been quiet since they left Tombstone. As soon as Captain slid the door shut, she finally spoke up.

"I think we should get off at Yuma. I don't trust Eight." She slid a wire brush down each chamber of the cylinder.

"Neither do I, but I'm tired of running and starving and being on the road. This is easy."

She frowned. "Easy? He's luring us into the

slaughterhouse. He might even be responsible for your pa's disappearance."

Shuffle crossed his arms, feeling her doubt jab into his ribs. "He might be untrustworthy, but he's not the one who attacked the expedition. Why would he ruin it before getting the treasure?"

"He'll try to ruin us when we find it, that's for sure. Why wait for his move?" She pieced her revolver together in a blink and reloaded it, one bullet at a time. "I say we hop, and search for the gold before we head to California."

Maybe she was right, and they should slip away while they still had their hides.

Except now they needed a fifth card to find the treasure. Which meant they'd have to find Dad first.

"I'm out here for my dad. And he has the missing piece. I just know it. Without him, we'd be lost."

"But imagine how impressed your pa will be if we solve his puzzle on our own."

Her insistence flicked at his ear. "No."

"Come on. Let's ride into the unknown. We even take the old bullet with us."

Shuffle slapped the table. "You can leave at Yuma. Search the desert. Find the treasure. I'm staying, all the way to San Francisco." Since they'd found the last card, she had been acting strange. What was her deal?

Popping her head up, Katana turned toward the window.

Beyond the long curve of the track, something bright flared in the distance. In the dark, it stood out like a warning.

Captain slammed the door open. "Gather our things. We've got trouble."

* * *

With Katana secure in his bag, Shuffle hustled to the treasure car with Atalanta and Captain. Mr. Eight, the steward, and three burly men armed with rifles and shotguns were waiting there.

"The engineer says there's a fire on the tracks." Mr. Eight hung up the cone and moved away from the panel's receiver.

"By the looks of your security, it's more than a tree burning from a lightning strike," said Captain, checking the ammo in his repeater.

The train slowed, shuddering. It groaned and shrieked to a stop.

"Bonfire. We've encountered this kind of thing before from rail bandits." Mr. Eight pounded his ram's head cane on the floor. "But we've faced worse odds and beat them back. Right, men?"

The security trio grunted. The biggest one, a mountain of a man, crossed two scatterguns behind his head. "They're gonna get a reckoning." He left the treasure car, with one guard at his flank.

Captain nodded at Shuffle before leaving with the third guard for the rear of the train.

So much for fast and easy.

"Don't worry, kids," Mr. Eight said, as he cleaned his glasses nonchalantly. "No harm will come to us. The car is steel reinforced with tempered windows."

Shuffle fidgeted, peering at the walls, the roof, the door. He couldn't tell if they were more secure than normal. By the looks of the white-knuckled grip Atalanta had on her pistol, he shouldn't trust Mr. Eight's blowhard confidence.

Tink.

Mr. Eight flinched. "What was that?"

"Jumpy?" asked Atalanta, smirking.

Tink. Tink.

Tink tink tink tink.

"It's rain," Shuffle said.

Soon, the sprinkles turned into sheets hitting the roof all at once. Then the pop-pop of gunfire punctuated the droning downpour. Shuffle hated that sound.

Atalanta positioned herself flat against the wall. "Are you good?"

"Yeah, I'm spectacular." He held Katana close. Hopefully, the storm and Captain would drive away the bandits.

Crash-boom. The treasure car lit up in blue light, and the windows rattled.

The rain, the thunder, and the gunfire mashed into

a single sound broken up by yelling. Shuffle wedged himself into a corner, trying to make himself small. He knew he shouldn't cower, but he couldn't help it.

Atalanta looked through the window as a bullet grazed off the pane. No surprise, she didn't flinch.

Mr. Eight trembled. "Can you see anything?"

"Movement. Coming closer." Suddenly she backed away as though a rattlesnake had uncoiled right in front of her. "Oh no. The passenger car."

"What is it?" Shuffle pressed himself hard against the wall, not really wanting to know.

She whipped around. "Dynamite!"

An explosion rocked the car. Debris flew everywhere. A piece hit Mr. Eight in the head, and he crashed into his shelf of artifacts. Atalanta stumbled into Shuffle, and they hit the floor. The bandits must've blown up the connected passenger car. The two security guards, even the steward and the engineer, were probably dead.

No treasure was worth this.

Another blast shattered the door. Six-Plum Skylla entered the treasure car, holding a cavalry sword in one hand and, in the other, the elephant gun, its barrel still smoking.

Last Shuffle saw of her, she'd been shot off her horse in Santa Fe. Instead of being six feet under, she stood there in her oxblood chaps, dripping with menace and rain.

Atalanta spun to her knees and reached for her revolver.

"Don't do it, girl." Skylla dropped the elephant gun and took a big step, pointing her sword inches away from Atalanta's neck. "I want two things, Jones. The cards. And the old man's head."

She wanted Captain dead? Was it because he was the one who shot her? Shuffle had to settle the bad blood before any of it was spilled.

"What do you mean, cards? Don't you want Cassandra's Warning?" Maybe she'd fall for the bluff since the *Trojan Horse* card wasn't needed anymore. He could lose it without losing the map pieces, and she'd forget about Captain and leave.

"No, Jones. All of it. You've found others. I want them."

A cold wind carried a metallic, wet smell through the car. Rain poured through the busted door and the holes in the roof. With Skylla wise to the treasure cards, could it get any worse?

Shortstack, wearing dynamite in a bandoleer, stumbled into the treasure car. Her face was cauliflower white. "We've got wounded. They can't ride on their own. And the storm—the monster. It's coming."

Shuffle stood with his hands up. Now that she was distracted, Skylla might just give up. "I lost the cards to a gambler."

Switching the sword to her left hand, Skylla drew

her black-steel revolver. "Not what I heard, Jones. Or should I call you Savior of Silver City? Or do you prefer Titan of Tombstone?"

Titan of Tombstone? Shuffle chewed on his lip to keep back a grin. That sounded kind of aces.

She cocked the hammer back. "I'm losing patience." The rain stopped, but the wind continued to wail.

"This is it," Atalanta said, rising to her feet. Shadows hid her eyes. "I'm sorry."

"We have to leave!" Shortstack pulled at Skylla. "Forget the boy. The monster . . ."

The muscles and veins in Skylla's neck stiffened. She aimed the gun. "GIVE ME THE CARDS! NOW!"

Shuffle braced himself. "I don't—"

Turning her back on Skylla, Atalanta shielded him. A lightning flash lit up the car. A pall of agony shrouded her face. Was she shot?

"I'm sorry," she said. "This isn't how it was supposed to happen."

"What are you talking—?"

The wind whipped her hair. Her yellow bandana flapped like a surrender flag. She drew him close and pulled out his deck.

Shuffle gasped, as if his cards were the plug that kept his chest from bleeding out. And she'd ripped it away. Reeling, he grabbed her arm. Atalanta broke his grip and shoved him down. He braced against the wall, the floor, whatever he could hold.

"I have them." She held up the deck like a prize. "Am I in?"

"Hurry! It's almost here," shouted Shortstack as she leapt out of the car and into a wall of noise.

"All right." Skylla holstered her gun and tossed a badge with a skull and five arrows at Atalanta. "You ride with me."

Atalanta pinned the emblem to her shirt. Its dull gray surface had dried blood on it.

Shuffle felt his strength wane. "What are you doing?"

Atalanta ran out, not looking back.

Mustering all the strength he had left, Shuffle stood. "Stop. I trusted—"

Skylla struck him in the gut with the hilt of her sword. He crumpled to his knees.

"Good luck, Jones." She disappeared into the thrashing wind.

This couldn't be happening. Not Atalanta. Had she been lying all this time?

He climbed to his feet, holding his stomach. The worst pain was higher up. He stumbled to the opening, hopeful all of it was a ruse and Atalanta had come back. Instead, past the smoldering wreckage and about a mile away, a beast of nature—a tornado—chewed its way through the landscape, heading right for him.

CHAPTER 42
A STORM OF EPIC PROPORTION

The twister rose through the fading daylight to the dark heavens like an inverted mountain, spitting lightning and devouring everything in its path.

Shuffle fell to his knees, clutching the bag that held Katana. The tornado might as well eat him, too. It was selfish to keep her, but he didn't want to let her go. He peered into the bag. She was curled up, her hairs standing on end. Maybe she wanted to stay.

Drenched from the rain, Captain returned from the caboose. "Jason, get up. We need to find cover."

Shuffle didn't budge. He pressed Katana against his chest.

"Where's the girl?" Captain nodded toward Mr. Eight. "Is he dead?"

The girl. She was a liar. A traitor.

Captain grabbed Shuffle under the arm and lifted him to his feet. "Double time, Jason."

A blast of lightning and thunder shook the car. A scatter of whinnies came after, and just outside the windows, the horses raced off.

"They'll survive on their own," Captain said.

There was no hope then. It was over. No cards. No friend. No way to get to Dad.

The wind howled as it surged through the car, whirling sharp chunks of debris from wall to wall.

Captain tightened his grip and dragged Shuffle toward the back exit connected to the caboose. "Whatever happened doesn't mean it's the end. But it will be, if you give up. Now move your feet."

Shuffle forced his legs to go. Captain was right, it wasn't over. He still needed to find Dad. Brooding over the cards or Atalanta wouldn't help, and he'd come too far to be defeated. But if he didn't find cover and do it fast, the fight he had left in him would be for nothing.

There was supposed to be nowhere safer than the treasure car, but an opening the size of a bear gaped, and the windows bowed like twigs about to shatter. If only they were in a real vault, or something as strong.

Katana leapt out of the bag, skittered across the floor, and hid behind the steamer trunks. Trunks with redwood panels, iron bands, and impact-weave!

Shuffle broke free from Captain and retrieved Katana. "Good girl."

The wind growled, pushed, and pulled.

"Over here!" Shuffle held fast against the lashing and found the trigger panel. The lid opened. He lifted out the vase and set it aside, then removed the box's velvet lining, exposing the impact-weave. "Put him in."

Captain dumped the rail baron into the chest. "How will he get out?"

"We'll open it after the storm." Shuffle placed the vases under Mr. Eight's folded arms and shut the lid.

"What about us? What if we get separated?"

Shuffle opened the other trunk and pointed. "Look, there's a trigger pull. And the trunks are bolted to the rail car."

Captain nodded, setting his repeater beside the trunk.

"You first." Shuffle turned around and rifled through the debris.

"What are you doing?" yelled Captain, standing inside the trunk and cradling two more Chinese vases.

Shuffle kept digging. Some things were worth saving. The wind wailed, sending splinters of wood and metal buzzing through the car and tearing through his clothes and cutting his skin. A cracked beam flew by his head, crashing into the wall.

Bad ideas came to him all the time. This was one of the worst, until he found it under the rubble on the floor—the Mask of Agamemnon. He dug it out and raced back to the iron box. Dad would've done the same.

Captain barely fit, squeezing against one side of the trunk with the vases tucked against his stomach.

Shuffle pressed against him, holding Katana.

The lid closed, and the lock engaged itself as the wind hit the loudest.

The trunk vibrated, resisting the storm. The redwood panels creaked. The iron bands and steel rivets moaned.

Shuffle took a deep breath, smelling sweat and blood and fear.

The tornado struck, like a hungry animal ripping into flesh.

He became weightless as the tornado lifted the train. He felt his stomach go one way while the rest of his body went another. Everything began to spin and flip, and he wanted to puke.

Even though it was dark inside the trunk, he shut his eyes. He tensed up, blocking out the sound and the pressure, focusing on every bit of muscle and bone to become like steel, holding Katana and feeling her shape and heartbeat.

He needed to survive so he and Dad and Mama could make up for lost time and have a future together. So he could be there when Captain called him Shuffle, and he would call him Granddad. So he could see Atalanta look at him with those mythical brown eyes and tell him why the heck she stabbed him in the back.

The tornado roared.

He roared back.

CHAPTER 43
TRAIL OF DESTRUCTION

Shuffle gritted his teeth as an invisible force pulled at him. He braced Katana.

They crashed. Something popped. The box cracked. The cushion vibrated against his back; the impact-weave must've taken most of the shock.

When everything stilled, he opened his eyes to the dark of the steamer trunk. "Captain, are you okay?"

His granddad grunted. "I'll live. What's your status?"

Shuffle focused past the ringing in his ears and the fury in his blood. "Let's see—Atalanta backstabbed me, stealing the cards and riding off with the enemy. A tornado tossed us around like a picked-to-the-bone carcass. I've got a headache and my stomach hurts where Six-Plum hit me with her sword. Other than that? I'm good."

Katana meowed a long, desperate cry. She had the right idea: time to bust free from this metal coffin.

"I hear ya, girl." Shuffle slid his hands along the impact cushion for the trigger mechanism. "Captain, feel around for a lever."

Captain shifted. "Nothing."

After a minute, Shuffle found the latch behind him. He pulled; it clicked, but the lid didn't open. He tried it again, pushing against the curve of the lid, but the trunk didn't budge.

"I can't brace myself to push any harder," Captain said.

"Great. Add to our tactical situation that we're trapped in an indestructible box, probably going to suffocate to death."

"Then figure out a solution." Captain wiggled, then grunted. It sounded like he was in pain.

"You all right?"

He sighed. "My collarbone. It's broken."

Dang it. The situation couldn't get any worse.

Shuffle closed his eyes and focused again on his body, realizing the trunk was upside down.

"Captain, can you shift your weight?"

"Affirmative."

Shuffle curled into a ball and flipped backward to his feet. He pushed hard against the bottom of the trunk, and it tilted. Captain matched him, grunting. The trunk teetered and then toppled over, landing right side up. Shuffle braced his shoulders against the curve of the lid, pulled the lever, and pushed with his legs.

The lid opened. Sticky, wet air whooshed inside the trunk like a big, lifesaving breath.

He stood and helped Captain up. Wreckage lay all

around them, but the Chinese vases remained unbroken. Their steamer trunk had separated from the floor, which hung inches above their heads. The tornado had flipped the train car and dumped them who-knows-where. The car had collapsed into a pyramid of bent iron and splintered wood. Thankfully, it didn't cave in and bury them in a shallow grave.

Unfortunately, Captain had left his repeater beside the box, for fear of it going off accidentally. Now, his favorite rifle was lost in the rubble or in a faraway place. He still had his revolvers, which would come in handy.

Knocking and muffled shouting came from the other steamer trunk still bolted to the floor, hanging upside down.

"Let me out." Mr. Eight pounded on the box. "I demand to be released or I will have someone annihilated." His voice cracked. "Please."

Shuffle reached up and pressed the hidden panels. The lid opened, and Mr. Eight fell out, clutching both of the vases.

"Ow."

"Sorry. Gravity's an uncaring bully." Shuffle helped him up.

"Young Mister Jones, what happened?" Mr. Eight looked around at the low-hanging ruins of the train. "The bandits, did they do this?"

"No, something much worse." Shuffle rifled through his bag for an extra shirt as Katana popped her head out and meowed. He tied the shirt around Captain's neck and shoulder, stabilizing the elbow.

Captain nodded. "You did good, Jason."

Mr. Eight fixed his glasses. "Tell me who's responsible for this outrage, and I'll have them—"

"Annihilated?" Shuffle handed the Mask of Agamemnon and the other vases to Mr. Eight. "Good luck with that."

✳ ✳ ✳

Shuffle managed to climb out a small hole in the wreckage. After carefully widening the gap, he freed Captain and Mr. Eight.

The parched earth sucked in water left behind by the storm. Cacti, tall and short, lay crushed and strewn everywhere, bleeding pulp. The wind whistled and whipped through the cool air. The sun burned like a shimmering ball to the west, and miles away to the east, the tornado continued on its path of ruin.

"I don't believe it. The storm threw us a long way. We aren't anywhere near the railroad," Captain said.

Shuffle picked up an unbroken dinner plate from a pool of mud and then dropped it because, really, it didn't matter. "Good thing it didn't dump us over a ravine and into a river. We'd be crushed or drowned or both."

Mr. Eight wandered the debris field, hugging his treasures—now bundled in a sheet—and sobbing like a baby who'd dropped his silver spoon. "Medea . . . my poor Medea."

"You can always buy another train," Shuffle said. The rail baron was lucky; some things weren't as easily replaced. Money couldn't buy back what he had lost, what had been broken. There was no adhesive or rope or nail that could ever fix the bond that Atalanta's lies had ruined. It was all a ruse, and she had played him with a perfect hand.

At least it had turned out that Mr. Eight wasn't the double-crosser. He wouldn't have hired Skylla to destroy his train and make off with the cards . . . unless they backstabbed him. But that was unlikely. The gang seemed dutybound and—it hurt to think it—somewhat honorable. He couldn't say the same for Atalanta.

Despite the carnage at his feet, he was alive. Was Atalanta, and should he even care? A twist of pain stung his chest, and he gritted his teeth through it. He wasn't going to let hurt feelings finish him off, and he sure as heck wasn't going to give up on finding Dad.

Captain nodded toward daylight. "Let's head that way. We'll make camp before it gets dark."

"Good idea." Shuffle put Katana on his shoulder.

The three of them (and Mr. Eight) rallied together and headed west.

Soon, the flatlands turned hilly and mountainous, and after an hour of quiet feet-dragging through the chewed-up desert, they came across a wagon road snaking around a prickly pear–covered butte.

Cries of pain broke the silence.

Shuffle stopped. "Someone's in trouble."

"You're right. They're saying *jio ming*," Mr. Eight said, hiding behind Captain. "*Jio ming* means help."

"Then come on." Shuffle charged down the road, frightened of what he might find. But after what had happened with Atalanta and the tornado, he didn't want to be scared. He didn't want to be useless. Forcing himself to move, he clenched his jaw and his fists, and ran to help.

Katana held fast to him, digging her claws into his coat. Captain caught up and kept pace. Shuffle looked over his shoulder; Mr. Eight stayed rooted in the dirt.

After hauling butt fifty yards on rocky ground, they rounded the corner.

"Jaguar," whispered Captain, barring his good arm across Shuffle's chest. "Stay back."

A great beast stalked toward a nearby cave. Shuffle could only see one man at the entrance, poking out a long pole for protection, but there were others, their frightened voices mashing into a garble of sound. The animal padded forward. Its muscles rippled, making the black spots on its orange fur swim like roses in the wind. Except, nothing pretty would happen if that predator got to the cave.

Katana jumped down and skittered off.

The trapped people screamed, "*Jio ming, jio ming.*"

But the jaguar preyed closer—ten feet, eight feet, now six feet away.

The man at the mouth of the cave stepped out and swung his pole around like a sword. He wore a loose-fitting jacket and pants, not much protection against the cat's claws. Two other men bounded out of the cave. They thrust their poles into the ground and swung upward in an arc high above the jaguar. They landed on the other side, kicking up dirt as their feet touched down. The leader backed away and guarded the cave.

The great cat tracked the pole jumpers, slinking down low in leaping position.

The two brave men scattered in opposite directions, yelling to goad the jaguar. The cat lurched at one, but the man leapt away on his pole, safe from the deadly claws.

But he landed awkwardly and tumbled down part of the slope. The jaguar whipped around and charged.

Shuffle pointed. "Do something!"

Captain fired a shot in the air.

The jaguar hunched low and stiffened. It turned its head, looking straight at Shuffle. The jaguar snarled, and its golden eyes glimmered. Becoming kitty food would not be a grand way to go.

Captain aimed his gun forward and blasted a cactus near the cat.

The jaguar flinched into a spin, and one of the men

smacked it with his pole. The big cat cried out, raced away from the cave, and disappeared.

Figuring the area was now safe, Shuffle hustled up the rocky hill. "You can come out now."

The man in front crept out of the cave, his pole still in a defensive position. The two jumpers joined him, holding their poles at the ready, too. After a quiet moment, five other people ventured out; two were children. One of the boys ran up to Shuffle and hugged him.

Nothing like a warm embrace to remind you you're alive. Shuffle gave the kid a squeeze. "It's okay, big guy."

Captain walked up and nodded a greeting to each one of the weary folks.

Meanwhile Mr. Eight waddled up the incline. He handed Katana over, and she climbed onto Shuffle's shoulders.

A buzz stirred among the acrobats as they looked at Shuffle and Katana. Their eyes brightened with inexplicable joy.

The two kids flipped into a handstand and started walking on their hands, chattering excitedly.

"What are they saying?"

"Seems like you remind them of a legend," Mr. Eight said. "They're saying, The boy and the black cat. Like Sun Wukong, the Monkey King."

Shuffle laughed. He wasn't a monkey with super strength or masterful fighting skills. Maybe they were talking about Katana, since the Monkey King had transformation powers, too. "Ask them why they're calling me this."

The rail baron spoke to the troupe's leader. After a minute of vigorous chitchat, Mr. Eight turned back to Shuffle. "It's because of your growing legend. It seems they've heard of your travels to California, which strike them as much like Sun Wukong's journey to India to reclaim the Buddhist sutras."

A fuzzy feeling, not Katana's fur, began to tickle up Shuffle's neck. *Legend. Journey.* They were words he never would have associated with himself before that night he snuck out the window. They were words connected to real heroes. Well, now that he was known as the Titan of Tombstone, perhaps they were apt after all.

But the journey wasn't over, and he had suffered the mother of all setbacks. Could he even do this—go where actions mattered most—without Atalanta? He'd have to. No one else believed Dad was alive, much less attempted to find him. Until Dad was back home safely, titles and tales would have to wait.

CHAPTER 44
WORSE THAN A NIGHTMARE

The travelers explained their situation. They were part of an acrobatic troupe called the Star Dragons. After performing in Tucson, they'd headed to San Diego for a boat ride to San Francisco. One of their wagons broke down, and a group of them stayed to fix it while the rest went on ahead. Luckily, they found the big cave before the storm hit. It had a deep chamber with room for everyone, their horses, and the small wagon. Their other, broken-down wagon was destroyed in the tornado, but it seemed losing one schooner wasn't going to stop the acrobats from getting home.

Shuffle and his companions spent the night in the cave with the acrobats, and the next day began with a harsh yellow sun rising in a sleepy sky.

Once they broke camp, two of the acrobats rode the extra horses, and the rest piled into the wagon, as hopeful as anyone could be. It was bracing to see their enthusiasm with such a rough road ahead.

Two days of travel on a cart made all the difference.

Walking to California wouldn't be good for the boot leather. Strength returned, as did hope of making it to San Francisco. It helped that Mr. Eight knew how to speak the acrobats' language. Apparently, the rail baron employed Chinese workers to help build his private line.

"Best workers I've ever seen," Mr. Eight declared, as proud as if he'd labored alongside them. "They're experts in the business, coming from years of experience with the big railroad companies. Tireless fellows, even though they often did dangerous work like lay rail on high bridges and use dynamite on sheer rock cliffs."

When Shuffle didn't say anything, Mr. Eight added, "My railway didn't require those often-deadly tasks. And I paid a good wage."

All that goodwill had apparently earned him the vases, gifts from his employees.

That still seemed odd to Shuffle. He'd never thought to give the baker a present, despite the man being a fine employer. Apparently, Mr. Eight wasn't the kind of guy to turn down a gift.

Today, the acrobats seemed to enjoy his banter, and that kind of levity did help with the jostle and heat of the road.

On the third morning, Shuffle sat up front, not wanting to look back. Now that he was sort of a celebrity, he got to control the ropes and drive.

Captain rode shotgun, since he knew the route and was armed. Shuffle liked having the company. It kept his mind off a certain someone. Best of all, he was on the move toward the one treasure that had any worth.

The morning sun blazed, beating down hard. The worn blanket of dirt spread out endlessly, broken up by cactus and thorny shrubs.

Shuffle kept his eyes on the trail, snapped the ropes on occasion, and steered the horses when they hit a bend. The crunch of rock underneath the roll of the wheels became a repeating rhythm.

"Are you still angry at me?" Captain kept his eyes forward, his stare cutting to the shimmering horizon.

Shuffle shrugged.

"Is your mother?"

Shuffle gulped hard, finding his throat tighten. He didn't know why he felt nervous all of a sudden. "Far as I know."

Angry was understating it. She held the grudge as close to her heart as a pistol to its holster.

Captain turned, now looking at Shuffle full in the face. "I came out here to find you. To make amends for not searching for your father when he went missing."

"Mama called you a coward." The last word came out strangled as his throat tightened even more.

His granddad tilted his hat up, exposing his face to the light. "It's true. I gave her money to hire the Pinkerton detective—"

"A lot of good that did," said Shuffle, forcing out the words. He wrapped the reins around his fists. Money paled in comparison to effort.

"A worthless gesture, but it was all I could muster. I didn't have the strength nor the will. I couldn't do it. Not even for my daughter." The old man wiped the barrel of his pistol, rubbing a shine on a single spot. "I added the ghost of your father to the ghosts of my comrades and of my enemies. They haunt me every day."

Shuffle uncorked his canteen and took a swig, his hand shaking. More water spilled down his chin than went down his throat. Something was wrong when a man as tough as Captain feared phantoms.

"You're not a coward," Shuffle muttered. "You're the Hornet of Shiloh."

Captain winced. "Don't . . . call me that."

It seemed being a hero wasn't all it was cracked up to be. Thinking back about some of the war stories, the ones with the lifeless bodies strewn all over the battlefield, Shuffle realized those tales of battle had been colored in something other than the truth. By the pained look on Captain's face, all that killing had cut deep.

"Listen up," said Captain, "what I had to do at Shiloh didn't amount to what you're doing now."

Ahead, something small writhed on the ground. Shuffle rolled past it—a rattlesnake swallowing a hawk. It was feeding time.

"*She*," said Mr. Eight from the back of the wagon. "Snake."

"Snake," repeated the kids sitting on the tailgate with him.

Mr. Eight turned around, grinning. "Did you see that? Reverse circle of life almost. Quite amazing."

It happens all the time, Shuffle thought. Nothing special about that.

Captain brought his story back with a sigh. "When I received the telegram about you running off, I didn't hesitate. I came out here to bring you home, to make amends with you and your mother, and hopefully to die free of ghosts."

Shuffle took another drink, barely feeling the water go down, barely feeling anything. He was numb to all the lies. Nobody's been who they've claimed to be or who he thought they were. Except for Skylla, everybody has been a paper doll of their true selves.

But what Captain did or didn't do was in the past. And now, no matter how much it hurt, he was being honest. And he was trying to set things right, and bring Dad home, too. That had to be worth something. That had to be worth forgiveness.

"I'm proud of you, Shuffle. You're the bravest young man I have ever known." Captain lowered his hat brim, hiding his eyes.

"Thanks. That means a lot." Shuffle dug through his bag and found the photo of Mama. The creases had deepened and there were new rips at the edges, but the damage didn't take away from her happiness shining off the paper. After one last look, he handed it over.

Captain lingered on the picture. "Do you think she'll forgive me?"

"When we find Dad, and we come home together . . . yeah, she will. I bet all the gold in the world she will."

* * *

"OW!" Mr. Eight popped up from behind a cactus. "Blasted needles!"

The group had stopped to set up camp, and the rail baron went out for a latrine break. It appeared he just got pinpricked where the sun don't dare to shine.

Shuffle chuckled. He couldn't help it. The slow crawl on the acrobat's wagon was taking forever, three days and counting. A good laugh was just what the doctor ordered.

Even Captain broke out a smile. His collarbone seemed to bother him less, and he hadn't had to shoot anybody lately.

The Star Dragons were doing their part in lightening up the mood. First of all, they were great hosts, sharing their food and water and, on occasion, putting on a show. They had to stay in practice, and they enjoyed having an audience. The leader would flip back and forth between two horses. The kids stood on their hands while they balanced spinning plates on their feet.

With Mr. Eight's help as a translator, Shuffle taught a few of the acrobats how to play Mythic. They caught on quick, executing their deck's strategy without a hitch. The leader recognized the card back and said something to Mr. Eight in an excited tone.

"He says their troupe is going to perform at a celebration for the game in San Francisco," Mr. Eight told Shuffle. "It's the one-year anniversary, and the creator, Stan Slythe, has engaged the Star Dragons for the occasion."

Shuffle couldn't believe the coincidence. Nor could he believe the audacity of that snake Slythe, who'd not only taken credit for Dad's idea but was now living it up on the anniversary of his theft.

Later in the day, they came across a signpost that stood at the side of the road, pointing west. *Yuma, twenty miles.*

Finally, something real worth cheering about. A town, hopefully one with a train station where Mr. Eight, if he kept his promise, would put them back on a locomotive to California.

Shuffle sighed. He was back on track to complete his quest.

"We're close," Captain said. "Half a day's ride, even at our pace. Just one more night in the desert."

After setting up camp and eating a dinner of dried fish and steamed rice, Shuffle curled up in his bedroll.

He closed his eyes, hoping to dream about Dad at home or Theseus in the Labyrinth or Oda Nobunaga in battle, instead of Atalanta hanging under a llama or wearing a yellow dress or waiting for him at Yuma. Soon enough, the crackle of the fire, Mr. Eight telling his ghost stories in Chinese, and Katana's purring lulled him to sleep.

* * *

"Get up."

Someone grabbed Shuffle and yanked him out of his bedroll. He woke up in a snap and fought back, but his attacker's grip was too strong. She shoved him to the ground, inches from the campfire. Though the flames had died down, the heat still burned, and bitter ash blew in his face. He pushed himself away, nearly coughing a lung out. This had to be one of the worst ways to wake up!

The *chink-chink* of spurs drew his eyes away from the ghostly ribbon of smoke rising from the embers.

Six-Plum Skylla stepped out of the deep dark and into the pale glow of the fire. "This ain't a dream, Jones."

It wasn't even a nightmare, Shuffle thought. It was worse. He looked around, his eyes adjusting.

Several of the Star Dragons and Mr. Eight were kneeling in a line, their arms bound by rope behind their backs and their mouths gagged by cloth. Big Hair stood over them with a blazing torch in one hand and her elephant gun in another. Cries came from the wagon where the kids and their parents were being held prisoner by Gatling Gal, armed with a rifle.

Was Atalanta around? That snake. She must be hiding in the shadows, but who really cared? There were more important lives to worry about.

Including Captain's. He had first watch. Maybe he saw Skylla coming and hid. He and Katana could be out there, biding their time for a rescue. Captain could spring into action any minute and take down Skylla and her gang. He could be—

To the side, an unmoving lump became visible in the darkness as it took in the light from the campfire.

"No, no, no." Shuffle crawled to it. "Granddad. Are you okay? Answer me!" He held back his hand, afraid to touch his granddad, afraid to know if it was really him. "Captain? Please, be all right." But not knowing was worse, and he reached out. Captain felt warm, and he moved.

Blood trickled down his head and across his eyebrows. "Shuffle, promise me, when you get the chance, you'll leave me and run."

"What? No. We'll get out of this—"

"You run." He coughed, wincing with each gasp.

"But we need to stick together." Shuffle grasped Captain's arms. Together, the two of them were adventurers. Alone, he'd just be lost.

"Promise me."

Shuffle forced himself to nod. "I promise." He pressed his forehead on Captain's shoulder, bracing against the painful tremors that came with his decision.

"These are nice pieces," Skylla said, spinning Captain's guns like she owned them.

Shuffle stood to his feet, facing Skylla. "Why don't you just leave us alone?" She had the cards—Atalanta had seen to that. No more was needed, bad blood or not.

Glancing over to Captain, the bandit leader felt the bullet hole in her vest, the place where Captain had shot her. "It's not over, Jones. Where did she go?"

Shuffle scowled. "Who? My cat?"

"Don't be stupid." She pushed the brim of her hat with the pistol. "Where is she?"

"Atalanta? She's with you now, isn't she?" Shuffle looked away, confounding thoughts rising in his mind like smoke signals. What was Atalanta up to? Was she playing two decks of lies against two fools?

Skylla dropped Atalanta's badge of the skull and five arrows in the dirt. "Don't be coy, Jones."

Lady Feather rode up. "He's arrived and will meet us at the rock."

Skylla grabbed Shuffle. "Load up the old man. I got the boy."

CHAPTER 45
GOOD-BYES

Behind the mountains to the east, the morning sun rose, and a ruddy sky with it.

Skylla tied Shuffle's arms behind his back and lifted him onto a horse. "We're going a little ways north, Jones. Excited?"

North was all right, but it wasn't west to California, where he needed to go. It wasn't where Dad was being held captive.

Big Hair climbed on, taking up most of the saddle. With the bandit pressed up against him, he was trapped like a sticky burr in wool.

Captain had it worse. His arms and legs were bound, and he was draped across the rear of Gatling Gal's horse on his stomach. He deserved better.

They thundered away in a cloud of dust, leaving behind the Star Dragons and Mr. Eight, still tied up and gagged.

And Katana—poor cat, she wouldn't understand. Shuffle looked for her as he was leaving the campsite, hopeful he'd see her one last time. She would be invisible in the darkness, except for her yellow eyes if the light hit them just right. But they never shined, and he hadn't found her by the time they were a mile gone.

Soon, the whole world seemed bleached out by the light as it painted everything in the colors of bone and ash.

Shuffle hid his eyes in the shadow of his hat, scouring his mind for well-timed moves or clever escapes. But he came up empty, and he didn't have a card at the bottom of his deck to get him out of this mess. A divine favor from Athena, like spears of lightning from the heavens, would be fantastic. Heck, a stroke of dumb luck, like Skylla and her gang falling off their horses because they forgot to latch their saddles, would work, too.

Maybe he could do whatever Atalanta did to get away from Skylla. Then again, the liar probably hadn't been trussed up like a roast chicken. She likely just snuck off with cards while the bandits were busy counting their bullets. It was a good play. Sure, it was underhanded, but what double-cross wasn't? Or was it a triple-cross? Good for her. It was vintage Odysseus.

Stop admiring her tricks, he thought. She probably never cared for anyone other than herself. After all, she was free, probably hunting for the treasure, while he was hogtied.

For the next few hours, he played out scenarios in his head, but they all ended up with him being run down or cut down or shot down by Skylla.

Eventually, they climbed up a winding path on a red hill dotted with yellow wildflowers. He shivered as a sharp wind cut into his bones. The ground leveled off, and the path straightened. Hours later, the road turned crooked again as it wound downhill. Insects clicked from their hiding spots, and two ravens on a cactus squawked at him. After one last bend in the trail, they entered a river valley. Cliffs on one side, a rocky beach on the other.

Roaring white rapids crunched against the boulders jutting out of the river. A mist hovered in the cool, wet air.

On the shore, a man stood atop a massive black rock.

✳ ✳ ✳

"Fun and games are over," Skylla said, riding alongside Shuffle.

The bandit sitting behind him, Big Hair, laughed loud enough to be heard over the roaring of the white rapids.

The other bounty hunters, Lady Feather and Gatling Gal, trailed behind, with Captain still hogtied across Gatling Gal's horse.

Following a spiraling downward path, they clopped to the shore where the stranger waited. Entering the river valley seemed like stepping into a room; the high climbs on each side of the river made the world around Shuffle narrow, less open for escape. Escape options seemed to be limited to climbing uphill, going down-river, or straight-up winning the inevitable fight.

The man waved as they approached him.

Shuffle gulped, certain it wasn't meant to be a friendly greeting. The bandits responded with a little more giddyup, picking up the pace.

Big Hair slowed her horse to a trot like she was parading. She stopped in front of the giant rock the man was standing on.

The man—a clean-shaven, slick-haired stranger—looked Shuffle up and down. "So, this is the Titan of Tombstone?"

Enough with the titles. Why did everybody think he was some sort of hero?

Shuffle craned his neck to see eye-to-eye. "What do you want?"

"The same thing you do." Slick rapped his fingers on a gem-studded holster.

"I doubt it."

Skylla circled around on her warhorse. "He claims he doesn't know the girl's whereabouts."

Slick slid his hands up his suspenders and gave them a snap. "Well, you weren't persuasive enough. Let him down."

"I'm gonna miss the company," Big Hair said, as she tossed Shuffle off the saddle.

He crumpled into the moist, pebbly dirt. Something jabbed against his leg. A pointy rock, maybe. He rubbed at the sore spot and found his pocket knife. The bandits hadn't searched him. He had a play after all.

"Easy," Lady Feather said. "You might mess up his face."

"That's right. It's not the way to treat a potential business partner." The man jumped down from his perch and offered his hand, a gold ring glinting on his pinky finger.

Shuffle climbed to his feet without any help, and ran to his granddad, still tied up on the horse. "Captain, are you okay? Granddad, please."

Sticky black clots clung to Captain's hair. Crusty blood streaked along his face and beard like a dry riverbed. Besides his busted collarbone, what kind of damage did he have on the inside?

Captain winked. "Playing possum."

Big Hair yanked him off, and he groaned as he hit the ground.

Shuffle gritted his teeth and slammed his shoulder into Big Hair, but the hulking bandit didn't budge. She just laughed. Maybe she'd like a knife in the leg instead?

"Now, now, he's been through enough." Slick leaned in close, the scent of cinnamon and tobacco riding the slither of his breath. "It appears my associates are bent out of shape for one reason or another. I can straighten them out if we work together. I know you're after treasure. The same cache your father was looking for. I invested in his expedition, you know."

So Slick had known Dad, had been another financial backer of the search. He backstabbed the group to keep all the treasure for himself. These money men really were the worst.

The man rolled up his shirt sleeves. "We'll be on the same team, and there won't be any more bickering. Just righteous harmony."

Righteous, my boot.

"I don't have the cards and don't know where the girl went. She tricked me, so I can't help you. Leave us alone. I just want to get to California." Shuffle helped his granddad up, careful with his arm and shoulder. If Captain was in a lot of pain, he didn't show it. Even if he could fight through it, though, his toughness might not be enough.

"Penny," he rasped. "My Penny." The picture of Mama had fallen out of his pocket onto the ground. "I want to look at her."

Shuffle set it face up. There was a time when Captain and Mama were close. They needed to reunite for the chance to be like that again.

A long shadow, as tall as a redwood, drew over them.

"I'm not buying it," intruded Slick. "You know where the girl went, or at least you know something. You had the map pieces in your possession. Don't deny it—you've seen the landmarks."

"Not all of them. I never found the last part of the

map. And I can tell you this: without it you'd only be wandering the desert. I can't help you." Shuffle turned away and helped Captain sit up while bracing his grand-dad's head. Captain looked so broken.

"Why do you want to get to California so bad?" asked Slick, the river mist making an unnatural halo around him. "What could be so important that you'd pass on the chance for a lifetime of riches?"

Slick must not know that Dad was in San Francisco. Maybe the killers he'd hired had told him everybody was dead and the treasure was gone. After all, if Slick had realized Dad was alive, he would've tracked Dad down instead of hunting for Cassandra's Warning. There'd be no need for the map if he had access to the one person who knew the treasure's location.

"I'm keen to see the ocean. Now kindly leave us alone." Shuffle winked at Captain, who forced a smile through a wince.

"I haven't been fair," Slick said. "To make the smart choice, you need to be informed."

Shuffle shivered as the dread clinging to the mist of the rapids crawled up his skin.

"Come on, let me show you something." Slick strolled off, his alligator-skin boots crunching against rock. "Don't worry. The old man will be all right."

"Give me a minute." Shuffle slipped out the knife from his pocket and opened it.

Off to one side, the lady bandits conversed with one

another, pointing and nodding at the rapids. Slick kept hiking to wherever he was going.

Confident he wasn't being watched, Shuffle palmed the knife and placed it handle first into Captain's stiff hand.

Captain's fingers curled around the knife, and his face changed, resembling the soldier of old. "You get back to your mama."

"I will, and so will you."

He withdrew the knife and began cutting the ropes. "Tell her I . . ."

"No. You'll tell her yourself."

Captain's breathing steadied. "Remember what you promised."

"But—"

"Go now. He's waiting. Don't give them cause to come over here." Captain smiled.

Fighting the urge to stay, Shuffle forced one boot in front of the other.

Slick waited on the other side of the black slab jutting out of the bank. "Look there." He pointed at a rough patch on the granite where a symbol was etched in the stone.

"Spanish cross," Slick said. "And this square below the cross indicates treasure. This riverbank is where your father's expedition found the cache." He put his arms out wide and presented the place like it was his kingdom. "This is where dreams are made real."

Shuffle rubbed the etching, wishing he had been

with Dad at the moment of discovery. It must've been exciting, following one symbol to another, across the country, until finally finding this secret spot.

"Unfortunately, your father's triumph didn't last long. This way." Slick marched off the beach and up the bank's edge.

Shuffle glanced back. Captain sat very still, hopefully cutting his bindings without any problem. Hopefully ready to spring into action.

Rocks jutting out of the cliff wall acted as steps for the steep climb. The path zigzagged to the top, about twenty feet high. Peering over the edge made the river below seem a mile down. That'd be one heck of a drop. Shuffle took a big step away, not wanting to be pushed over. "I enjoy a good hike, but I can't say this was one of my favorites."

"I'm like you. Many years ago, my loved ones were taken from me. My inheritance, too. I regained most of my fortune and claimed my revenge." Slick wiped debris off something on the ground. "This should get us on the same page, and you'll understand why we should work together toward the same goal."

Three headstones lay flat against the ground, and each one had a recognizable name.

Bicker. It was the last name of the trail boss hired by Dad to drive the expedition across country.

Bloom. Dad's mentor, leader of the expedition.

Jones.

"Lies." Shuffle kicked away a fallen tree branch. An empty grave. An empty threat. "He's not—"

"You're out here looking for him, aren't you? There's no use denying it now. You don't have to waste your energy circling like a vulture looking for scraps."

"You're the vulture."

"Help me, and you'll get your share. Tell me where the girl went." Slick rapped at his holster again but ended his rhythm with the snap of undoing the strap. "Or disappear in a shroud of misfortune."

A scream came from downriver.

Captain was on his feet and had Gatling Gal by the arm. He swiped her gun away and knocked her out with the pistol. He turned and fired.

Pop pop. Two shots.

Big Hair and Lady Feather fell.

Slick drew his gun.

Shuffle tensed, and the edges of the world darkened as if he'd put on blinders. His chest heaved, and he could only hear the *whoosh* of his breath.

The branch felt slick and cool and heavy in his hands as he picked it up. He swung it. It cracked against Slick's head. The man crumpled.

The river splashed against the rocks, and the mist cooled the air.

Shuffle looked at the broken branch in his hand, amazed how he had picked it up and smashed the marbles out of Slick, without even thinking.

No time to dwell on it; he needed to escape with Captain. Dropping the branch, he turned to go back down to the riverbank.

Captain faced off against Skylla.

Pop pop.

A red spray misted the air behind Captain, and he toppled.

Shuffle froze.

Everything but Captain, lifeless on the ground, seemed to disappear. The clear, zoomed-in focus was too real, and it burned.

Something broke across Shuffle's line of sight, snapping him out of his daze. Skylla charged toward him on horseback.

Shuffle ran, like he'd promised.

Pkkr. A shot whizzed by and hit a tree.

The ridge's edge drew near. Slick began to stir.

Pkkew. Another bullet zipped past.

Dad was still out there. Shuffle had to believe it. He had to prove it.

So, he jumped.

CHAPTER 46
THE RIVER

The water hit hard.

Shuffle held his breath as he plunged into the cold, humming dark. He didn't sink very far before the river dragged him away. He clawed and kicked, fighting not to drown. The current tore him from the light. His chest burned, begging for air, but he knew if he opened his mouth, he'd suck in water and die.

No way that was happening while Dad still lived.

Using every bit of his body, every bit of his strength, Shuffle fought his way to the top, breaking the surface. He fought to stay afloat, gulping in air as the river swept him downstream.

Gaining his bearings, he spotted the black rock. It was far and getting farther by the second. Granddad was somewhere over there, too, getting left behind.

A rider on horseback crested a high ridge on the riverbank—Skylla, the killer. Fortunately, she got smaller as he was pulled to who-knows-where. Good riddance for now, but it wasn't over, not by a long mile.

The river thrashed, and the whitecaps thickened. The water slapped him in the face and spun him around in a twist. The rocks were the worst, hidden and unforgiving. He dodged them, flailing and kicking like a wild cat in a tin bathtub. He swam for shore, but the river roared as it clenched its jaws around him, sucking him away. There had to be a waterfall at the end.

Shuffle pulled and kicked, swimming harder. His arms and legs burned, wearing him out, but the safety of shore grew closer. He could almost reach out and grab land, until the river turned him away with one strong swipe, and he smacked headlong into a rock.

A burst of white pain flashed as he shut his eyes to the sharp ringing in his head. His body stiffened, and as the white faded to black, he began to sink.

✳ ✳ ✳

Something slammed against Shuffle's chest.

He coughed hard, and it hurt as though his insides were busting out to get revenge.

He gasped, spitting water that burned coming out. He half opened his eyes to a distorted, swirling world. Was this heaven?

Two shadows loomed. Dad? Granddad?

The piercing ringing came back, and Shuffle shut his eyes, fighting the pain.

Voices echoed inside the dark.

"Captain."

The ringing changed to a sustained, high-pitched whistle.

Captain.

The dark grew heavy.

Captain.

The dark screamed.

* * *

A horn bellowed, and slowly, the world came back.

Shuffle blinked away the blurry darkness, focusing on a crack that cut across the ceiling like a forked lightning bolt. His head throbbed, but he'd had worse. Despite the pain in his temples, he sat up, finding himself on an unfamiliar bunk. He realized he was barefoot, his socks and boots sunning on a rack by the window. His hair and clothes were mostly dry.

The musty room smelled like fish and old books. On a desk nestled in a corner, a glass of water glistened with condensation. Suddenly thirsty, Shuffle reached for the drink and found a note beside the glass.

Meet me on the bridge. Captain Pollux.

* * *

Shuffle stepped out of the cabin onto the deck. The sun and wind swept across his face, both warm and cool at the same time. Below, the river lapped against the boat, calmer than he remembered, and it was a mile wide, with tall red cliffs on both sides. He looked down the deck and figured out he was on a steam-powered paddleboat.

After getting directions from one of the crew, Shuffle found the bridge.

A brick house of a man helmed the wheel. His forearms flexed even with the slightest of movements. "Welcome aboard the *Nemesis*. How are you feeling?"

"I'm fine." Shuffle felt the side of his head where he remembered hitting the rock. "Still a little shaken."

"You're lucky. Two Mojave fishermen found you half dead. They saved you and brought you to the docks. I told them I'd take you to town."

"You'll have to thank them for me." Shuffle leaned against the wall for balance as he was hit by a sudden spike of dizziness.

"Got family around?"

Shuffle turned away and wrapped his arms around his chest. "I'm alone."

Back home after Dad was gone, Shuffle always had Mama to warm up to or Katana to snuggle up with, when the Mourning Glory blues hit out of nowhere. But now, the reality of his predicament, with no friends and no family, tore through him.

"What were you doing in the river?" Pollux asked.

Shuffle faced the window, imagining Granddad gently holding the faded picture of Mama, which turned into the pocket knife. The waking dream enveloped him, and he teetered, conflicted whether to tell Granddad to cut the rope or not. Too late. Granddad aimed a gun, his knuckles white. His hand was fast and steady. He squeezed the trigger.

The boat's horn blared. Shuffle snapped out of his thoughts, and a cold dread surged through him. He fought away the welling tears by closing his eyes and picturing Granddad with the sun on his shoulders and a wry smile just underneath his gray mustache.

But a mist flashed in the darkness behind Shuffle's eyelids. Red and bursting. He slid to the floor and hid his face in the crook of his arm, crying until the red mist disappeared.

CHAPTER 47
WAY OF THE LONESOME

The next morning, Shuffle watched the sunrise off the starboard bow as the riverboat, *Nemesis*, neared the town's pier. The cool air began to give way to a creeping heat.

After docking the ship, Pollux escorted Shuffle off the deck and pointed the way to the marshal's office. "Good luck to you."

Shuffle sighed. Good luck had been in short supply lately. And no amount of strategy or quick thinking had made a lick of difference against all the misfortune plaguing this hunt.

Well, one thing did matter—sacrifice.

Without Granddad's selfless act, this whole quest would've drowned there at the river, by the black rock, at the hands of Slick and Six-Plum Skylla.

Shuffle waved good-bye to Pollux and headed for the marshal's office. He needed the law on his side—if nothing else, to find Granddad and bury him with full rites befitting an honorable man.

Head down and eyes up, he weaved through the streets crowded with strangers, possibly teeming with hidden killers and thieves. Determined not to get caught unaware again, he paid attention to people's eyes and head turns. He watched for tells and body language. He checked reflections off windows and peeked around corners for anyone following him. After being jumped by Skylla and her gang enough times, he figured there was no such thing as being too careful.

He tensed up even more as he neared the marshal's office. He didn't want to relive what'd happened by talking about it, but it had to be done. His chest seemed to weigh a ton, and he slowed his breathing just so it wouldn't hurt.

Eventually, he made it up the stoop and through the door.

Beside a half-empty gun rack, "Wanted" posters of hard-as-horn criminals covered the near wall. One of the faces seemed familiar. Shuffle drifted closer, the killer's cold eyes drawing him in. Then the face appeared to change, and now Skylla stared right at him.

"Need something, son?"

Shuffle tore away from the poster and took a calming breath. A quick glance back at the poster confirmed it wasn't Skylla, though she oughtta be on it. *Dead or Alive.*

"Well? Spit it out." The lawman twirled his white handlebar mustache.

"Captain Pollux said the marshal would help me."

"Take a load off." He pointed at a chair on the other side of a weathered old desk. "What can I do for you?"

Sitting down, Shuffle told him everything, even the painful parts.

The marshal chewed on his lip, his mustache tilting like a seesaw. "A man came by late last night, demanding I search for a boy and his grandfather captured by bandits."

"A man?"

"At first, I didn't recognize him. He was dirty and disheveled and raving." The marshal rapped his knuckles on the desk. "But when he calmed down, I realized it was the man who brought the railroad to town."

"Was it Mr. Eight? Edward Eight?"

The marshal nodded. "I guess that boy is you?"

"Yes! You believe me."

"I sent two deputies to the desert. Mr. Eight didn't say anything about the river."

"He didn't know where they took me."

The marshal dug his elbows into the desk. "In any case, the thing about this man and the bounty hunters. It ain't gonna fly."

"It's the truth. The man hired Skylla and her gang. The man ruined my dad's expedition. They're why I left home, why I'm—"

"Whoa, slow your wagon roll, son. Conspiracy to a kidnapping and to murder is a major allegation. And you don't got a name."

"Sir, I'm not lying, and I can describe him for you. Describe him for a 'Wanted' poster."

The chair creaked as the marshal sat back, his arms crossed. "I'll send the deputies up the Colorado to bring your grandfather back. I'll post bounties on Six-Plum and her gang, but I can't do anything about the no-named man without evidence."

Retrieving Granddad was the main priority. Skylla and Slick's comeuppance could wait. Hopefully, not for long.

* * *

Shuffle stepped out of the marshal's office and into a wall of heat. He rolled up his sleeves and unfastened the top button of his shirt as he thought about what to do next. One thing was for sure, he'd have to let Mama know by letter or telegram. Not a pleasant prospect either way.

The air shimmered from the heat.

Deciding that finding something to drink oughtta be the next step, he wandered down the dusty road in search of some lemonade.

Two boys tumbleweeded out of the general store, their voices echoing as they hurried away. In their excitement, one of them dropped something, and it skittered end over end at the spear-tip of a hot wind.

Shuffle stepped on the piece of litter as it came at him. It fluttered for a moment before going stiff. He picked it up. *MYTHIC* on black paper. And on the back,

Stake your claim to adventure and to dreams made real. Stan Slythe Publishing. San Francisco, California. He crushed the wrapper, then let it fall to the dirt.

Down the street, a blue and white mirage, swimming in a sea of drab brown and gray, came toward him. He blinked, hoping he wasn't still loopy from hitting his head on the rock. The figure drew closer, and with one hard look, Shuffle realized it was Mr. Eight.

"By gum, Mr. Jones!" Mr. Eight put his arm around Shuffle's shoulders and gave him a shake. "Those gun-toting beldams didn't eat you alive! Let me guess, you outsmarted them, and the good Captain finished them off with a one-two-three." He made gunshot noises.

Shuffle shook his head. "Granddad's . . . he took a bullet so I could get away."

"Those murderous—" Mr. Eight's face turned a reddish orange, like a yam about to explode. "They'll swing from the gallows." He gave Shuffle's shoulders a hearty squeeze. "I'm sorry. I didn't know him long, but I could tell he was a rare coin."

"Thanks, Mr. Eight." Shuffle wiped the sweat (not tears) off his face. "I see you got a new cane. And some new duds. I like your hat."

"Had to. Couldn't stand wearing dirties." He straightened his white felt bowler and tugged at the drape of his blue pin-striped jacket. "Unfortunately, it's hotter than a furnace."

"How about the Star Dragons? Are they okay?"

"Why, yes. They're as tough as they are flexible." Mr. Eight chuckled. "They met up with the rest of their group and left by train early this morning."

Shuffle grinned. Finally, something to smile about, and he rubbed his fingers as though he had cards in his hand. A train was just what he needed. Lemonade would have to come later. "Mr. Eight, will you still honor our agreement?"

"Agreement? Oh, of course. You need a ride. I will get you home. I'm sure you miss your mother."

"I do. I really do, and I want to go back." Shuffle looked at his dirty boots, then to his whitening knuckles as he made a fist. "But not yet." He met Mr. Eight's eyes. "The deal was two pieces of treasure for a ride to San Francisco. By train and by boat."

"That's correct, but what about the marshal?"

"I can't wait any longer. I need to get to California."

"What about your grandfather?"

Shuffle glanced away. "And that's where I have to ask you for another favor." It hurt to even think about it— leaving Granddad behind and not being at his burial— but saving Dad was top priority.

Mr. Eight frowned, then took off his hat and put it on his chest. "Of course. I'll make sure the good Captain gets proper rites and a funeral befitting an honorable warrior."

"Thank you." Shuffle extended his hand.

Mr. Eight grabbed it and pulled him close for a hug. "Let's get you on a chariot, Mr. Jones."

SAN FRANCISCO BULLET POINTS

SLYTHE CELEBRATES A MYTHIC ANNIVERSARY

Publishing powerhouse Stan Slythe is celebrating the one-year anniversary of the wildly popular card game Mythic this Friday. "People love the fact that it's easy to learn and hard to master," said Slythe. "It has depth, like apple pie."

When asked about using known criminals as spokesmen for his game, Slythe replied, "Gunslingers sell. Good or bad, these men of the west are living legends. Everyone wants to be larger than life, and whether you're a banker from New York or a farmer from Iowa, you become limitless when you play Mythic."

Festivities will begin at 9 a.m. in front of Cronos Emporium, where the first Mythic cards were sold. At noon, an eight-seeded tournament will be held at Oni's Saloon, with the champion receiving a cash prize of $100. To finish off the celebration, a private party for Stan Slythe's close friends and business partners will be held at his estate on Spirit Hill. The famed Chinese acrobat troupe, the Star Dragons, will perform for the privileged attendees.

DASH DARKWOOD ADVENTURES: THE NORTHERN WILD

In this latest installment of thrilling tales, Dash Darkwood searches for a mystical totem in the Canadian wilderness, where he wrestles a wendigo, rides a condor, and encounters a forest siren. Meanwhile, his nemesis, Dr. Norris Grinder, has a new weapon capable of destroying a whole forest, and he will not hesitate to use it on Darkwood.

DOUBLE DISASTER

YUMA, Ariz.— Notable rail tycoon, Edward Eight, 63, states his private train was derailed by bandits in the Gila Desert last week. Moments after the attack, a massive tornado barreled its way toward the locomotive, chasing away the would-be thieves and destroying the train.

"I lament losing my one-of-a-kind marvel of engineering, but I'm grateful to have survived. I would've perished if it weren't for brave and quick-thinking passengers," said Mr. Eight.

The would-be robbers were not apprehended.

CHAPTER 48
DRAGONS AND CATS

Shuffle strutted down the platform from the deck to the pier. After riding a train from Yuma to Los Angeles, he'd taken a ship the rest of the way. Mr. Eight had set him up on a passenger liner, *The Dauntless*, twice the size of Captain Pollux's riverboat. Despite the decent accommodations, two days on the ocean was more like two years, with all the teetering and tottering.

But now, finally making it to San Francisco, he felt right as rain.

For about half a minute.

A sneering man with unkempt hair and matching ratty beard shoved over a Chinese man minding his own business. It was probably meant to look like an accident, but he put his shoulder into the push and didn't even apologize. The people nearby ignored it like the harbor's salty stink. Before Shuffle could move to help, the Chinese man picked himself up and continued on his way.

Not wanting to linger any longer, Shuffle made his way through the wharf as a cold fog rolled in from the bay and made the air damp. He drifted through the mist, remembering his escape from Skylla's gang at Cici's ranch—knocking out Shortstack with a rock, Atalanta blowing stuff up with a methane bomb, Granddad blasting Skylla off her horse. They were all encouraging memories, the kind he would need to survive this mess.

A newsboy shouting about Mythic brought him back to the present. He bought himself a copy of the paper the newsboy was hawking, which carried a story about Mythic's one-year anniversary.

His best shot at finding Dad would be to find Stan Slythe, the so-called creator of Mythic. Wherever Slythe was, Dad was sure to be close, since he was providing Slythe with original ideas and artwork for the game.

The article reminded Shuffle that the Star Dragons would be performing at Stan Slythe's estate. Odds seemed good that Dad would be there, too, either as a guest—or as a captive.

✳ ✳ ✳

Outside the wharf district, Shuffle caught a ride on a cable car. It trundled up and down rolling hills past houses with pointed roofs, colorful paint jobs, and bay windows like some of the homes in Mourning Glory. He closed his eyes, imagining the green shutters and red door of his house. Inside were his bed, his books, and his cards. And Mama was home, humming her favorite hymn.

A little bell rang, and the cable car driver waved. "Your stop. Chinatown."

Shuffle hopped off the trolley and looked for his destination.

The driver pointed down the street. "You have to walk the rest."

Shuffle sighed, watching the cable car take a crossing street and roll out of sight.

Heading up the sidewalk, Shuffle couldn't help but notice ugly posters plastered on the building's walls. Some of them were cartoons, colorful and sickening. One depicted Uncle Sam, in his brightest red, white, and blue, tossing a Chinese man away from the gates of Liberty. Another was a sign, in bold letters bleeding at the edges, stating: *Chinese Must Go.*

Horrified, Shuffle hurried to the Chinatown entrance, a green-shingled, towering archway, the Dragon Gate. Beyond the gate's shadow, a cobblestone street stretched to a faraway point, buildings crowding both sides, sidewalks teeming with people. Taking a deep breath, he strode through the Dragon Gate, dead set on finding the Star Dragons.

The acrobat troupe was a power play—one of the essential cards of his strategy to get him into Stan Slythe's place. They were going to perform there, and what better way to infiltrate a guarded mansion than with the hired entertainment? It would be like the Greeks sneaking into Troy in the horse, but hopefully with less killing.

Chinatown bustled—people playing tile games and Mythic at the edges of alleys or buying and selling sizzling food at curbside stalls. Shuffle's stomach rumbled as spicy, meaty smoke wafted from the entrances of windowless buildings. Talking and whistling and random noises bounced off walls hung with white paper lanterns and red-and-yellow ribbons.

Using the newspaper article that mentioned the Star Dragons, Shuffle asked for directions from anyone who would pay attention to him. One person pointed him to an orphanage. Another fellow led him to a reptile store. It continued like this—one wrong way after another—until he ended up at an alley smelling like rotten eggs.

It was a long path with lots of dark places to hide. Surely, they weren't thinking he was stupid enough to walk into an obvious ambush.

But what if this alley led to the Star Dragons? Not all shadowy, stinky pathways were deathtraps.

Full steam ahead, he pressed his hand against his bag, where his calming force normally slept. It was empty, but that didn't stop him.

Teeth clenched, he headed to the end of the alley, where it became obvious his friends weren't waiting.

The pall of the alley grew darker and deeper, and he couldn't help but quiver, feeling lost and alone, until something blurred across the path.

Small. Four legs. Pointed ears and a tail sticking straight up to a hook at the tip.

He followed the cat out of the alley that opened into a busy street.

The cat weaved in and out of the crowd, her black fur shimmering.

He gasped as if he'd been hit with both barrels.

Katana?

The cat appeared on the sidewalk by a lamppost, then disappeared around the corner.

Could it be? He chased, saying *sorry* and *excuse me* as he bulled through the people in his way.

The cat pranced onward. Shuffle neared the black, silky fur, closing in on the flickering tail.

Closer.

He slammed right into someone.

A colossal Chinese man looked down at him.

"Sorry." Shuffle shrank, slumping his shoulders and bringing his arms inward for defense. When he realized he wasn't going to be stomped on, he held out the ad. "Do you know where—?"

"*Tianlong*," the giant said, snatching the paper. "*Zhidao Tianlong*." He handed it back and pointed to a four-story building with a sign containing Chinese characters Shuffle recognized.

Shuffle looked back and forth from the ad to the sign, comparing the symbols. They matched.

"*Xie xie*," Shuffle said, remembering how to say thank you.

The giant bowed before lumbering away.

Shuffle pumped his fist, certain he'd found the place.

And the cat? He looked around for her. No sign. Maybe it was her, but that could've been wishful thinking. For now he let go of the notion and walked across the street to the Star Dragons' building.

The ten-foot door creaked and moaned.

Inside, the room was pretty much the whole building, four stories tall, at least a hundred feet deep and a hundred feet wide.

Some of the Star Dragons flipped cartwheels and walked handstands. Others climbed up and slid down silk drapes that hung high from the ceiling. And of course, a few of them bounded across the room on their bendy poles.

Shuffle took a deep breath. "*Ni hao.*" His voice boomed through the whole room, bouncing off the walls.

The acrobats stopped even before the last echo ended. The two kids jumped when they saw him and ran to him for big hugs.

Shuffle put his arms around their shoulders. "Missed you, too."

"Welcome," said an old Chinese woman. Her slate-gray robe shimmered as she moved. Dragon embroidery within gold bands decorated the sleeves and collar. "My name is Meng Jiangnu. My family told me what happened. They feared for your life. But it appears they had nothing to worry about."

"I had some luck and a whole lot of help. I came here for a favor, but I also have a couple of questions."

"Yes, of course."

He felt awkward, asking a stranger about these unsettling things going on that really had nothing to do with him. He was no longer a kid, when it might've been acceptable to blurt out whatever came across his mind. But he wanted to know if his friends were in trouble.

"I noticed . . . I don't know . . . anger toward Chinese people. Not here, but at the wharf and, well, every other corner."

Her easy-going demeanor seemed to take on an invisible burden. "Ah, yes. You see, young man, after the railroads brought so many of our people here, jobs became scarce, bringing ill winds that carried white people's fears and hate. They're afraid our men will take their jobs, among other things. And they hate whatever is different." She grasped one of the boy's hands. "With that hate, the future winds sway grimly."

Shuffle nodded as though he understood. He did in a way. He knew Granddad had lived through a whole war that was fought because of fear and hate. What Shuffle didn't understand was the blatant ugliness. The unapologetic show of it all.

Dad had taught him that each culture had their own mythologies, making their stories special, but no matter how different the gods, the monsters, and the heroes were, mythology was a tapestry of a collective world. *We're all human—unique and equal,* Dad would say.

"But the wind doesn't always bring bad tidings. We are staying," Meng said. "We perform because that is what we do. That is what we love."

"And your family is amazing!" Shuffle told her.

Meng bowed in acknowledgment, her countenance brightening. "And your second question?"

Hopefully, the Star Dragons had better news about this one.

"My cat." Shuffle knelt to eye level with one of the boys. He didn't want the alleyway cat to be a shade of his loneliness. "Is she here? Katana, my cat."

"*Mao,*" said one of the boys, his eyes shining.

The other boy bounced in place. "*Mao. Mao.*"

They grabbed Shuffle's hands and pulled him to a back room filled with equipment.

On a sunny patch by a closed window, a black cat lay curled like a little gift waiting to be opened.

"Katana?"

The cat raised her head, her pointy ears standing straight up. She casually blinked her big yellow eyes.

Shuffle went down on one knee. "Hey, girl. Giddyup, kitty."

Slow and slinky, the cat stretched out her legs, back, and tail and then came toward him. She weaved around his leg, rubbing her fur against him, before climbing up his back. She nestled down on his shoulders, purring.

CHAPTER 49
PARTY TIME

The girl in the mirror looked back. Powdery white makeup with pink blush. Ink-drawn eyebrows. Deep red lips. A black wig braided into two spiral buns.

To finish off the look, Shuffle put on a blue head-dress embroidered with a gold dragon and embellished with gold tassels. He stepped back and looked at the whole getup. The jacket, a blue-and-gray cotton piece with dragon patterns on the sleeves, fit perfectly. The pants and shoes did, too. He checked out every angle, unsure he could pull off being a Chinese girl acrobat. *Face of Deception: Hero may activate without being countered. Discard after hero scores.*

Katana watched from a ledge. Her tail hung over the edge, swinging like an easy-going pendulum.

"What do you think, girl?" He stood at profile: shoulders back, chin up, and gut sucked in.

She slow-blinked an answer.

"I miss my hat. And I don't like these shoes. Atalanta would've laughed." He tugged at the wig, making it itch

298

worse. No matter how clever it was, the dang thing was torture. "It's gonna work, right?"

Katana yawned and stretched.

He slipped his hand through her fur, and confidence rippled from his fingers to the rest of him.

* * *

Shuffle waited with the Star Dragons at the back gate of Stan Slythe's estate.

The sun began to set, turning the sky pink and violet. The tall gaslight lanterns turned on, glowing amber. It was finally time to push all-in, no turning tail, and to start the first part of the plan.

He kept his head down and his posture small as iron-packing guards inspected everyone and everything going into the grounds. But it wasn't as easy as a lice check. The wig itched like Hades, the collar dug at his throat, and his sweat began to run down the makeup. Worst of all was his job: pushing the cart of fireworks. It could explode at any moment. Probably sensing the danger, Katana wriggled nonstop, inside his shoulder bag.

One of the guards knocked on the cart. "What you got in here, little girl?"

Shuffle bit his trembling lip, pretending not to understand.

"Open it."

Shuffle kept his eyes on his tiny silk shoes.

"Well, you gonna do as you're told?"

"Excuse my granddaughter," said Meng. "She knows very little English." Shuffle glanced up and Meng opened the cart lid, exposing the load of explosives.

The guard's eyes grew as big as wheels of cheese.

Meng smiled. "Mr. Slythe ordered fireworks for the celebration. What kind of party would it be without Sky Blooms and Hanging Crackles?"

"A boring one," the guard said.

Meng batted her eyelashes. "May we pass?"

The guard nodded and waved everyone through.

* * *

A steward ushered Shuffle and the Star Dragons to the west end of the compound—a villa of multi-storied buildings with clay roof tiles, smooth plaster walls, and iron balconies at each upper-floor window. One third-floor balcony had a red Mythic banner draped across its bars.

Shuffle helped the Star Dragons get ready for the performance near the open-air plaza the size of four schoolyards. A humongous stone fountain stood center stage, a gathering spot where fancy guests mingled as waiters served dainty food bites and a string quartet played slow songs. A bearded fellow dressed up like Zeus poked fake lightning bolts at random people as he stalked through the crowd. What a dumb gimmick. Shuffle didn't know whether to scoff or laugh. At least he wasn't the only person in a costume.

Shuffle handed out dragon-decorated paper fans, while keeping an eye out for Dad.

What if he couldn't recognize Dad? It had been three years. The desert, the time apart, anything and everything could've changed him. Dad might be a different person, not just in looks but in heart.

Perhaps Dad didn't come home because he had a better life in California.

No.

Dad would never stay away, and he was not under that grave marker in the desert.

Determined to trust his gut, Shuffle continued his search, while trying to stay inconspicuous as he handed out fans. *Keep your head down but stay vigilant.*

But after a while, he was down to a handful of fans, with no sightings of Dad to show for it.

"Excuse me, young miss," said a man. He said something in Chinese.

So much for going unnoticed. Shuffle turned, keeping his head down.

The man bent over slightly, trying to make eye contact. Eye contact?! Shuffle trembled, afraid the man would see right through the makeup. One slip-up, one little tell could mean a lasso around the whole plan.

Fighting through his now shaky knees, Shuffle handed out a fan.

Taking it, the man said something else in Chinese and bowed, before turning around to leave. Shuffle glanced up in time to see an old scar streaked along the side of the man's head like a dry riverbed cutting across the desert.

Katana popped her head out from the bag and meowed.

"Shhh. We need to keep a low profile." Shuffle slid a finger against her face, and his confidence began to return. "We're on a stealth mission."

The sound of breaking glass pierced the crowd noise.

"Dang it, boy. Watch where you're going!"

At the center of the commotion, a large man, dripping wet from a disastrous spill of drinks, towered over a young serving boy picking up the broken glass.

The man dabbed himself with a napkin. "You ruined my waistcoat. It's worth more than your life."

Shuffle squeezed through the crowd to help, but when he got to the edge of the circle formed around the mess, he realized he'd attract too much attention. He didn't want anybody to get hurt, but he also didn't want to get busted.

Thankfully, the server finished cleaning up and left. He kept his head down, but in his hurry, he ran into Shuffle.

"Sorry," Shuffle said, even though he was the one who'd been bumped into.

The serving boy stopped and tilted his head, almost glancing back.

Realizing he'd just messed up his disguise by opening his dumb mouth, Shuffle snapped open a folding fan and hid his face. Hopefully, the boy would just go away. One little slip could be a big problem. What if the Trojans had believed Cassandra? The Greeks' last thoughts as they were burned alive in the horse would've been "Well, dang, it was a good plan up to this point."

After a moment of hiding behind his fan, he took a peek. Thankfully, the serving boy was gone.

Someone tapped Shuffle on the shoulder. This time, he kept his fan up and his mouth shut as he turned around.

"There will be a speech," Meng said. "Maybe by your father. At the fountain."

Shuffle took in a deep breath, steeling himself to finally see Dad.

CHAPTER 50
FLASH AND GRAB

A man stepped forward onto the balcony with the Mythic sign.

Shuffle gasped, bracing Katana against his chest.

It wasn't Dad.

But it was someone familiar.

"Welcome, everyone, to my humble abode! As the creator of Mythic, I owe a debt of gratitude to all you game players for making this possible. Without you, we wouldn't be having this celebration."

That oily, drawling voice filled Shuffle's ears with sickness.

It was undeniable as mold on bread.

The man on the balcony was Stan Slythe. Also known, in Shuffle's mind at least, as Slick.

Slick wasn't just the treacherous backer of Dad's expedition. He was also the man who'd stolen Mythic.

Draped in hoity-toity bib and tucker—a shiny jacket with coattails and a fancy top hat—Slick waved his arms as he congratulated himself for all his wonderful achievements. Dad should've been the one giving the speech and basking in the glory. It was *their* game, and they should be celebrating.

Revelers crowded the fountain, forming a suffocating, buzzing mob. Shuffle squeezed his way to an open spot to catch his breath and make sense of it all.

Slythe controlled Dad, the one man who knew the hidden treasure's location. He didn't need the map cards.

Yet he was clearly desperate for them. He hired Skylla, and she hunted for them across country. He couldn't be a true card collector who cared for the game. Surely, he didn't care for Maker's cards. He was after treasure.

Then why keep Dad? Was it just for creating the game? Mythic couldn't be making Slythe *that* much money.

There had to be a reason, other than the lie that was buried under the headstone by the white-water rapids.

"Soon there will be new cards. New heroes and monsters," Slythe said. "This expansion will showcase new art, open up new strategies, and, of course, provide new ways to win some money."

The crowd cheered. Shuffle would want nothing more than new cards, but not if Dad was locked up and being forced to make them.

Slythe flashed his pearly whites. "Folks, we can't forget why we're here today. The new is all well and good, but we're here to celebrate a whole year of fun and profitable times."

Whoops and whistles from the crowd made Slythe grin even bigger. He was a bona fide, ego-loving money-grubbing snake.

"It all began with this," Slythe said, raising a card in the air. "A Maker's card."

Even at this distance, Shuffle could see the card clearly. *Cihtym*. The deity card of the four-color four-suit strategy. The fifth and final card in the treasure map.

"You won't find one like this in any of the packs or decks. No, you'll find better." The card caught the light before Slythe placed it in a silver case, which he then slipped into his inner right pocket. "Stake your claim to greatness."

Slythe finished up his speech by telling everybody to form a circle around the courtyard. When the space was clear, the Star Dragons kicked off their show.

Shuffle stood off to the side with Meng, watching her family perform while fighting the urge to charge into the building. After searching all evening for Dad, he'd come up empty. The only way to get him back was for Slythe to give him up. And the only way to get Slythe to release Dad was to drive a hard bargain.

So Slythe had the key piece of the treasure map—the one with X-marks-the-spot. Without the surrounding landmarks on the cards Atalanta had taken, he still wouldn't be able to pinpoint the treasure's location. But without the Cihtym card, Slythe would be truly up a creek.

That's why Shuffle decided he was gonna steal it.

As the Star Dragon boys danced across the courtyard, setting off small flashes with trick flowers, an idea formed in his head.

Eventually, Slythe appeared in the courtyard, slithering out a guarded door. Aside from the outer gates, it was the only one under watch. It must lead to Slythe's hidden vault or tower dungeon. Maybe Dad was in there. Slythe wormed his way to the courtyard, front and center to the entertainment. The Star Dragons did their cartwheels, handstands, backflips, and pole flying.

Shuffle tapped Meng's shoulder. "Now or never."

She handed him a delicate paper flower. "Squeeze the stem until you feel the glass crack. The chemicals will release. Don't put it too close; he may not like the flash."

Trick flower in hand, Shuffle pranced his way to Slythe.

Slythe's jacket was unbuttoned. Good. Easier to steal the silver pocket case, just the way Atalanta had stolen the deck and the treasure cards. Distraction and sleight of hand.

Shuffle twirled nearer. Sweat began to run down the side of his head, and he could feel it pool under the itchy wig. Gritting his teeth behind a smile, he fought hard not to yank the headdress off. *Dang it, this better work.*

The crowd *ooh*ed and *ahh*ed. He didn't look at what they were watching; he kept his eyes on his prey. Slythe. Inside pocket. Silver case. The last treasure card.

Fireworks flashed and crackled.

Slythe clapped, now at arm's reach.

Swooping in close, Shuffle guided the flower into Slythe's view, catching his attention, and clamped down on the stem. The glass bulb cracked. Shuffle whisked the flower to the side, and Slythe followed it with his eyes. It burst into a yellow light.

Shuffle slid his hand into the jacket.

The silver case cooled his palm.

CHAPTER 51

FOUND OUT

Shuffle hid the silver case in his sleeve.

Slythe waved him off, unwise to the pilfer. Sucker.

A rocket whistled overhead and exploded into a shimmering, crackling flower. Shuffle backed away, feeling the same kind of fireworks in his hands. He weaved through the shoulder-to-shoulder crowd, accidentally bumping into a few people. His headdress and wig went crooked. Fortunately, he caught them before they fell off, straightening the getup as best he could.

When he found a dark area near the back wall far from all the hoopla, he opened the silver case. Inside was a brass three-hooped key, but not *Cihtym*, the last treasure card. Slythe must've switched the card for the key. Shuffle slapped the case shut. Of course, the job wasn't going to be easy.

Still, a key meant a door or a safe with something valuable locked away. Something being guarded. Only one building had guards posted, and it was the one with the Mythic banner draped across its highest balcony.

Shuffle stowed the silver case in the bag with Katana and kept the key in his pocket. It was time for more banditry, starting with the guard at the door. Shuffle grabbed a large rock from a flower bed, certain he could knock the guard out. Nobody would see; everybody was watching the show. Sure, he'd rather be clever and trick the guard by drawing him away with a feint or a distraction, but playing a Chinese girl kinda ruled out talking. Rock-skull-bash was the best course of action.

Hiding his hands and the rock in his sleeves, Shuffle headed toward the guard, just around the corner, in the light, where everything could go wrong.

He slowed. There could be a better way. Without violence. Without risk.

Maybe he could—

A shrill whistle.

"You there. Girl." A woman's voice, not Meng's. Under the light of a bursting red firework, Skylla approached him, her hands on her iron.

Shuffle backed away. He needed to turn and run.

Eyeballing him up and down, Skylla smiled. "You amaze me, Jones. I thought the river had you. But seeing you here, now, in that getup, well, I ain't surprised one bit. Not after all the excitement we've been through together."

Turn and run for help. Now.

"Don't move, or you'll get what the old man got."

Shuffle froze. Not from obedience or fear, but from something heavy and deep and red in his gut. He didn't want to escape anymore. Instead of running, he tightened his grip on the rock, until it felt like a part of himself. A part he wanted to send crashing into her face.

"Nice look. The wig gave you away, though." She drew a pistol and tilted up her hat with the barrel. "Real hair don't move around like that."

He dug in his heels, ready to launch. She just needed to come closer.

"What are you doing here, Jones? Revenge? Want to get back at Slythe? Is he the top of your bill?" She paced toward him. Her oxblood chaps swayed, and her spurs chinked.

Closer.

She spun the gun's chamber. Her eyes reflected the red from the light of a firework flash. "Or am I your most wanted?"

Close enough.

Shuffle swung the rock. It smashed into her jaw. She stumbled but stayed on her feet. The curve of her body slackened, then seemed to slowly turn rigid, like a bowstring being pulled back, ready to loose an arrow. She rubbed her chin, then spat out a bloody tooth.

He reared back for a second, maybe knockout blow.

But with a quick swipe, Skylla struck his arm, and he dropped the rock. She grabbed him and jammed the barrel into his ribs.

"I don't think Slythe would want a dead kid to ruin his party," she said, cocking the hammer back. "But what's another dead Jones to him? And really, I don't care."

He clutched his bag, pressing Katana close. Again, he didn't want to die alone.

"Hey, lady. Can you hold this for me?"

Out of nowhere, the serving boy who had run into Shuffle earlier shoved a large, dome-covered platter into Skylla's chest. White smoke steamed from a small hole on the top of the cover. Skylla dropped the tray, her bloody face twisting, as she kicked off the lid.

Inside, a tangle of fuses and fireworks sizzled.

The boy tackled Shuffle.

The fireworks exploded.

CHAPTER 52
REUNIONS

Shuffle dared a peek at the explosion. Flashes of fire and lightning shot out as though a thousand dragons were having a coughing fit. But he couldn't take his eyes off the light even as a blue fireball screamed past. *Almighty Wrath: Destroy everything on the playing field.*

"Get your head down." The serving boy glared from underneath the cover of his arms, while yellow sparks showered him.

The pops and bangs kept firing as gray, bitter smoke choked the air. Okay, maybe the kid was right. No sense losing an eye to a Sky Bloom. Shuffle turned away from the angry barrage until the last whistling rocket fizzled.

When the smoke cleared, he sat up, keeping his wig and headdress from falling off. He looked in his bag. Katana meowed.

Not everyone had fared well.

Skylla lay motionless on her side, stinking like burned bacon. Her arm was bent behind her head, and her leg was kicked out like an L. Shuffle kept his eyes on the smoldering heap for a moment, wanting to cheer, but his gut turned.

The guard ran up. "What in devil's iron happened?"

No one else showed up. The folks had to be wrapped up in the acrobatics and the real fireworks show.

"She's hurt," the serving boy said, climbing to his feet. "Help her."

Covering his nose and mouth with his hat, the guard inched toward Skylla. "That's bad. I'm going to get—"

The kid slammed the rock across the poor guy's head, knocking him out, and then began rifling through the fallen guard's clothes.

"Whoa! What the heck?" Shuffle grabbed the boy and swung him around. First Skylla and now the guard—did this kid have some kind of vendetta against grownups?

"Isn't your voice a little low for a China doll?"

A burst of yellow light illuminated a familiar face. A girl's face. The constellation of dark freckles. The cool, sharpshooter eyes. The smug grin.

Shuffle sucked in a spike of air, his chest clenching at the sight of her. "Atalanta!"

"Don't—don't make fun of my hair."

Shuffle focused, realizing her braids were gone. Her haircut looked like a butcher job from a half-asleep dentist.

"What are you doing here?" He pointed at the guard. "You just—"

She jiggled the ring of keys.

"And the fireworks. You—"

She nodded toward the carnage that was Skylla.

"Yeah, but you—"

Katana jumped out of the bag and began weaving around Atalanta's legs. That made two traitors.

"I missed you, kitty." She put Katana on her shoulders.

"Oh, heck, no. Don't conspire with the enemy." He snatched his cat away. "And you. Why are you here?"

Atalanta shrugged, then reached into a nearby potted plant, pulling out her gun belt. After strapping it on, she hustled to the door and began trying the keys on the lock.

Shuffle followed her, feeling the push of her treachery and the pull of her presence. He wanted his friend back, but he needed answers. "Talk to me, dang it. Why are you—"

She dropped the keys. "Hey, you messed me up."

"No, you're just fumbling," he said, watching her sway and tilt and shiver. "No, you tried that one already. No. The other one."

"How do you know? And I ain't fumbling!"

Shuffle leaned against the door. "Then why are you shaking?"

"Because it's taking all my will not to punch you."

"Punch me? I should be the one to give you a knuckle sizzler. You betray—" The door opened, and he fell backward. He reverse-somersaulted to his feet. Giddyup.

They were inside now, standing in a large entryway—too dark to see much. Atalanta locked the door behind them, then spun around and embraced him. "I'm sorry."

He stiffened, feeling every thorny vine of her betrayal wither, all but one—Granddad died because of her.

"Stop it." Shuffle tore away. "Captain's dead. Skylla killed him. Because you ditched us." He stuck a finger in her chest. "Because you took the cards."

"Captain's dead?" Her head drooped. "I didn't know. I swear. You gotta understand, I had to leave. That moment on the train, Skylla would've killed us all if I hadn't taken your cards. And when I double-crossed her, I thought she'd hunt *me* down, not go after you and Captain."

She grimaced, as though she had drunk sour milk. The regret seemed genuine, and really, she wasn't the one who pulled the trigger. Skylla was the cold-blooded killer.

"The old bullet and I hardly saw eye-to-eye," she said, "but I respected him. He was one tough duster."

"He saved me so I could save my dad." Shuffle crossed his arms. "But why are you here?"

She shrugged. "To help you with whatever half-cocked plan you've got now."

He sighed. He should dump Atalanta like she dumped him on the train, but it felt too dang good to be with her again. "How can I trust you?"

Atalanta sighed. "Look, you want the whole truth? A couple years ago, I saw Skylla and her gang collect bounty on five outlaws. Ever since then I wanted to be a part of her group. I showed them I could ride, shoot, fight. I even begged Skylla, because I had no one else. When I overheard them talking about some boy with clues to a treasure, I thought I could win them over by scoring the gold first."

"That's why you were so keen on finding the treasure."

"That's right." Hard to see her face clearly in the dark, but her voice was quiet and unguarded. "But everything changed. All I wanted since the cut-off was to have an adventure, treasure or no, with you."

The way his chest ached made him want to believe. All that time spent riding the dusty trail, through forests and mountains and deserts, meant the world to him. He wanted to remember all the fun and excitement, the way they'd shared confidences and had each other's backs, not the load of lies.

Well, he couldn't forget the lies, but maybe they didn't have to be the full story. After all, Dad had chosen Alec, Cici, and Doc to keep the treasure cards, not because they didn't make mistakes, but because they did their best to prove their quality. Trust wasn't expecting someone to be perfect; it was believing they'd make the effort to do right.

Atalanta put something in his hands. "They're all in there."

Shuffle nearly crumpled, bracing the weight of his cards, the weight of her contact. He held the deck against his chest, and her eyes in his. They might have a fighting chance after all.

Atalanta glanced through the windows. "The show's almost over. We don't have much time. What's your plan?"

"I have Slythe's key." Shuffle tapped his pocket, making sure he still had it. "I'll find Dad, or get whatever is locked up, with this key. Slythe will make an exchange."

"What if he don't?"

"Well, I have a plan for that." He didn't.

He expected Atalanta to call his bluff, but instead she tiptoed to the double doors at the far end of the room. She cracked them open and took a peek. "Ready?"

He nodded, stowing his deck and treasure cards in his bag. Atalanta pushed through, gun drawn. Katana sneaked past and disappeared into the dark.

The room opened all the way to the ceiling, four stories high. Barred ledges ran along at each level. A winding staircase led up to the next floor. A giant stone statue of a blue deity stood center stage. It sported a crown of skulls and held a tall spear. Its three-eyed, fang-bearing face was a mug he wouldn't want to see in his sleep.

"Where do we start?" Atalanta asked.

Shuffle caught movement on the second story; Katana was tightrope-walking across the handrail. "I'm going up. Check around here, maybe for a cellar."

"Right." She came up to him and adjusted his headdress. "I liked your hat better."

"Me, too." Shuffle bolted up the stairs to the second floor. Katana hopped off the rail and continued down the overlook walkway before slinking through an open door. Shuffle followed her into a dark, musty room that smelled like Dad's old antiquities books.

"Katana," he whispered, hopeful she wasn't going to cause trouble. "Where are you, kitty? Giddyup."

Faint pops of light came through a window, and for a moment, he saw cards, lots of them, tacked onto the wall, spread out on a table, and piled on a desk.

Unfortunately, the light went away, and darkness drowned out everything.

Shuffle needed to see again, to confirm he had just stumbled into the room where all the Mythic cards were made. Even as his eyes began to get used to the dark, he could only make out big shapes. He stretched his hands out, feeling his way. He brushed up against a stack, knocking it over. The flutter and slide of thick paper stock echoed. Sorry for making a mess, he tried piling them together by feeling for the sharp edges and corners.

The lights came on.

Shuffle froze. How did the wall sconces just turn on like that? Was the place wired with electricity?

No time to ponder it. Shuffle looked down at the cards. They were Mythic cards, all right. Some of them looked hand drawn, like test cards. Shuffle picked one up—*Young Jason. Chiron's Pupil.* The space for special abilities was blank, but the card had a hand-drawn picture of a boy long gone, a picture that looked like him as a ten-year-old. Did Dad draw it?

The lights flickered and buzzed before going out. Darkness again.

And footfalls sounded from near the door, coming closer.

"What are you doing?" A man's scratchy voice.

Shuffle spun around but couldn't see much more than the man's outline.

The man said something again, but in Chinese. Of course. The Chinese girl disguise. It must be the man from the courtyard who had asked for a folding fan, the man with the long scar.

Shuffle thought hard for the words for lost and help and sorry. He should know sorry. Did this guy know Dad? Maybe he could help . . . if he wasn't one of the bad guys.

Squinting in the dimness, Shuffle scanned the desk for a weapon—a letter opener or a fountain pen, something sharp—just in case.

The light fixture above the desk sparked and

crackled, on and off, eventually leaving them in the dark.

"So much for new advances," the man said, his voice hoarse. "Electricity is a modern marvel but not quite ready to spread its glory."

The lights bloomed on.

"I'm still working on that one." Moving closer, the scarred man pointed at the card Shuffle was holding. He scratched at his bushy beard. "*Qing*. Please, may I?"

Shuffle pulled it away, wanting to keep it. It could be another clue to help him find Dad. If anything, the card was a piece of Dad's artwork, and that alone made it special. But a confrontation with one of Slythe's friends might ruin the chance to find Dad. Shuffle had no choice but to give it up. After one last look, he handed it over.

"*Xie xie*," the man said, stowing it into his pocket. Shadows and light deepened the lines of his face and the crevice of the scar along his head. He tapped at the hanging lamp until it and the rest of the sconces brightened. He turned away and focused on the cards, making everything nice and tidy.

The organizing of the cards struck a familiar chord. Neat stacks in rows of faction and ability. Each card seemed to mean something to him. Especially *Young Jason*.

As if to ruin everything, Katana hopped up and sat down right smack dab in the middle of the desk.

"Holy!" The scarred man jumped back. Katana folded her legs underneath her stomach, now looking like a bread loaf with a tail.

Shuffle dropped his face in his hands. He'd always thought she was a lucky charm. It seemed time to rethink that notion and rename her Miss Fortune.

"Aren't you a pretty one," the scarred man said. "I got my son a kitten just like you."

CHAPTER 53

MIRACLE

The light sconces buzzed as they filled the room in a warm glow.

Shuffle fought through a tight, dry throat. "Her name is Katana."

The musty card room flickered with light from the fireworks and the testy lamps. The off-and-on illumination was enough to see the scarred man's face underneath his beard.

"What?" The scarred man's voice trembled. Maybe he was confused. That was understandable, with Shuffle dressed as a Chinese girl who sounded like a boy speaking English. Or maybe because it had been too long since they'd seen each other. Way too long.

"Dad, it's me. Jason." Shuffle pulled away the wig and headdress.

Dad stood there, his mouth slack and his hand frozen inches away from Katana's fur. He was alive, and not a whispering shade.

This should have been a glorious moment, not some uncomfortable face-off.

Dad stepped back, yanking his hand away from Katana as though she were rabid. "Impossible. Is this some kind of cruel hoax?"

Shuffle recalled the day Mythic came to Mourning Glory. He had thought the same thing—impossible. The card game was supposed to be lost, forgotten, dead. Was it the same with him showing up like this?

"Please believe me. It's me. I had to dress like this to get in here." He held out his arms to show the whole costume. "It's just a disguise, not a trick. Please, Dad. It's Shuffle."

Dad clutched his head and gasped. He fished through his coat, pulled out a small, dark bottle and took a swig. His face soured before he fell to his knees.

Shuffle ran to help. It seemed Dad was broken. His memory. His body. His whole being appeared to be a lesser version of who he used to be. His dad shouldn't be scarred and weak and on his knees.

The room lit up to full brightness, and he could see every speck of gold in Dad's brown eyes.

Dad looked up. "Is it really you?"

"Yes." Shuffle wiped the rest of the makeup from his face. "And you're my dad, Euless."

"My god. You are Jason." Dad grasped Shuffle.

He fell into his dad's arms. After all this time out on the road, all the running and dodging and gaming, he had finally found Dad. He pressed his face against Dad's chest, focusing on the warmth he had missed. Tears began to swell. He closed his eyes tighter, yet the tighter he clamped down, the quicker the tears slipped out. He figured finishing his quest was worth a few tears of joy.

But something nagged at the connection. All this time he thought if Dad wasn't dead then he was being held prisoner. But seeing him like this, unchained and well-to-do—was it possible that Dad wanted to stay away?

Shuffle winced. All the unanswered questions slid in between his ribs like a slow knife. "Why didn't you come home?"

Dad's eye's glistened. "I thought you were dead."

CHAPTER 54
THE TRUTH

Dad trembled. "I read the newspaper story. The sheriff confirmed it. You and your mama were killed in the raid. I saw your graves."

Shuffle slapped the desk, startling Katana. There was only one wormy scoundrel who'd use the dirty tactic of a fake grave. "They were lies, Dad. Tricks."

The lamplight continued to randomly brighten and dim.

"You never sent for us," Shuffle said. "We never left home."

"That can't be right. I was told . . ." Dad pressed his temples, then moved his hand to his scar.

To leave a mark as big as the Mississippi, the injury to his head must've been terrible. No telling how much damage was done. "Dad, what do you remember from the raid?"

"Not much . . . I was shot."

Shuffle shuddered, feeling a phantom impact hit him in the head. Imaginary gunfire echoed. This whole quest had been filled with violence. And certainly, there would be more bloodshed before the end.

Dad tried combing his hair over the scar with his fingers, but it didn't hide anything. "I can recall stopping for supplies in Texas, but that's it. Everything after is a blank. An empty hole. But sometimes I have dreams. Nightmares."

"How did you survive?"

"A man brought me to a doctor," Dad said. "The man helped me through this whole ordeal. Still is."

"Helped. I don't think so." Shuffle made fists. "Is his name Stan Slythe?"

"That's right. This is his place. He takes care of me. He gives me medicine when the pain hits. When I hurt."

"Because he needs you," said Shuffle, rubbing his knuckles. "Slythe's playing you with a stacked deck."

"But he finances Mythic. That's what kept me going after I found out you were dead. I'm creating our dream project."

"It's part of his scheme," Shuffle said. "And the medicine. I bet he controls you with it. Keeps you needing it . . . until you can remember."

Dad looked at the bottle, confusion in his eyes. "Remember what?"

"The treasure, Dad." This whole mess had to be all about the gold and the artifacts and the wealth. The worm needed Dad to remember where he hid the treasure or the map pieces. But because Dad was broken, it was taking Slythe a long time and a lot of trouble to get all the pieces together. "You found the Spanish treasure. Athena's Aegis. All of it. And then you moved it, hid it somewhere so that a dirty double-crosser like Slythe couldn't find it. That's what he wants you to remember."

Dad shook his head slowly, as if this were all gibberish to him, and raised the bottle to his lips. Shuffle took the elixir and whipped it across the room. The glass shattered, bleeding dark brown syrup on the wall. The medicine must keep Dad from leaving, because the pain had to be unbearable without it.

Shuffle stood and urged his dad to his feet. "We'll get you more medicine, Dad. Better medicine, from an honest doctor. But first we've got to get out of here. We've got to go home."

Fireworks flashed and boomed in rapid beats, rattling the walls. The finale had begun. Time was almost up.

"Wait," said Dad, clutching his head. "This is—I need a minute."

It hit Shuffle that it wasn't going to be easy to hustle Dad out of here. And even if they got off Slythe's estate without being caught, Slythe could come after them. He'd gone to great lengths to track down Shuffle already. What was to stop him from recapturing both him and Dad?

They needed a bargaining chip. Shuffle revealed the key. "Do you know what this opens?"

Dad lit a nearby kerosene lantern and took a close look. "That's Stan's. How did you—"

"I stole it. But Dad, he's not your friend. He's a liar, and he tried to kill me."

A flash strobed the room in red. Dad's eyes opened wide, taking in the color. His mouth dropped open.

"I wanted to take what Slythe has and swap it for you. You can get your life back, Dad."

Silver and green bursts shook the walls.

Dad took a deep breath. "The key opens a safe. Up on the third floor. Whatever's in it might help me remember."

Gold shimmers crackled outside the window.

Shuffle grabbed Dad's hand. "Let's go get it."

✶ ✶ ✶

Shuffle led the way, with Katana meowing from his shoulder. Dad followed, bringing a kerosene lantern from his workroom. Hopefully, Atalanta was still downstairs and out of trouble.

"In there." Dad pointed to the room at the end of the dark hallway.

A smoky odor hung in the air of what looked like a bedroom; a canopied bed dominated the space, and monster-face masks protruded from the walls.

"I think this is it." Dad lifted the lantern near a mask with three eyes and a pair of spiraled horns. He pointed at its gaping mouth. "Slythe sticks his hand in there."

Shuffle peered into the maw, finding a keyhole and a small lever. He fed the key to the mask, turned it until it clicked to a stop, and pulled the lever down. A mechanism clacked, and the mask loosened from the wall. Shuffle sighed. It didn't spit fire or chomp down on his hand. He withdrew the key and opened the mask like a door, revealing the inside of an iron safe.

A gold bar shimmered, and stacks of greenbacks took up most of the space, but none of them were the real treasure. What he had come for leaned against the back corner—*Cihtym*.

Shuffle handed it to Dad. "Bring back memories?"

"*Cihtym*." Dad smiled. "Four-color strategy."

"Turn it over."

"X marks the spot," he said in a whisper as his eyes pored over the map piece on the back. "The treasure. Dr. Bloom and I—we found it?"

"Yes, you did. And I have the other pieces to make the whole treasure map. Maybe then you'll remember the rest."

A scream from outside pierced through a nearby open window. In the courtyard, the crowd stood frozen with their heads turned toward a commotion. A woman on the verge of collapsing made her way to Slythe, who was standing near the fountain. The sobbing woman pointed toward the back wall, probably where the guard and Skylla were poorly hidden. Too bad there hadn't been time to stash them somewhere else.

Shuffle grabbed Dad by the hand. No doubt the whole place would soon be crawling with trouble.

CHAPTER 55
THE BACKUP PLAN

Shuffle held his breath as he rounded the corner and ran down the stairs. Having the last treasure card didn't mean it was over. Until he and his dad were long gone from Slythe's fortress, they weren't safe.

Dad shambled down each step, trying his best to hurry while keeping the kerosene lamp steady, but it appeared his condition didn't allow him to move any faster.

They stopped on the second level. While Dad caught his breath, Shuffle looked out the open window. The courtyard was empty and quiet. Meng and the Star Dragons were nowhere to be seen.

Instead of taking the stairs to the first floor, Dad limped down the hallway.

Shuffle caught up to him. "Where are you going? We need to leave."

"I have to get something." Dad patted Shuffle's hand. "It will take two shakes."

There wasn't time for two shakes, but Shuffle choked up and couldn't say no.

Banging and yelling thundered from downstairs. He ran to the walkway and gripped the rail.

Electric lights illuminated the first floor, but they didn't make the place any safer.

"Atalanta!" Shuffle called out. "You down there?"

Atalanta popped out of a side room and slid to a stop at the three-eyed statue. "I barred the doors and shuttered the windows, but they'll be through any minute. Any smart ideas?"

He stifled a cringe. His backup plan needed a backup plan.

"We'll escape from up here." At least his voice didn't crack from the weak crud he was selling.

But a brilliant idea came to mind. They could go back up to the third floor and use the large Mythic banner to lower themselves down to safety. Dash Darkwood got out of trouble like that all the time.

Down the hallway, Dad's light glowed from the card room. Hopefully, he'd found what he needed, because time was up.

Shuffle hurried to the room. "Ready to—"

Dad knelt crumpled against his desk, clutching his head. The light from the kerosene lamp made the cuts of his pain look deep.

The bottom of Shuffle's stomach dropped like a bad bet. He flew to Dad's side.

Trembling, Dad reached for a notebook on the floor by his legs.

Shuffle retrieved it. "Is there anything else? What can I do? How can I help?" Maybe he made Dad worse by getting rid of the elixir. "Do you need your medicine?"

Dad clamped down on the bridge of his nose. "Are you my son? Are you Jason, and not some fake?"

Shuffle forced himself to speak steadily. It was his turn to be the person Dad could trust and lean on. "Yes, Dad. It's the truth. I'm here for you. Me and Katana."

Gunshots rang from downstairs. Shuffle jumped. He would never get used to that sound. Closing his eyes, he prayed for Atalanta, while helping Dad to his feet.

"I believe you," Dad said, clutching the notebook as he steadied himself. "I've written things that have come back to me. They might help me remember."

"Like Cassandra's Warning?"

"Yeah, how did you know?"

"Never mind that." Shuffle didn't want Dad to know he'd unwittingly sent a killer to their house. "Anything else you need to take? Any of these cards?"

"No. I can make them again. I can make more."

Dad's hard work hung under pins like the bugs for science at school. His ideas would be trashed by Slythe or stolen by some hired scab to finish the game. Either way, it hurt to see them go.

As they turned to head out of the room, Atalanta appeared at the door. Blood trickled from her lip and she held her hands up.

She lurched forward, pushed by a guard holding a gun to her back. Behind them lurked Slythe.

"Took two out before this one sucker-punched me," Atalanta said, spitting blood on the floor.

"Shut up, killer." The guard jabbed the pistol in her back.

She glared at him. "They ain't dead, but you won't be so lucky when I take my gun back."

Slythe spun his revolvers and pointed them from his hip. "Skylla said you were a little wildcat, but you oughtta know that having nine lives is just a myth."

There were too many threats, too many barrels being aimed. Shuffle stiffened his back and put his weight on his toes, ready to strike. Or to run.

But Dad collapsed.

CHAPTER 56
OVER THE EDGE

Shuffle spun around and dropped to his knees beside Dad, who had crumpled to the floor. "Please, no. Please, be okay."

Atalanta reached out, but the guard pistol-whipped her leg. She fell to one knee.

"Looks like he's in bad shape," Slythe said, holstering one of his revolvers and taking out a small vial. "Euless, didn't you take your elixir?"

"We dumped it." Shuffle sneered at the scoundrel. "You're controlling him with poison."

"I'm not poisoning him. He's too valuable. But you, boy," said Slythe, pointing his pistol at Shuffle, "you've no doubt been slipping him venomous lies."

"You're the liar."

"Euless. I have some elixir if you want to feel better," cooed Slythe, before clucking his tongue sharply. "And the boy, he's an impostor. He's after your treasure. Your game. Don't you see, Euless. He wants what you've made, and he's trying to pry it out of you by dishonoring your poor son in heaven."

Atalanta stood. "What a stinking load—"

The guard struck her again, but this time she stayed on her feet.

A high-pitched tone fed into Shuffle's head. If there was a time to be like Granddad, it was now. To fight, no matter the cost. How many steps were between him and Slythe? How many bullets could he take before he reached the scoundrel's throat? He dug his feet into the floor, ready to find out.

"Jason," mumbled Dad. "Jason. I believe you." He sat up. "Stan, you're the liar. I don't want your medicine."

Shuffle helped Dad stand, his eagerness to fight cooling. An escape opportunity better come up, because a hate-fueled suicide charge wasn't the best play.

"That's a shame." Slythe pocketed the elixir and drew his other iron. "I know the girl doesn't have the cards. So it comes to this: give them to me or she dies."

An ultimatum. A life for the cards. This whole trip out west had been full of stinking liars armed to the teeth with these kinds of dang threats, but Slythe was likely to pull the trigger.

"Look, I'm not here for the treasure." Shuffle pleaded with his hands and steadied his words. "I'm just here for my dad. Let us go—me, Dad, and my friend—and I'll tell you where I stashed the cards."

"I make the demands. Not you." Slythe raised both guns, one at Atalanta, the other at Dad. "This time my aim will be true and will deliver a killing blow, instead of complicating things."

Shuffle stood in the way, realizing that Slythe was the one who'd shot Dad in the head. He wasn't about to let that stinking horsepile do it again. "You'll get the dang cards, just——"

"He has them there," spurted Atalanta. "In his bag."

An all too familiar pain sank in between Shuffle's shoulder blades. "What are you doing?"

"I don't want to die. Mister, I gave the cards to him." She turned and made eye contact with Shuffle. "Just in case."

The dagger turned into a flame of an idea. Atalanta wasn't giving him up; she was giving him a spark—to light the firework she had given him to stash, *just in case.*

"Okay. Fine. You win. You make the rules. Let me find them." Shuffle put his hands into the bag while looking for some way to light the explosive. A kerosene lantern glowed from the desk. "Dad, can you get me that lamp?"

A smile crept across Atalanta's bloodied face.

Shuffle tasted the salty sweat budding on his upper lip as Dad held the lantern close enough to see inside the bag. He angled it away from Slythe and revealed the dynamite-sized firecracker to Dad.

Katana cut across the floor in front of Shuffle. "Well, well, what do we have here?" asked Slythe.

Everyone's eyes followed the cat as she slunk to the

dark side of the room. Shuffle lifted the glass enclosure of the lantern, exposing the flame, and lit the boomstick.

Slythe chuckled, still focusing on Katana. "Looks like you're saddled with some bad fortune."

"Nope. She's my lucky charm." Shuffle hurled the sizzling firework at Slythe.

Atalanta elbowed the guard in the head; he fired his gun as he fell unconscious.

The bullet smashed the lantern out of Dad's hand.

A blue and yellow explosion blasted Slythe. *Fire of Retribution: Defeat enemy hero that scored earlier in the game.*

Gray, acrid smoke consumed the room. Shuffle swatted at it until he could see.

Leaning on his desk, Dad gave a nod. Atalanta retrieved her gun from the guard, who was out cold. Near the doorway, Slythe steamed like a roasted pig.

But the smoke darkened and grew more bitter. Crackling and heat radiated from nearby as a fire began to spread among the paper and cards on the floor to the ones on the desk and table.

Shuffle hooked Dad by the arm and pulled him toward the exit. "Come on."

"Wait. My notebook." Dad stopped and stumbled.

Climbing the walls, the blaze swallowed the tacked-up cards.

"I'll get it." Shuffle passed Dad over to Atalanta. He wasn't going to have him in any more danger. "He needs help walking, but don't dally."

"Come on, mister," Atalanta said, putting Katana on her shoulder and taking Dad's hand. "I don't want Shuffle angry at me."

"Who are you?" asked Dad.

"I'm your son's right hand of vengeance. And a friend." She shot him a nod; Dad returned it before they descended the stairs.

Shuffle pushed through the black smoke, moving closer to the fire. Dad needed his dreams and memories to become whole again. He braced against the heat and found the notebook.

As he turned to run, Shuffle noticed two guns on the floor near the guard, who was coming to. He kicked the guns across the room and yelled at the guard. "Get out of here. Now!"

Once the guard caught sight of the fire, he scrambled away, whimpering.

The heat bore down hard, hotter and meaner. Shuffle fought against its push, tasting ash in the air. Fingers of flame crawled across the ceiling, reaching closer. There was no more time to waste.

He stepped over Slythe and out the door, but the villain grabbed him.

Shuffle stumbled into the overlook hallway. A fist slammed hard against his face. A red flash. A heavy weight crushed the air out of his chest. Slythe straddled him, the fire reflecting in his eyes. He raised his fist.

A white flash. Shuffle clenched his jaw from the pain and put his hands up. His arms took the next blow.

A gunshot popped. Slythe cried out and grabbed his shoulder, stumbling backward.

An opening appeared in the smoke, revealing the stairs, the way out. Shuffle ran for it.

Slythe charged like the Minotaur, head down and growling.

As Slythe barreled into him, Shuffle ducked, took Slythe's weight and momentum, and heaved him over the rail.

Slythe yelled.

All the way down.

To the three-eyed statue's spear.

CHAPTER 57
THE *ARIADNE*

Under a high-noon sun hiding behind lazy clouds, Shuffle and Dad waited at the Yuma station for the *Ariadne*, Mr. Eight's new train. Mama was coming.

The train whistled and steamed as it chugged to a halt along the open-air platform.

Shuffle reached over to hold Dad's hand, but Dad pulled away. Since leaving San Francisco, Dad had struggled with everything. Most of the time it was because of the pain. Sometimes, it seemed like he was lost. A stranger in a strange world. It was understandable, after everything had happened so fast. And the head wound still plagued him, fogging up his mind on some days and twisting it in knots on others.

Dad smiled, but it didn't seem genuine, like he was holding back his feelings. The one time he let loose his thoughts, they were on the boat to Los Angeles, in a private cabin. After waking up, Dad seemed to snap, and he yelled, "Not my son!" It took an hour to calm him down.

Maybe he would never be the same.

Thankfully, there hadn't been another incident like that, but Shuffle had realized the shattered pieces of the past few years wouldn't be so easy to fit back together. Dad's healing was going to be slow and crooked. On a day like today, Shuffle could only hope to get things moving in the right direction.

Soon, the train doors opened.

"Will she recognize me—and I, her?" Dad gripped his cane as he watched passengers pour out.

Shuffle went to hold Dad's hand again but stopped short. "Yes, on both accounts, Dad. I just know it."

The stream of folks began to die down. A young couple hopped off, laughing. The fella grabbed his lady and swept her off her feet. An old woman, wearing a large hat with peacock feathers, crept out of the rear train car. She straightened her crooked back just a bit before scooting away.

Had Mr. Eight given them the wrong day? There could've been a mix-up at Silver City. At Tombstone.

Dad tapped his cane against the platform. "Perhaps she changed her mind."

That couldn't happen. Not after all they'd gone through. In her letter agreeing to come to Yuma, she seemed excited. Then again, a couple thousand miles, four-plus years, and Bronson could have messed with Mama's decision.

Shuffle kicked a rock off the platform. It plinked off the train's iron cattle-catcher.

Then Mr. Eight stepped out of the first-class car. He helped Mama down. She wore a white-and-orange dress, brand new by the brightness of it. At first, her eyes were to her feet, but then she glanced up.

Dad braced himself, two hands on his cane. "That's Penny." He let go with one hand and put his arm around Shuffle.

"It is. It's Mama." Shuffle wanted to run to her, but he stayed, as Dad's pillar.

Mama approached, slowly at first. Then she seemed to pick up speed. Her shoes clapped against the wood boards. The ruffles on her skirt fluttered. She stopped short, but close enough for Shuffle to see her green eyes. Close enough for him to embrace her.

Dad joined in, and the three of them held each other. "I'm sorry, Penny," Dad choked out.

She gave him a look that would've shaken the world off Atlas's shoulders.

CHAPTER 58
GAME ON

Nothing like a tall glass of lemonade to squelch the dry Arizona heat, a tad over a hundred degrees outside.

Inside the Rising Sun Saloon, where the "first-ever ceiling fans in the West" spun overhead, the temps proved more bearable. But instead of prickly pear needles and rattlesnake fangs, the saloon hid shifty eyes and prying ears.

Shuffle took another sip. Sweet and tart. If only the saloon had ice chips to put in their drinks, the lemonade would've been perfect. It was better than nothing, and once on the trail to the Mojave, lemonade would be a scarce treat, unless . . . he smacked his lips at the thought of getting some bottled up.

Across the table, Atalanta slurped her drink. She scrunched her face. "Sour as heck."

"Then lemonade suits you perfectly."

"I do have a sweet side," she said, emptying her glass with a final gulp. "You got any of that ginger candy?"

Shuffle retrieved a small burlap sack from his bag and tossed it over. The Star Dragons had given him some treats for the road, but he was grateful to Meng and her family for more than sugar-coated, bite-sized slices of ginger. He owed them more than he could repay.

"Spicy. Sweet. Just like me," she said, popping one in her mouth. "But make fun again, and you'll find out how sour I can get."

Shuffle smirked. "I'm shaking in my spurs."

Atalanta stuffed a couple of candies in her front pocket before giving up the sack. "You better be. It'll be a long ride to the Mojave if you're on my bad side."

Two tables away, a man with flies buzzing around him tilted his head as though he was listening in. From a dark corner, a dusty cowboy glanced at them from under the brim of his ratty hat.

"Keep it down," Shuffle whispered.

"I dare anyone to cause trouble." She pushed away her glass to make room for her rifle. Well, it was Granddad's repeater. Mr. Eight had found the gun when he and a railroad crew scavenged the rubble of the *Medea* train wreck. The rifle fit her like a longbow fit Artemis, and Atalanta cried when he'd given it to her, though she would never admit it.

Coming back to Yuma hurt; memories of gunshots, the jump, and the cold white water came back with the blinding sun and the searing heat. But at least Mr. Eight did Granddad right by having his final resting place under a giant yucca palm tree that stood like a soldier, arms up in victory.

A simple gray granite slab with orange and azure speckles served as the tombstone; *Captain William Ithaca —An honorable soldier, husband, father, and grandfather* was engraved on its glassy surface. Maybe Granddad wouldn't have cared where he was buried or what the headstone looked like, but it fit the kind of man he was. If only he had gotten to make amends with Mama before he died.

The *chick-chick* of the repeater's lever brought Shuffle back from his thoughts.

"You think we're gonna find it?" Atalanta looked down the sights, pointing it at a deer skull hanging on the wall.

At a nearby table, two men in long dusters—which was odd because it was hot as heck—began whispering over their plates of chicken bones.

Shuffle leaned in close. "Keep blabbing it out, we won't find nothing but the bottom of a shallow hole."

"Don't fret." She rubbed a shine on the stock. "Ain't you a little excited? You must be keen to see Athena's sword, spear, what was it?"

Shuffle couldn't help but blurt out. "Athena's shield!"

Atalanta frowned and gestured with her sharpshooter's eyes to a trio of iron-packing travelers at the bar.

Shuffle slapped his head, hiding his eyes, feeling dumber than the deuce of clubs.

"The gold isn't yours to wager," Dad said, sliding into a seat at the table. He banged his cane on the floor. "It's going to the university."

"And the artifacts will go to museums," Mama said, taking the other empty chair. A scent of roses perfumed the dusty air.

Dad wiped the table clean and unrolled the treasure map of the five Mythic cards, his hands trembling. Some days he was fine; on others, the side effects of his head wound wrecked him.

Mama seemed to notice it, too, and she grasped his hand until he stopped shaking.

"We'll have to take another route after this point," Dad said, pointing at a boulder landmark. "Bandit activity has gone up in that area."

"Fine with me," Atalanta said with a shrug, although she was probably disappointed about avoiding a potential dustup.

Katana leapt onto the table and sat on top of the map. *Butt marks the spot.*

Shuffle leaned back in his chair. "So, Dad, are we ready for a treasure hunt?"

"Packed and set to go. But I was thinking, we have time for one more thing." He pulled out a Mythic deck from his jacket.

Atalanta slapped her hands together. "Come on, Miss Penny. Care for a challenge?" She took Mama and Katana to an empty table for a duel of their own.

Now with his dad to himself, Shuffle drew out his *Athena* deck with a new, one-of-a-kind, Dad-crafted *Odysseus*. "Game on."

ACKNOWLEDGMENTS

To Dawn Frederick, I'm grateful you never forgot about my pitch, even though I took three years to finish the manuscript. Thank you for taking a chance on me and for being *Cardslinger's* champion.

Thank you, Amy Fitzgerald, for your enthusiasm, insight, and guidance. It's been a pleasure, an honor, and an education working with you. Your editorial savvy shaped this book into its finest form.

To Laura Westlund and Kim Morales, your art and skill have done wonders for this book. Libby Stille, thank you for being the ace up my sleeve. And to the rest of the team at Carolrhoda and Lerner Publishing, your books are amazing, and I couldn't be happier to be a part of your wonderful list.

To Heidi Mann, your eagle eye spotted a mistake that made it through hundreds of readings. Disaster averted!

To Mónica Armiño, I couldn't have wished for a better cover artist. Your work is magical.

To Mary Kole, your knowledge and skill with your

manuscript honing steel gave me the confidence to send out my story into the wild.

To DFW Writer's Workshop, you guys are the cluster bomb of critique groups, and without DFWCon and the gong show, I never would have connected with Dawn. To SCBWI North Texas and Novel Nineteens, you're the best shadowy organizations.

To my writer friends—Kellye Abernathy, Dani Baxter, Diana Beebe, Gerardo Delgadillo, Anne Denise Dupont, Sean Easley, Amy Kelly, Alexis Lantgen, David Lin, Sarah Mensinga, Jared Pope, Emily Roberson, and Holly Rylander—you helped me through terrible drafts and gave me invaluable feedback and advice. Thank you.

To the grognards of the North Texas Gamers, huzzah! Thanks John Boone and Nevin Ball for joining me down that Magic: The Gathering rabbit-hole way back when. Without all the gaming and the card collecting, there would be no Mythic in Cardslinger. And I'd probably be a million dollars richer.

To my family in Michigan and Texas, I cherish your love and support.

To my kids. Conner, your smarts and creativity are at a mythic rare level. Your letter to the villain made it into the book, and it garnered smiley-faces, lols, and hearts from everybody who's read it. Shuffle aspires to be like you. Charlotte, your fierceness and talent are great bonfires, wild and bright, and your love for kitties brought Katana to life! Because I respect and love you both so much, I will always try my hardest to crush you when we game.

Above all, to my wife, Jodie, your selflessness, grace, and love are everything. You encouraged me to follow my dream, and when I despaired with writer's block and rejections, you kept my spirits up. Thank you for reading and being unflinchingly honest, for being cool with every new game that somehow appeared on our shelves, and for filling our home with laughter and silliness. You are incandescent and singular. You are my life. I love you.

ABOUT THE AUTHOR

M. G. Velasco's middle-grade adventure stories feature clever kids facing perilous situations in unique settings, sometimes with llamas. He earned a Bachelor of Science in Microbiology and worked at a pathology lab, which was not gross. Not gross at all. As a retired stay-at-home dad, he lives in North Texas with his wife and two kids and hoards strategy games. *Cardslinger* is his debut novel.